YOU AND ME, BELONGING

YOU AND ME, BELONGING

AARON KREUTER

TIGHTROPE BOOKS

Tightrope Books
#207-2 College Street,
Toronto Ontario, Canada M5G 1K3
tightropebooks.com
bookinfo@tightropebooks.com

EDITOR: Deanna Janovski
COVER DESIGN: David Jang
LAYOUT DESIGN: David Jang

 Canada Council   Conseil des arts
for the Arts   du Canada

 ONTARIO ARTS COUNCIL
CONSEIL DES ARTS DE L'ONTARIO
an Ontario government agency
un organisme du gouvernement de l'Ontario

Produced with the assistance of the Canada Council for the Arts and the Ontario Arts Council.

Library and Archives Canada Cataloguing in Publication

Kreuter, Aaron, author
     You and me, belonging / Aaron Kreuter.

Short stories.
ISBN 978-1-988040-41-7 (softcover)

     I. Title.

PS8621.R485Y68 2018   C813'.6   C2018-902533-6

Praise for *You and Me, Belonging*

"In writing that crackles and smoulders and leaves you checking your pants for burn holes, Aaron Kreuter maps the veinwork of the Jewish Toronto experience. Swill a bottle of honey, get haunted by Anne Frank, ride a waterslide into the unknown. On the surface, these are stories about suburbs and movie theatres, jam bands and A/V kingpins—beneath it all there's a riptide of hectic passion and desperate intimacy. *You and Me, Belonging* steals beauty from wreckage, stashes love in all the right places." —David Huebert, author of *Peninsula Sinking*

"Aaron Kreuter's new collection is fresh and exciting. His enthusiasm for his characters and their stories draws the reader in and beckons continuation page after page. His descriptions are colorful; his dialogue is realistic. Kreuter really captures the whole jamband scene—our feelings, our joys, and our difficulties." —Christy Articola, editor and publisher, *Surrender to the Flow*

CONTENTS

Restaurants

I had only been at the restaurant for three weeks when I slept with Samir. It happened in the underground storage room after my shift, a cramped, dimly lit space with shelves of flour and canned goods on one wall and cubbies, laundry bins, and stacks of clean towels and aprons on the other. "I've never slept with a Jew before," Samir said as he pulled my underwear down to my ankles. "That's funny," I responded, sliding out a foot, lying down on the cold cement, our clipped banter charging the sexual currents whipping through the room, "I've never slept with an Arab before." He positioned his doughy body on top of me, both of us already damp with perspiration. "Let alone a Palestinian," I grunted.

"Well, it's your lucky day then," he breathed.

When we were finished, I threw my apron into the laundry, stuffed my work clothes and shoes into my cubby, put on my jeans, laced up my boots, and walked with Samir out the side exit to smoke a cigarette on the sidewalk. He was halfway through a double, and I wasn't on again until Monday. We stood there together, smoking in silence, men in suits rushing past in the slanting evening light. It was the first time since we had met that we weren't at each other's throats.

Sitting on the Metro on my way home, the thought occurred to me that in some strange way, I had slept with Samir to get back at Arthur. I was still supremely pissed off at him for making me transfer from La Retro to BunBuns. "I need you to whip up the front-of-house there, Sarah," he had said at the beginning of what would turn out to be my last shift at the capital of Arthur's restaurant empire. "Show them how it's done. You start tomorrow."

I was shocked. "I thought you moved Kevin there?"

"Kevin can manage inventory and replace old bread on the sandwiches, but nobody can keep the ship as even-keeled as you.

You start tomorrow."

That was it. (That was Arthur.) I had been waiting tables at Retro for two years and didn't think I would suddenly be working the cash at the small financial district soup-and-sandwich place with table-and-counter seating for twelve that was Arthur's newest acquisition. But Arthur had been good to me, and I couldn't help feeling a sense of loyalty, so I figured I would tough it out for a few weeks before demanding to be switched back. If he refused then, I would quit. The city was full of restaurants that would die for a waitress with my experience.

The train stopped at Préfontaine, and I got off. It was a fifteen-minute walk from the station to my small third-floor walk-up, where I'd lived since I left Hampstead. The neighbourhood was the polar opposite of where I'd grown up in every possible way: working-class, Catholic, and French, it was made up of narrow streets of skinny squeezed-together townhouses. My dad was furious when I told him my new address, which was precisely the reaction I was going for. Out here, far away from the large, bloated houses of Hampstead, no one knew me. I was anonymous. I unlocked the door, flipped on the light. David, my boyfriend of just over three years, head waiter at La Retro, would be over soon. I lit a cigarette, stood at the window, watched the street darken, imagined Samir telling his friends about me, bragging about how he's ravishing the enemy.

I laughed out loud, but then, seeing David turn the corner, I stopped.

Samir was walking on De Maisonneuve, on the way from the restaurant to the two-bedroom apartment he shared with his mother, two younger sisters, and three cousins. It had been six hours since he had sex with Sarah, the new Jewish girl, and he was awash with strange feelings. He had not been expecting the sensations that had thrummed through him; he still felt them, even now, hours later, diminished, yes, but still there. And on the floor at work when he was supposed to be counting cans of pop! He hadn't even been on his break.

What had he been thinking? If this got back to Arthur, Samir didn't know what he would do. Samir wanted to be confident in Arthur's trust and love for him—he had started him as a busboy when he first arrived five years ago, after all, with a family to feed and no money to feed them with—but he couldn't help thinking that the solid ice of Arthur's love was no match for the heat of Arthur's temper. Samir had seen it many times, assistant managers and head chefs reamed out, fired in front of the entire staff, banished to Toronto. Arthur could rage in English, French, Spanish; he could even swear a little in Hindi. It was one of the many ways he kept such a firm grip on his employees, his steadily expanding culinary domain, something Samir respected him for immensely—so, again: what had he been thinking?

Samir laughed. He knew what he had been thinking. The two of them were down there, and they fucked. It's what happens. There wasn't much thinking involved.

Not that Samir ever thought he would sleep with a Jewish girl, especially not here. But, as cynical as he was, as hardened to the world's cruelty as he imagined himself to be, he could, apparently, still be surprised; the moment he climbed on top of her it ceased to matter what she was. And another surprise: who knew that Montreal was so Jewish? In some indefinable way, it was more Jewish than Tel Aviv, a city Samir knew well, where he had learned to cook as a teenager, working in the kitchens along the beach. This was before things got bad and then worse and then, somehow, even worse. This was before they left to become refugees in this island city full of refugees— Palestinians like him and his family, but also Somalis, Koreans, Colombians, Iraqis. Before they landed here. Montreal, Province du Québec, Canada.

Samir walked by the Best Buy, resisting the urge to go inside. Samir's three cousins—talkative, good-natured boys, who quickly adapted to Canadian life—were obsessed with *Empires of Magic*. They spent all of their free time working on their avatars, completing missions, exploring the virtual online world of Faldaria. They only had one clunky computer at the apartment, though, part of the package they received from the refugee centre when they first arrived, and they all had to share. Last week, instead of studying for his economics midterms and outlining final history-of-law essays, Samir let them make him his own *Empires* character—a wizard, complete with floppy hat and wooden staff. He had loved having the three of them hanging on his arms and neck, instructing him on the ins and outs of what seemed to be an exceedingly complicated game, located in an enormous country, full of hills and forests and towns and unending opportunities for adventure.

He hadn't said anything yet, but he was planning to buy them another computer, a laptop. He had a friend who worked in Concordia's tech department—a fellow Palestinian, born and raised in the Lebanese camps—and they had a bunch of old computers they were selling. He was going to get Samir a good price; though with his studies, his mother, all the young ones, saving up for anything other than food and school supplies was going to be tough. He was going to try and bring home more food from the restaurant, but really, besides a few more three-day-old sandwiches and bottom-of-the-pan brisket meat, there were no more corners to cut. He was already clocking sixty hours a week, plus his classes, plus schoolwork, plus everything else.

All this to mean that he shouldn't sleep with that girl again. Why put everything at risk? The city had been good to him. The country had been good to him. Most of all, Arthur had been good to him. Why jeopardize it with sex?

I partied a little too hard over the weekend, David and me drinking a bottle of rum, bar-hopping on Saint-Laurent, eating ice cream off each other in the dawn light. We hadn't had a wild night like that in years, and even though the guilt increased with every pull of rum, every downed pint, even though I felt myself cringing at the way David spoke to the waitress at Bifthèque, the way he boasted about his academic accomplishments to the undergrads at the table next to us, even though the sex—when it finally arrived—was boringly vanilla, leaving me cold and unsatisfied, even though standing on my balcony in the light of a new day, smoking the last of my cigarettes, David sprawled naked, sticky, and asleep on my bed, I saw clearly for the first time that something was missing in our relationship—by far the longest and most serious of my life—even through all of that, I was still drunk enough to have had a good time. But, come Monday, I was understandably in a shitty mood. Samir and I didn't say a single word to each other the whole eight hours we were working together, but at the end of my shift we were back on the rough cement. I wasn't expecting a repeat, and I doubt he was either, but there we were: it was even more furious, more crazed, more mountainous than the first time. Minutes after we had finished, Julie walked in; we were mostly dressed, still breathing hard, standing at least. She didn't say anything, but it must have been pretty obvious what she had almost stumbled upon.

I doubted she would tell anybody. We'd known each other for years, had both started waiting tables for Arthur at the same time, had worked together right up until Arthur transferred her to BunBuns immediately after buying it. Like Julie, I knew practically everybody at BunBuns before I had transferred, except the gaggle of awkward, interchangeable busboys that Arthur moved around like pawns. Except Samir.

I had heard of him, of course. Arthur's newest protégé. Samir had come up through another of Arthur's restaurants, Monsieur Winston, out in Laval. A big man with what I've heard people call olive-coloured skin—though I've never seen any olives that were the same roasted brown—he was a serious, quiet worker, though when he did speak it was often cynical, rude, cutting. I had heard whispers of a rough past, something about his father, the Israeli army, but tried not to think about it. Israel had nothing to do with me. Israel belonged to my father, to David, to my ex-Hampstead classmates who went on Birthright, got into yelling matches at Concordia, moved there, who turned religious so hard and so fast that within five days they were utterly different people. I had avoided all that since I was thirteen and stopped going to after-school Hebrew classes (classes whose only educational benefits occurred with Jeremy Kraftchuk in the second-floor bathrooms). Israel, and the arrogance with which it was spoken of by the men I grew up with, was one more reason behind my desire to get out of Hampstead and never go back.

Truthfully, I actually found those first few shifts at BunBuns a welcome change from the hustle of the floor at La Retro. Julie and I chitchatted, brought up drinks from the storage room, worked the till, changed the techno-house CDs when they started to skip, counted the money at the end of the night. The tips weren't great, but besides the lunch rush there was plenty of time to hang out, unless Arthur was there with a client or with any number of blond-haired women he seemed to cycle through endlessly.

On my fourth shift, the last of my first week, Kevin sent Samir to La Retro to pick up more brisket for the sandwiches and told me to go along with him. Nothing was said on the ten-minute walk to the restaurant, but on the way back, thirty-pound boxes of meat in our arms, Samir asked where I was from.

"Well, I live in the east end now, but I grew up in Hampstead." I didn't usually admit I was from Hampstead, but I felt inexplicably challenged.

"Uh, I knew it," he said.

"Knew what?"

"That you were Jewish."

"Yeah, so?"

"So nothing. Why are you working here? Is your daddy not giving you enough money? Are you not his little princess?"

I was so stunned that for a moment I was speechless. We kept walking with the boxes of meat.

"What the fuck business is it of yours?" I spat.

"Relax, relax," Samir said, smiling, proud that he had gotten to me.

I quickened my pace and started walking in front of him. Bastard. Should I go back and slap him? I've slapped men for far less. I shifted the meat and walked with strong, purposeful strides.

He thought he had Jews pinned. That because he came from over there, he knew all about us. The infuriating thing was, he wasn't so far off: my father was definitely wealthy, though he hadn't given me much money since I dropped out of university and moved to the east end. Which isn't to say we got along before that, because we didn't: If he was unhappy with my grades, I would fail harder. If he didn't want me to get my ears pierced, I would pierce my ears, my cartilage, *and* my eyebrow. If he thought I was hanging out with a bad crowd, I would pick the worst of the bunch and start sleeping with him (or her). If I had known how much he would like David, I probably never would have started dating him. As far as my father was concerned, David was the only thing I was doing right, David who hailed from a working-class Jewish background in the West Island, David who had paid his way through the MBA he was months away from finishing by serving at La Retro (with the full support of Arthur, a vocal believer in education), David who was the Jewish apple of my father's overly particular eye, the only reason he hadn't yet disowned me completely. Samir couldn't have known that I hated Hampstead probably as much as he did, that most of the people I went to high school with, whether on their way to being doctors or lawyers or inheriting the family business, left a bad taste in my mouth (when David first started hanging out with us in Hampstead, he was like nobody I had ever known, sweet and intelligent and reckless). I didn't doubt Samir came from a rough place, but what did it have to do with me? He was so smug, so cocky in his suffering, in his oppression. I decided then and there not to talk to him unless absolutely necessary. Unless the restaurant was burning down and he was in the way of the fucking fire extinguisher.

Ten days after the walk with the boxes of meat, we found ourselves on the storage room floor.

Samir had witnessed Arthur's fury on more than one occasion. At Monsieur Winston, he had pushed Samir from his station during the night rush, and, unhappy with the sharpness of the knives, started hurling them against the wall. "Can't do anything with these fuck dull fucks!" he had screamed. Samir had been terrified, but minutes later Arthur was calm, chatting with Samir, garnishing the chicken. How many firings had Samir been privy to? How many meltdowns on the Korean guy who delivered the vegetables?

When Samir wasn't working, going into the storage room with Sarah (which had now become a regular, anticipated occurrence), trying to focus on his homework but instead watching his cousins play *Empires*, he imagined Arthur freaking out on him, firing him. He couldn't stop; he closed his eyes, and there was Arthur, ending him with a merciless string of screamed words, spit flying. He knew it was only a matter of time before his little liaisons with Sarah got through to him. Samir was suspicious of everybody: Kevin was a vindictive prick, both Patels (Vikram and Dale, cousins) wouldn't blink twice before throwing him under the bus, and Julie, that look in her eyes when he asked her to restock the sandwich bread, that was trouble.

But he couldn't stop. Sarah had him hooked. He never would have expected to have feelings for a girl like her—cold and hard in public, but wild and giving when they were alone amid the soiled aprons and two-fours of diet soda. Just thinking of their love-making filled his stomach with overly carbonated soda water.

And that was not the only thing weighing on him. Last week, on a whim (after Sarah, supposedly on a five-minute smoke break, pulled him into the freezer and went down on him instead), he had gone into Best Buy and bought a computer. The fastest processor, the biggest screen, the best graphics card on the market. No used machines for his family. Not anymore. They were going to get to explore Faldaria in all its geographic, lag-less splendour. So, not only was he half in love with Sarah, not only did he go about his day in constant fear of being fired, not only had the worrying shaved his usual five hours of sleep down to a thin three, but now he had an extra thirteen hundred dollars on his credit card that he had no way to pay for.

Samir thought of his father—something he tried not to do too often. Sitting at a cafe on the water, smoking his hand-rolled cigarettes. The man spoke in proverbs. *Do not drink from a well and throw a stone into it.* Well, there was no way around it. He was drinking deeply, and the stones, smooth and hot in his hand, seemed to have a will of their own.

Last night we closed the restaurant together, went downstairs, and made a bed of aprons with pillows of dishtowels. Afterwards, knowing we were alone, that nobody was going to come looking for a can of tomato paste or a box of salt, we stayed on the floor longer than usual. He was holding his arm up above us, and I had my hand on him, was tracing his burn scars with my fingers, a line on a map.

"Your battle wounds," I said.

"Your brothers and cousins did this to me," he said, smiling. Our sex talk had become more and more political, a raging, delirious back-and-forth on the Israeli-Palestinian crisis amid grunts and moans, but this was the first time he said something like that once the heat of our demented coupling had subsided. I punched his arm. "No, no, of course not. I joke. Mostly the oven, oil, pans that were hotter than they looked."

"What about this one?" I said, pointing to a circular discolouration a few inches above his elbow. A strange place for a burn.

"Snowboarding," he said, readjusting his body into mine.

"Snowboarding? In Gaza?" I said, surprised.

He pulled his arm away, his face hardening. I stared at him, but his face stayed impassive. That was probably the first time in my entire life I said the word *Gaza* aloud. "Fine, whatever," I said, jumping up, angrily looking for my clothes. Samir stayed on the floor while I dressed, staring at the exposed pipes and asbestos ceiling. Eventually he got up, swept the aprons and towels into his arms and dumped them in the laundry.

"When we first came here," he said, softly, as if he were speaking to himself, "my little sister asked me what the one thing I wanted to do most now that we were in Canada was, and I said snowboarding. 'So let's do it,' she said. We had been here for only a few weeks, but we got onto a bus and went up to Tremblant. I fell off the chair lift on our first run, gashed open my arm on somebody's ski pole. I never got myself to go to the clinic."

We were standing beside each other now, under the bare light bulb. Samir was still naked. "I'm sorry," I said, feeling terrible, touching his arm.

"You and your Jewish guilt," he said, smiling.

"Go to hell," I said, though I was smiling also.

On the Metro that night, I debated with myself, once again, about what I was doing. What *was* I doing? I was cheating on David on an almost nightly basis, that was what I was doing. And yet, the thing was, after the first couple of times, I no longer felt bad about it, not that the guilt was so terrible to begin with. Was I a bigger bitch than I had realized? Or was something else going on? A few nights ago, David and I had gone drinking with some of David's West Island friends, Brent and those assholes. When the conversation inevitably turned to Israel—the point of the night when I would usually tune out, go for a smoke—and Brent started spewing his usual racist diatribes, I found myself arguing with him, yelling about military occupations, historical facts, the need for empathy, surprising everybody, not least of all myself. Is that what this is about, the weird look David gave me when Brent said,

"Whoa, Sarah, what has gotten into you? Spending too much time at Concordia?" I couldn't tell. Maybe. One thing I was sure of, though: without my noticing, the feelings I used to have for David had shrunk to almost non-existence. Before David, I had never thought of myself as someone who liked to be tied down, and now, thanks to the explosive sex I was having with Samir, I saw the three years with David as an aberration, a blemish on my freedom. I knew I should just end it with him, but something was holding me back, and I couldn't figure out what it was. Was it that David was the last connection I had with the part of my life I had spent the last five years actively trying to get away from? Was that it? That I wasn't yet ready to make the final, decisive cut?

I thought of Samir's face after the one time he came in my mouth. He looked so sheepish, so innocent, like a child who, knowingly disobeying his parents, gets caught eating ice cream before dinner.

I smiled to myself, alone on the Metro.

He had to admit it to himself. The warm hollow in the pit of his gut was not a stomach ache, the humming he felt in his bones was not exhaustion: he had fallen in love with her. He was smitten. Her white skin, her piercings—seven in the left ear, five in the right, a small stud in the left nostril, the scar of a ring she once had on her right eyebrow—the feel of her body under him, on top of him, entwined with him as she cut his back with her nails as she thrashed through the third orgasm of the afternoon (his father again, with him constantly these last few weeks: *The eye is the one that eats*). Even her meanness to him when they were upstairs, pretending to be co-workers. The time he came up to her with a choice piece of brisket, and she said she was a vegetarian. "How spoiled of you," he responded without thinking, terrified until Sarah smiled her wicked smile at him. The time—downstairs, again, always downstairs—he said, "Don't start thinking this makes up for the oppression of an entire people," freezing up with fear after he said it (Sarah probably thinking he was coming), but she just laughed and started going harder. The sight of her working the till, her hands moving faster than should be possible, counting change with incredible speed, yelling "Where's the chicken club?" cleaning the espresso machine, shoving the busboy out of the way and scrubbing the pans herself, hauling two enormous bags of garbage on her back, holding her own with all the men of the restaurant. That first time he came inside her and his whole body emptied out, his history and sorrows and worries purged for what felt like the first time.

When they arrived in Montreal, Samir had three goals: to protect what was left of his family; to make enough money to support those in his care; and to get an education, in order to better serve the first two. Women simply did not figure into it, not now—later, maybe, when he had his degree, a kitchen of his own, when his sisters and cousins were well into university, maybe then he would consider finding someone, sharing a partnership, a family.

And yet, here he was.

Then there was the big question, nagging, getting louder: how did Sarah feel about him? As far as he was aware, she wasn't seeing anybody else, though he had to admit he really didn't know. He never paid any attention to the restaurant gossip, and though he talked about his personal life, his family—too much, probably—when they were in the storage room, she never did. He thought of asking Vikram or Dale, nonchalantly, knowing he would never actually make himself so vulnerable to their derision. He couldn't help it: he had been fantasizing about bringing Sarah home, introducing her to his mother, his sisters. They would love her; he was sure—how could they not? The boys would make her an *Empires of Magic* profile, and together they would conquer the kingdom of Faldaria, unite the elves and the warlocks, bring peace to the entire digital realm.

He was, in fact, going to ask her at their next shift together. Friday. He was terrified. He had lived through occupation, bombings, the scarcity and leanness of being under constant siege; he had survived moving to a new country, becoming the head of the household, his first job interview with Arthur, but he had not known fear like this. Adding to it all was his certainty that any day now the rug would be pulled out from under him at work. It felt like a definite inevitability. But what would he do if he got fired? Find a new job? Arthur had many connections in this city, could keep him out of the kitchen forever if he wanted to. His father came to him again: *Whatever is written on the forehead is always seen.* Arthur knew. He must know.

He had to do something.

But what could he do? Samir was not the kind of man to not listen to his heart, and his heart was stuck on a single tune, on one repeating note.

The note was Sarah.

After two months at BunBuns, I had had enough. The work was fine, the sex with Samir was the best I'd ever had, but the tips were shit. Basically, there were none. The ten, fifteen dollars Kevin counted out of the tip jar at the end of every night was barely enough for a pitcher of beer. At La Retro, I could pull in two, three hundred dollars on a Friday alone. I had told myself I would tough it out for a handful of shifts, but somehow eight weeks had passed. It was time to speak to Arthur.

The next time I saw him was a morning shift. He had shown up with a client, some nondescript white man in a suit, as he sometimes did, and was frying some eggs for them behind the counter. A middle-aged man at the height of his success and power, I watched him from the till, his clean-shaven, old-world face, the fierce intelligence of his always-watching eyes hidden behind drooping lids that would shoot open like cartoon window blinds when he was angry. Since Arthur guarded his origins with the same ruthlessness as he ran his restaurants, nobody actually knew what he was—Québécois, British, French, Eastern European, Middle Eastern—though everyone had their theories. He had hung his peacoat on the corner of the oven, had rolled the sleeves of his custom-made dress shirt to the elbows, revealing arms covered in black hair, a gold watch. For some reason, as I watched him cook I thought of my father, scrambling eggs for me when I was a child.

I pressed my lips together, walked up to him, smiled my biggest smile, and asked if I could switch back.

He refused.

"C'mon, Arthur. Please. What if I stayed here for the most part, but picked up one or two shifts at the restaurant?"

"I'm sorry, Sarah," he said in his vaguely British accent, expertly flipping the eggs, "but we need you here. What is it you don't like here, hmm? Is it Julie? Kevin? Samir, perhaps?"

I was flustered, but only for an instant. "What? No. It's the money, plain and simple. The money, or lack thereof."

Arthur wouldn't budge, repeating what he said whe

me I was transferring: it was temporary, my skills were r

trust him. I stayed pissed throughout the lunch rush, scre

when he made a brisket sandwich instead of a chicken. As

garbage out through the loading docks behind the restaura

admitted to myself how sick I was of working the till, how si ̣ _ was of

my apartment, of Montreal, of David. I would quit the restaurant, end it

with David, and just take off. I still had most of my bat mitzvah money

in a tax-free savings account, a few thousand dollars in a purse under

my mattress, some girlfriends living in Barcelona. Why shouldn't I? My

little east-end enclave was starting to be invaded by McGill students,

my father was calling more often, asking irritating questions about my

relationship with David, the world was open and I was stuck here selling

sandwiches. I was young and beautiful and free, fluent in English,

French, and Spanish, could find work in any restaurant in the world.

Samir's stories about his family, his obligations, made me see how

incredibly lucky I was: there was nothing tying me anywhere, to anyone.

I didn't tell anybody about my plans, not David, not Arthur,

especially not my father. The only person I felt bad about not telling

was Samir. Another surprise. Sure the sex was great, but it was purely,

deliriously physical, a fling to deal with the tedium of the till, the

kitchen, heightened because of the situation over there. It wasn't

like we were going to start introducing each other to our families or

anything. Samir and my father in the same room, the same house,

required feats of imagination I was not capable of.

I would miss those sessions on the floor, though. That first time

we hooked up, I was changing out of my work clothes, he was on

his hands and knees counting inventory. There was no tension that

needed to be broken, no long flirtation; or it was all tension, tension so

thick, so predetermined, so much larger than our little lives, that there

was nothing for it to do but crack wide open over us. I would be lying

to myself if I said the whole thing had no impact on me, because it

did: it made me want to get even further away from Hampstead, from

those who, without my consent, included me in their wars, their lies,

who pulled me into their complicity. Well, not anymore. If I was saying ɔye to Samir, if nothing else, I should thank him for that.

Tomorrow was Friday.

Quitting day.

You're walking down Sainte-Catherine, clenching and unclenching your fists, full of anger. Pedestrians make way for you like you're a tank. You can't believe it. You're furious. You didn't believe it when she had started acting different, distant, just thought she was being childish about switching to BunBuns. You didn't even believe it when the kitchen staff told you, their bastard eyes full of mirth. She's cheating on you, you know, your lady friend. Sarah. And with him. You didn't believe it—at first—when you walked over there on your break and watched at the fogged window as she walked to the back, touched his arm—did she touch his arm?—and a minute later he followed. Only once you were halfway back to La Retro, playing the scene over, did you start to believe, did belief break over you like raining napalm. And with him. Samir. You know him; of course, you know him. A quiet, hulking Arab who kept his hatred glazed over his eyes. It's not like you hate *all* Arabs, like some of your friends do. Of course you thought it was ridiculous when Brent wouldn't even go into that shish-taouk place because it was staffed and owned by "the enemy," *of course*. But they were the ones firing missiles into the heart of Tel Aviv, after all, weren't they? And now Sarah's screwing one of them. Why would she do this to you? And so soon before you finish your MBA? Sarah's dad's going to have a heart attack. And Arthur, Arthur's going to go ballistic. Arthur does not take well to insubordination from those he accepts into his ranks. You'll stand behind Arthur laughing as he deports his brown ass back to Gaza! Not that that's necessarily what you want, no. What do you want? You want revenge. You want confrontation. And what else, what else? You want to beat him bloody, that's what else. Sarah. Sarah. Why? And with *him*. She doesn't know, but you'd gone out and bought an engagement ring—the diamonds conflict-free, what a joke!—and were just waiting for the right time to propose; you had called her father to ask his permission, had gone over to his beautiful Hampstead house and had a beer, toasting to your future together. And then those bastard gossips in the kitchen had to go and ruin everything. You're seething. You've never felt like this before. All your life, you've done everything right, and now this. Everybody knew. They were all laughing at you—even Arthur probably knew. You'll get them. You'll show them all. You're a great guy, a great, great guy with a good job and seven-eighths of an MBA. Didn't you dig yourself out of poverty, wasn't the future yours, weren't you going to give her everything—a big house, a safe, powerful car, jewellery? Oh my God you love her so much. *Loved* her so much—right? Oh Christ. You can't shake the image of her caressing his arm, disappearing down the stairs; it's scarred onto your soul. Why would Sarah do this to you? What, in your entire life, have you done to deserve this?

David stops, takes a breath. He's at the restaurant.

Friday night, David came by the restaurant. It had been a quiet shift, overcast and blustery outside the glazed windows. The usual house music was on the stereo, and I was missing more than ever the light jazz of La Retro. Samir had been even more quiet, more gruff, than usual, his face covered in sweat. I had called Arthur the night before and asked him to come by the restaurant before he went to La Retro. I figured I owed it to him to quit in person. It was just me, Samir, and Julie when David stormed in, walked right up to the till, and asked, "How could you?"

His eyes were on fire, like I'd never seen them before. Did he know?

"What, what do you mean? How could I what?" I asked. I glanced at Samir, who was standing behind the counter, his back straight, his chest out, his eyes wet, everything suddenly out in the open. David followed my eyes, stamped his foot like a tantruming child.

"And with him? With, fucking, him?!"

David and Samir were glaring at each other. I could feel Julie standing behind me, her hands frozen at her sides. Samir could destroy David if he wanted to, though for all his bluster and vocal hatred, his weight and sweaty face, I was sure he didn't have that kind of violence in him. I felt surprisingly protective of him, wary of the way David was staring at him. How had I stayed with that self-satisfied asshole for so long? All the carefree swagger, the grinning boyishness of when I first met him was gone, and what was left was smugness, entitled, possessive smugness—how had it taken me so long to notice?

"David, it's not—" I began, but David jumped over the counter and lunged at Samir, who pushed David away like a bear shoving off a scarecrow. David pulled back and punched Samir square in the face. Julie was screaming now, and I was yelling at both of them as well, but David continued beating on Samir, punching his torso and arms. Samir was just standing there, taking it, his arms heavy at his side, his face fallen. Eventually David pulled back and clocked him again right in the face, under the left eye. He stopped after that, leaned his body into Samir's, panting, pushing into him with his shoulder. Thank God the small restaurant was empty. Julie, still screaming, grabbed the cordless phone and ran into the back.

"I don't believe you," David said to me, going to sit down at the counter, dropping his head into his hands, his sandy hair leaking through his fingers.

"I'm breaking up with you," I said to David's back. He didn't respond.

I turned to Samir, who had yet to move. His eyes flashed. "I'm quitting, Samir. I didn't know how to tell you." It was true, I hadn't known how to tell him, until now. There was a splatter of blood—Samir's or David's?—bubbling on the glass oven door. "I'm sorry," I added, softly.

"I'm going for a cigarette," he said, coming back to life, sidestepping the counter, going out, his body touching mine but not quite. "Watch the oven timer for me, please." His face was unreadable.

I was standing in the middle of the restaurant, at a loss. The techno CD had started to skip violently, the beat fragmented into an endless drilling barrage.

"I'm going away for a while," I said to David, not keeping the anger out of my voice.

"Go fuck yourself," he said into his arms.

I wanted to go and change the CD track, but I was stuck; I couldn't move. I glanced at the empty phone cradle, at the indeterminate shape of Samir standing outside the opaque windows, at the clock over the till. An hour and fifteen minutes before I could start closing up.

Arthur would be here any minute.

Amsterdam

The night before the three of them left Frankfurt, Greg woke up
covered in bugs. When Josh and Barry found him the next morning,
he was sleeping on the hostel common room's rutted couch, a sheet
of newspaper for a blanket, a Blue Jays hat covering his face. An hour
later, waiting for their train, he told them the story: after smacking the
little monsters off him and bolting from the room with a shriek, the
door had swung shut and locked behind him. Naked except for his
boxer shorts, keyless, he had gone downstairs to ask to be let back in.
He had found the receptionist sitting at the bar, staring at the crackling
storm outside the window. She slowly turned to face him, but he could
not get her to understand that he was locked out of his room, and after
ten minutes he had given up and gone to the couch.

"She must have been whacked out on something," Greg
concluded, the three of them sitting on a bench at their platform, their
rucksacks and day bags heaped beside them, "just a complete inability
to communicate."

Josh was laughing, shaking his head. He half didn't believe Greg,
though there was no reason to call him out on it—the image of him
half-naked on that couch, everybody sitting around him eating their
complimentary breakfasts, was enough.

"You should've knocked," said Barry, laughing so hard he was
almost crying.

"What, and disturb your nightly wet dream?" Greg said,
precipitating a swift shoulder punch from Barry.

"Etai sure didn't have a problem waking me the last night at the
kibbutz," Josh said. He told them again about being woken up to find
the serious-faced soldier leaning over him in his dark green uniform.
"Please let me have the room, Joshua," he had said in his accented
English. "Please. I am so horny." Josh had looked over Etai's shoulder

and seen Jordana, one of the girls on their trip, sitting timidly in a chair, her hands folded shyly in her lap, though he knew she wanted the room as badly as Etai did—about to bag an Israeli soldier, it was her lucky night.

"What happened with you and Shoshi, anyways?" Greg asked Barry.

Barry shrugged, grinned, released the shrug. "We dealt," he said.

"Bastard, nothing like a stacked Israeli girl with a semi-automatic," Greg said. "Fuck, what a country!" he added, slapping his jeans. Josh experienced the wave of uneasiness that, for the week they had been in Europe, rose up in his gut whenever Greg—and, to a lesser extent, Barry—brought up Israel. He shrugged it off. Greg put his head back, closed his eyes. "Let's just hope those tiny fuckers didn't lay eggs in our clothes," he said into the open air of the station.

A moment later, the train pulled up and they got on. They were now pointed, more or less, towards Amsterdam. Ever since the three of them had gotten accepted on the same Birthright Israel trip and decided to extend their return flight by two weeks, it was Amsterdam they had planned for, had talked incessantly about in their dorm rooms, had dreamed of. The fifteen days in Israel (the ten of the free trip plus another five in a hostel in Tel Aviv), the five nights in Paris and two in Frankfurt were all just preamble to this morning, the impending journey, and the following five days. Josh had planned the trip like this on purpose, to end with an extravagant blow-out in Amsterdam before flying back to Israel and heading home. The air tingled with excitement.

Twenty minutes and the train would leave the station.

A group of girls in the four-seater across the aisle were talking animatedly over their assortment of artisan meats, cheeses, and crackers spread out on their tray table. "These girls with their accents," Barry said, louder than necessary, grinning.

"Don't be fooled," Greg said in a forceful whisper, eyeing the girls as he stuffed his day pack under his seat, "they're the granddaughters of Nazis, after all." He sat up straight, stretched his hands above his head. "Fuckin' Germany," he declared, "why did we ever come here?"

The train started to move. Barry closed his eyes. As usual, he would sleep until they arrived. Josh stared at Greg, trying to decide if his oldest friend was being more obnoxious than usual, or if Josh was just extra anxious because this was the longest he had gone without smoking weed since he was thirteen. Sunlight flooded the car. Barry started to snore. "We're off," Josh said.

They exited the train station and found themselves in a large stone plaza, thousands of tiny leaves swirling low to the ground. From where they stood, the city opened out before them, each street a waterslide into the unknown. Josh took a napkin of handwritten directions out of his jeans pocket, and they crossed the plaza, entering the city.

At the hostel, a nondescript townhouse close to the station, there was a large clump of people at the counter waiting to check in with the owner, who was an Arab doppelganger of Jon Stewart. When their turn came, Josh signed them in, ignoring Greg's obvious discomfort, hoisted his bag, and led the way up to their room, Barry and Greg clomping behind him on the carpeted stairs. It was only the three of them in the six-bed room. Two of the bunk beds were in an alcove with a window opening onto an airshaft, the third against the opposite wall, a table and two chairs in between. Josh tossed his rucksack onto one of the bottom bunks in the alcove, and Greg slid his onto the bed opposite. Barry stayed by the door, dancing from foot to foot.

"Dudes, let's go. We can unpack later," he said.

Greg and Josh turned from their bags.

"All right," Josh said, "but I have to fill my water up."

"Ugh, *fine*," Barry said.

"We're close now, boys—imagine how sweet it's going to be," Josh said, mussing Barry's hair. "I don't think this city's prepared for what's about to be unleashed on them."

"Ah Joshie, you got our backs, don't you?" Barry said, grinning widely, giving a little dance.

The kitchen was a floor up from their dorm and looked brand new. Shiny appliances, long wooden counters, red-tiled floor and backsplash—it didn't fit at all with the rest of the hostel's carpet-and-peeling-paint aesthetic. It was empty except for a group of seven blond-haired guys sitting at the long wooden table at the far end of the kitchen, playing a game with many decks of cards and boxes of wine, laughing hysterically every time a card was played.

Greg opened the fridge and peered inside. Josh filled up his Nalgene. Barry stayed near the door and fidgeted with the drawstring of his sweatshirt, giving a start whenever the blond card players erupted with laughter. Still convulsing with giggles, they started speaking in a fast, guttural tongue. Greg looked at Barry over the door of the fridge. "Germans," he mouthed, his face an exaggerated mixture of hatred and silliness. Josh tightened the lid of his water bottle. Greg shut the fridge. They turned and filed down the stairs.

A block and a half from the hostel, they found what they were looking for: The Koala Cafe. They entered on a surge of rising excitement, nervous as if they were back at the park behind their elementary school smoking their first joints. The cafe was darkly lit, with patrons huddled in the booths along the back and slow reggae on the sound system. The girl behind the counter looked up as they approached, her eyes icy with apathy. A sign hanging next to the menu said in three languages, "No outside food or drink. No tobacco in joints."

"Uh, I'll take a gram of the Jack Hare," Josh said, looking at the menu. "You know what, make it two grams." The girl weighed it out, put it in a baggie, and handed it to Josh in exchange for his crisp euros, all without looking directly at him. Greg bought two grams of Red Sugar; Barry bought two of Blueberry Daze, and they split a pack of extra-long Skunk rolling papers.

They sat at a booth near the front, under a low-hanging lamp giving off thick orange light. Josh and Greg watched as Barry, with shaking hands, his hood off and sleeves rolled, broke up the weed, licked two papers together into an *L*, and rolled the joint. He used a strip of the cover of his Eurorail pass for a filter. When he finished, he held it under the lamp and turned it in his fingers. "Not my best," he said. He put the twisted end in his mouth and bit off the tip, spitting the extra paper onto the table.

He put the joint—their first in three excruciating weeks—on his lips and leaned in for the waiting flame of Greg's lighter.

After they left the cafe, they continued their walk away from the hostel.

"Ah, back to normal," Barry exclaimed, throwing his arms around Josh and Greg.

Josh chuckled slowly. "A bit more normal than usual."

"Imagine cafes like that in Canada!" Greg said, laughing.

They found themselves on a street lined with storefront restaurants, the sidewalks and cobblestone road thronging with tourists in thin rain jackets. A light rain tickled their faces. Greg stopped at a fry shack, ordered a cone of fries with mayo and a Coke. "Terrible dry mouth," he said, drinking half the cold red can with the first raise. The three of them finished the greasy packet before the end of the block. Barry proceeded to get a slice of pizza; Josh got another cone of fries and a dry falafel. Another round of Cokes. More pizza. They stood on the street eating, their hoods up.

Within forty-five minutes, they were in another cafe, rolling up the last of the weed. After reading the laminated menu aloud to Greg and Barry, Josh bought three grams of Prolix, a "stoney sativa-indica blend," and they were off. The stone streets began to fan out and connect to each other in a system that was both unintelligible and hilarious, the canals long strips of grumbling blue water. The fronts of the tall, many-windowed houses leaned forward at slight angles, the triangular brick roofs topped off with rusty hooks hanging from oxidized pulleys. They walked through crowded streets, bought a half dozen fresh stroopwafels, then, amazed at their sugary softness, bought another three batches. They laughed into the moist air, got high again and again, took turns pronouncing street names. Keizersgracht. Huidenstraat. Nieuwezijds Voorburgwal. Damstraat. Sour Diesel. White Widow. Big Buddha Cheese. Love Potion #1. Spirit of Amsterdam.

After aimlessly walking the city for the entire afternoon, they found themselves on the outskirts of the red-light district. The rain had stopped, and the sun was out. Still daytime, the district's main drag felt like any other of Amsterdam's canal-seamed thoroughfares: a jumbled mixture of commercial and residential, the buildings old, narrow, and tall, arched bridges connecting the two sides of the street. But the other streets did not have scantily clad prostitutes posing behind glass windows. Josh, Barry, and Greg walked down the drag barely able to control their eyes or their mouths.

Barry, who had been walking ahead, stopped at a window kitty-corner to a wide, curved bridge near the bottom of the street. Josh and Greg came up on either side of him: sitting on a three-legged stool was a woman in a red bikini top. A white blanket was over her legs, but her calves were in view, as well as the four-inch pumps she had on. There was also a clear view of her room: sparsely furnished, a bed with a thin mattress to her left, to her right a sink and a little counter with a teapot and a stack of books; what looked like a spice rack was mounted to the wall. The curtains that framed the window were black velvet and were tied back with thick black rope.

She smiled at the staring boys, tilting her head from side to side, making her hair swing against her face. Barry blew her a kiss, and the woman put her hand on the window, caught it in a closed fist, and put the fist between her legs, giggling inaudibly behind the glass. Startled, they scampered off.

Without a map, very, very high, getting back to their hostel was near impossible. In the end, Josh led them back to Centraal station—businessmen and newcomers mingling in the early evening light, their shoes clicking on the grey stone—and they retraced their steps from earlier in the day.

"Did you see the breasts on that one in the red?" Barry said as they stamped up the stairs. "I'd have her sit on my face and sing the national anthem." He got no response as they entered the kitchen, which was empty except for the Germans from earlier, who turned their blond heads to look at the three of them before going back to their cards. The boxes of wine had been replaced by cans of Amstel Light, and there was a girl with them now, wearing blue overalls and unlaced brown work boots. One of them—tall, lanky, a mop of sandy hair—was at the stove making hamburgers. The meat was in an enormous stainless steel bowl, and he was cooking them in a thick pool of oil on three separate pans, taking up the entire stovetop.

Barry and Greg collapsed on the couches near the TV, and Josh went to fill a glass with water. The burgers were cooking noisily, the smell of oily onions thick in Josh's nose.

Draining the water in three gulps, Josh slumped onto the couch, and the three of them sat for a while in stupefied silence, listening to the Germans eat and laugh. Barry's eyes were wide open. Josh's fluttered from closed to nearly closed. Greg was asleep. As the windows darkened, the kitchen filled with people. Josh heard, as if in a dream, French, Spanish, and Australian and British English being spoken. His head filled with the sharp sounds of vegetables being cut, food being fried, cabinets opening and closing, toasters dinging, wine glasses clinking, someone asking someone else to please pass the colander, with the smells of garlic, burning toast, smoked and unsmoked weed, the watermelony shower products wafting from the wet hair of the girls getting dressed for a night on the town.

As those with freshly prepared meals sat down around them, their plates on their laps, Josh, Barry, and Greg escaped to their dark dorm room and passed out on their unmade beds. They woke around ten, groggy and disoriented, climbed into their sweatshirts, and ventured out into their first Amsterdam night. The hostel manager was sitting at his desk watching a soccer game on a tiny television, his face a concentrated frown.

The next morning, they were up just in time to catch breakfast. Discovering that the kitchen was cordoned off for cleaning, they followed the stream of hostel guests to the ground floor. They loaded up their faded pink trays and sat down next to two Japanese girls who smelled of baby wipes.

"Remember those Israeli breakfasts we were eating a few weeks ago?" Barry asked, his mouth full of crumbly egg. "Three kinds of fresh cheese, all that finely diced salad, scrambled eggs, and those olives, those olives, fuck I'm going to cum in my pants!"

"Shut up," Josh said. He hadn't started eating yet, was cutting his egg into slices and making two open-faced sandwiches on his toasted pieces of whole wheat. Greg was spreading jam on a blueberry muffin. A big screen at the back of the eating area had on the international news, though the sound was off. "Don't mind him,"

Josh said to the girls, reaching over to grab the salt. The girls giggled, glancing at each other.

"What's planned for today?" Greg asked, tearing into his muffin.

"I thought we'd check out that house where Anne Frank lived," Josh said, cutting his sandwiches in half.

"What? Are you serious?!"

"Why wouldn't we?" Josh asked as he chewed. "We went to the Jewish museum in Paris, not to mention everything we did in Israel."

Greg made a face. "Yeah, but I know what happened to Anne Frank. She was murdered by animal monsters. What more is there to know?"

Josh looked down at his breakfast. Greg usually didn't give two shits what they got up to, as long as there was weed.

"Fuck yeah, let's do it," Barry said, breaking the impasse. "I'd love to check out Anne's old digs." He spoke as if he and Anne Frank were old friends, had known each other since kindergarten. Raising his fist, he smashed the eggshells on his otherwise empty tray, rose, and sprinted up the stairs. They packed their day bags and left the hostel, stopping at The Koala Cafe to smoke a joint—a blend of everything leftover from yesterday—before crossing a series of canals and emerging onto Prinsengracht, where, a block later, they stopped at the end of a long line. "This must be it," Josh said.

"Hold our spot, J-sauce; we'll be back in a few," Barry said, taking Greg by the arm and walking down the street.

Josh looked around. They were in a nicer part of town, the townhouses austere, the canal wide and calm, the sky soft and blue. Staring into the pates of the two elderly women in front of him, Josh found himself back on the beaches of Tel Aviv. It was only twenty days ago that he had first seen them: It was the second or third day of the trip, and everybody had just met. No one had slept since their plane landed, they had already drunk enough vodka to satiate an army, and it was their first scheduled free time. Half an hour in the sand. Josh was coming out of the sea when he noticed two kids kicking around a soccer ball on the beach. They were wearing jeans and white t-shirts, were barefoot, and were yelling at each other in what could only have been Arabic. The older Israeli women sunning themselves nearby—they could have been the same women in front of him now—did not look happy, and, when Josh was back on his towel and the kids' ball rolled into the sunbathers, they had started yelling at the kids in angry Hebrew before packing up their stuff and huffing off. Everyone on Josh's trip, including the leaders and tour guides, looked away. Later, as Josh was rolling up his towel, two uniformed police officers and a soldier had walked onto the beach and started talking to the two Palestinian kids, who listened silently, their faces both terrified and defiant. The cops were talking in low voices, pointing towards the water, then towards the high-rises of the city. Eventually they took them by the arms and led them up past the showers onto the boardwalk and out of sight. No one on the trip mentioned it, though Josh knew they had all seen it.

Josh was pulled from his reminiscing by the reappearance of Barry and Greg. Greg had his sweatshirt around his arm and was absently scratching his elbow. Barry grinned, his eyes glazed pink, the pupils metallic mirrors. He pulled Josh out of the line, which had branched out considerably while they had been gone. "C'mon, man. Greg will hold our spot." Greg smiled sagely, and they were off.

Barry took Josh halfway up the street and into a coffee shop that had a designated smoking area, a small glassed-in room near the entrance. It was nothing more than a glorified telephone booth, with three stools, a high narrow shelf, and a mirrored wall. Barry nodded at the bearded man behind the bar as if they had worked out some kind of agreement, and he and Josh went into the booth.

"What's that?" Josh asked as Barry took a dime bag of fine brown-coloured powder out of his jeans pocket.

"This is Icealator hash—remember, I bought it off that slick Italian guy at that retrofitted castle place last night?"

"Can't say I have a recollection of any of those things."

Barry was already sprinkling some of the hash onto the marijuana he had arranged on a doublewide paper. "Combine with a little Apple Jack, and you have a nice, pungent salad." It had been a little over twenty-four hours, and Barry was back to spinning joints out like an automated factory. He rolled, he licked, he twisted, he ran his fingers along its length, and it was in his mouth and on fire.

Coughing, grinning, tiny curlicues of black smoke wisping off the end of the joint, he handed it to Josh. "It's made from ice. Ach, ach. Ninety-eight percent THC," he said through the smoke.

"How did you and Carol end things?" Josh asked, ashing the joint.

"She lives in Calgary, man, that's how we ended things. Besides, I think she knew about Shoshi."

Josh looked at the spliff before putting it in his mouth. He saw Shoshi in her army fatigues, standing on a rock in the desert, machine gun strapped on her shoulder, backlit by the sun. Everything that happened during those ten sleepless days was beginning to clamour for attention.

"God, could that girl give head," Barry said, looking wistful.

Josh nodded, not knowing which girl he had meant, the Albertan or the Israeli.

He inhaled deeply.

By the time they got back, Greg was almost at the front of the line. "Why are your arms all red?" Barry asked. Greg shrugged. He was moving his mouth slowly, his hands twitching against his jeans.

The old ladies ahead of them entered the museum, tittering to each other, and a minute later Josh, Greg, and Barry paid their twelve euros and ascended the staircase as well. The museum was busy and slow moving, visitors walking through the exhibits, following the predetermined route through the house and around the secret annex before being spit out downstairs at a bookshop and a small theatre. It was very quiet.

At the top of the first staircase, the three of them separated, like they had done at every museum or art gallery they'd entered since landing in Europe. Barry glanced at the glass display cases and skimmed the explanatory notes as he weaved through and maneuvered around the elderly Americans, Japanese families, and camera-laden Europeans. He was through the stuffy museum in record time, sat in the kids' theatre, and slept through a video on human rights two and a half times while waiting for Greg and Josh.

Greg staggered around, unable to focus on the exhibits, hot bodies crowding around him. The confined air squeezing his brain, he bumped into a middle-aged man with a sky-blue kippah and wet eyes. The man looked up at Greg, startled. Greg shook his head in apology, turned, and bolted down the one-way stairs, crashing through the crowd; he burst through the entrance and onto the street, running down Prinsengracht at full gallop until he stopped at a fancy white bridge, panting, bent over, completely lost.

Josh took his time, floating above the dioramas, the short blurbs on the Frank family and the occupation of Holland. He stood in front of the family portraits, the pages from the original journal, transfixed, the faces and words resonating with profound meaning. He had read the journal in high school, and parts of it came back to him now: Anne's dislike for her mother, her ability to write about her inner life at the same time as she painted full pictures of the circumscribed world of the secret annex. What would Anne Frank have made of *her* Birthright trip? Josh thought, staring at her black-and-white image—the pre-dawn hike up Masada, the colour-coded map hanging at the front of the bus, the soldiers and their stories that made the guys and girls alike wet, the tour guides and their particular view of things. In the attic, overcome with uncomfortable emotion, he felt like he was about to fall off of a precipice, collapse into the undulating hordes pushing into the small space. When a hungry and sleepy-eyed Barry finally found him, he was signing the guestbook, sweating, fellow patrons walking past with their bookshop bags.

Back at the hostel, Josh went straight for the kitchen. He was still soaring from Barry's ice hash, and he needed water, bad. Topping the stairs, which he took two at a time, he smelled something buttery cooking; sure enough, the resident Germans were at their usual table, their lanky leader cranking out towers of coaster-sized pancakes.

Josh nodded slowly as he went towards the sink. They were talking about him, he was sure. Did they dislike him because they thought he was American? Did they know how high he was? Did they really come to Amsterdam to cook and play cards in a hostel kitchen?

Josh opened the cupboard and fumbled for a cup. His elbow connected with a dirty wine glass perched on the counter, and it fell off, shattering across the red tiles.

The Germans stopped their chattering and joined Josh in contemplating the shards.

"I've got it," the cook said, running over to the closet and pulling out a broom.

"Oh, thanks, yeah." Josh watched him sweep up the broken glass before ducking out of the kitchen and going back to their dorm room. He hadn't gotten a drink. His mouth was Styrofoam.

Barry was sitting at the small table, sorting bags of weed. Josh searched through his rucksack and sat down on his bed, Nalgene in hand. "Have you seen Greg?" he asked, taking a slug of the warm, briny water. All he wanted to do was lie down, get some sleep between himself and that house, reset the strange mood he had fallen into.

"He's in the shower," Barry said.

The door opened, and Greg came in, a white towel around his torso, his hair dripping wet. "Sorry about that, boys. That place really freaked me out. Those fucking murderers."

Josh grabbed his kit bag and towel from the top bunk, and the door shut to the sound of Barry's laughter, a joint in his upturned fingers.

In the shower, steeping in the hot water, Josh found himself continuing his daydream from earlier, still unbidden but now, alone and calmed down, not unpleasant. Anne Frank on Birthright. He imagined her arriving at the airport, shy but ridiculously perceptive, watching as the group solidified along clique and gender lines. He imagined Anne enduring the twelve-hour flight that ended in cheering and clapping as the plane touched down on supposedly sacred asphalt. He imagined Anne being whisked directly from the airport to Independence Hall, the video clip of Ben-Gurion declaring the state leading off an afternoon of speeches. The first day so crammed with museums and stories it was hard to keep it all straight. Three nights in Jerusalem, three in the north, four in the south, the seven soldiers arriving on the fifth day and staying until the ninth. The highly constrained journey through the Old City, the bullet holes, the lavish breakfasts, the ubiquity of machine guns, the night at the Bedouin tent, the warm desert wind, the serious sunrise conversations: Josh followed Anne through it all, distantly aware that this was, by far, the strangest sexual fantasy he had ever had (if that was even what this was).

Anne Frank not fitting in with the boys and their antics, their vodka, their drooling over the sunkissed Israeli women. Anne Frank asking their guide questions that he did not want to answer. Anne Frank the only one awake as the bus sped through the desert night, writing furiously in her journal. Anne Frank unsatisfied with the tours, the sights, the explanations. Anne Frank swimming in the mineral pools in Tiberias, all of them laughing and splashing in the shelf of water pulled out over the nighttime city, the lights from boats on the Kinneret blinking like stars, feeling for the first time in ten days the possibility of belonging.

Rinsing the shampoo out of his hair and lathering his arms, Josh was completely captive to the fantasy. Would Anne have fallen in love with the kibbutz they spent two nights on, the kind, old, weathered Israeli who gave them a tour of the banana grove? Would Anne have slept with a soldier? Would Anne have cried at the Western Wall, crammed into the small section set aside for the women? Would Anne have spoken up when the tour guide called the Dome of the Rock an "abomination"? Would Anne have let those soldiers drag those Palestinian kids off the beach without saying something, without doing something, without feeling something?

Anne would have known what to make of it all, Josh was sure, the beauty and the falseness, the heat and the separation, the sense that the Israel they were being shown was only the showroom of a very big house, the walls painted brightly, everything arranged just so, signs everywhere forbidding them, under any circumstances, from venturing into the attic, sneaking into the basement.

The water lost its heat, and within seconds Josh was being burned with cold. He pushed off the water and stepped out of the shower: clean, more-or-less sober, oddly satiated (even though he hadn't jacked off), thoroughly, unavoidably exhausted.

Their fourth and final night in Amsterdam and they were at a long rectangular table on the second floor of Third Bird, a large bar-coffee shop hybrid. They were many Heinekens into the night.

In the past two days, they had wandered far and wide. They ate their way down the winding spine of Chinatown, joined the bike lanes on rented yellow cruisers and pedalled through Vondelpark, stopping to smoke up at every lake, bench, and hill. Yesterday, standing on the street outside of a stone-walled library with a massive wooden door, having decided to skip the ridiculous ticket price and long wait of the Van Gogh museum, a local, her arms loaded with paper grocery bags, spat at their feet as she sidestepped around them. They smoked Master Kush at Hunters, Chocolope and Edelweiss at Grassroots. They vaporized Shark's Breath (Jamaican Lambsbread crossed with Great White Shark) at Flight Zone, smoked blunts of Desert Storm followed by pipe hoots of G13 at Bermuda with a group of affable Californians, did gravity bong hits of Kali Mist in their room, exhaling out the window, munching on stroopwafles. And every time they strolled through the red-light district, they would stop at the window across from the bridge, stare at the closed black curtains—"She's probably at her singing lessons," Greg would say, beginning to yodel, badly, as they walked off, Barry lingering behind before running to catch up.

Now, at Third Bird, Josh and Greg were talking to two Australian girls they had met on their way back from the bathroom.

"It's our last night in Europe," Josh was saying.

"Yeah, tomorrow we fly back to Israel, kick it for two days, and then back home for us," Greg said.

The girl with the straight brown hair, Remy, began to say something, but Josh interrupted her—"How much longer are you girls out for?"

"Well," began Alice, the one with wavy brown hair, "we've been in Europe for eight months. Two more to go, then on to Thailand for another two, then back to Oz to start uni."

"What's in Israel?" Remy said, as if it were the moon.

"Noth—" Josh began, but Greg started talking over him.

"We were in Israel on a free trip, and then we just extended our return tickets for a few weeks so we could come over here. Basically, a pretty sweet deal, though I can't wait to get back."

"Isn't it, like, really dangerous out there?"

"Nah, not really." Greg said. "Actually, it's paradise. That's what this whole trip was about, you know? To find out how the homeland keeps the world safe for us. And because we're Jewish, it's our right to be able to visit Israel, to live there, whenever we want—"

Josh sprang forward. "That's not exactly true," he said, almost yelling. Looking a little shocked, he sat back. "The paradise thing, I mean."

The girls nodded, glancing at each other. Greg looked blankly at Josh, who quickly began downing the rest of his pint.

Barry came up behind the two of them, smacking their backs. "Hey, boys—*hello*, ladies—I'm bored; let's go to the red-light district!" Josh and Greg made no immediate signs of movement. "Let's go! Let's go! Let's go!" Barry cheered, lifting them off their seats. The Australian girls half smiled.

"Bye!" Barry hollered, grinning full throttle, before they disappeared down the stairs.

"My arms are itching like crazy," Greg said as they walked the cobblestones of the district. It was after midnight, and the street was alive, in full disco-revelry, bass pounding out of windows, pink light bouncing off the sidewalks and shining on the water.

"Maybe it's that pot brownie you ate finally kicking in."

"Maybe it's those bugs from Frankfurt," Josh said, throwing it at him like an insult. They were yelling over the music and laughter.

"I fucking hope not. And hey, why did you go and blow it with those girls?"

"Me? You were being an asshole."

"Man, what's with you? Are you ashamed of being Jewish or something?"

"What? Not at all."

"What don't you get? If the Germans and Arabs had their way, we'd all be long gone by now—it's like our tour leader said, without a strong Israel, what's to prevent our enemies from picking up right where they left off?"

Josh stopped walking. He was so infuriated that he wanted to take a swing at Greg. He thought again of the beach in Tel Aviv, the cops taking those Palestinian kids away—if this was what

Josh was allowed to see, imagine what was going on *beyond* the circumscribed walls of Birthright? He thought of Anne Frank, his constant companion the past three days. He was sure she would side with him, not Greg. Until recently Josh—like Barry, like Greg, like everybody he knew—had taken at face value everything he had been taught about Israel. But almost from the second he arrived that started to change. For Greg, however, it seemed to have had the opposite effect. Josh looked at Greg, already less angry. He wished he had the words to explain.

Barry was jogging back towards them.

"Man, you've been acting weird ever since we got here," Greg said finally, slapping his jeans in frustration.

"Whoa, boys, chill, chill," Barry said, bringing them in with his arms, propelling them forward. "You both have been acting a little spaced out, ha ha. Who knew you were such lightweights, eh?"

Josh opened his mouth, but Barry brought them to a sudden stop. They were at the window belonging to the woman in the red bikini. Her curtains were open; there she was, in the same bikini top, looking bored. Barry took his arms off Josh and Greg and took a small step forward.

The woman, spotting the boys gawking at her window, got off her stool, opened her door and stuck her head out. "C'mon, big boy," she said in accented English. "I'll give you a deal if you bring your two friends."

The three of them looked around. Barry took another step, Josh and Greg followed, and together they stumbled through the open door.

The small room was warm and smelled like perfume and disinfectant, a mixture that Josh found powerfully intoxicating. The three of them stood awkwardly, at a loss as to what to do. None of them could look directly at her as she closed and locked the door. "You're ... very beautiful," Barry said, his eyes on the floor, the shyest Josh had ever seen him. She was young and pretty, with pale skin and curly black hair, not at all what they would have expected, more like someone they would have a crush on back home, if slightly older. Being there with her in her little room was unlike anything Josh had experienced before. He felt stuck in place.

"What are you reading?" Barry asked, stealing a glance at her. Josh hadn't noticed before, but there was a thick hardcover library book on the small nightstand; he tilted his head and read the title: *The Hannah Arendt Reader.*

"Oh, that? It's nothing, hot stuff. Just homework."

"You're in school?" Greg asked, speaking for the first time since entering her room.

She laughed at his astonishment. "If you must know, I'm doing my master's degree at Hamburg. I am here for a semester exchange."

"You're, you're German?"

She laughed again. "Something like that," she said, running her hand down Barry's arm as she stepped past him.

"What's your name?" Barry asked, his eyes back on the floor.

Pulling the curtains closed on the neon canal with a flourish, she said her name, and Josh blinked, almost falling down. "P-pardon?" he asked.

"My name is Fran," she said, but it was too late, Josh's mind had already taken off.

Fran sat down on the bed, and Barry went and sat down next to her. Josh and Greg stayed standing next to the window. Josh's face was white, and his mouth was slack (though his mind was whirring); Greg scratched his arms, looking half at Fran, half at the floor.

Barry cautiously moved his hand onto Fran's leg. Fran put a finger in her mouth and pulled her lower lip, a practised gesture that electrified the already tense room. "So what is it going to be, fifty euros for fifteen minutes or a hundred and fifty for an hour?"

Anne listening intently. Anne writing shorthand in her journal. Anne raising her face to the sun.

Fran laughed, grabbed Barry's hand, and placed it on her breast. "Look. Your friends are ready," she said, giggling, motioning towards Josh and Greg.

Anne looking out the bus window at dilapidated villages, huts made out of cardboard and tires. Anne sneaking into the Arab Quarter, the soldiers in green fatigues standing in twos, guns that stretched from their knees to their chins, meeting a friendly shopkeeper, buying a thin silver chain. Anne writing "birthright" over and over and over again in her journal until the word lost all meaning.

Barry stood up, exhaled, and unzipped his pants.

Anne cracking through the bright, loud surface. Anne rising above the noise, the arguments, the cacophony. Anne understanding.

A sudden flurry of movement yanked Josh from his fantasy. Greg had started to flip out—he was jumping up and down, flailing his arms, screaming in high-pitched bursts. Josh dove, trying to move out of the way, but Greg crashed into him anyways; Josh dominoed into Barry, Barry slammed into Fran, Fran screamed and shoved Barry off, scampering onto the bed as Barry spilled backwards, cracking his head on the side of the sink.

At the sound of Barry hitting the porcelain everyone stopped. Josh looked at Greg, who was standing with one hand on the doorknob, and then at Fran, who had reached out for the black doorbell-like button on the wall, her fingers hovering over it, her bikini top almost off. They stared at each other. Barry moaned from the floor.

"What's wrong with you, Greg?!" Josh screamed, jumping off the bed.

"Bugs—I saw a bug on the floor—I'm covered in them! I'm sorry, man, I gotta, I gotta …" Greg opened the door and tumbled onto the street, the noise of merrymaking reaching Josh's ears before the door fell shut again.

Josh turned to Fran. "Listen, I'm sorry. Greg's—my friend's a little, a little fucked up. All right? Right?" Fran looked at the door. She took her hand off the alarm, straightened up, and pulled the straps of her bikini back over her shoulders.

"Hey, what did you say? Fifty euros for twenty minutes? Here, here's a hundred, okay? We'll go now. We'll go." Josh put the money down on the bed. Fran brushed her hair out of her eyes; Josh pulled Barry to his feet. Barry stood, his eyes open, a gash on his head that was bleeding through his hair.

"Is he going to be okay?" she asked, half-closing her eyes in doubt. She went to the sink and filled the kettle with water.

"What? Yeah, he'll be fine." Josh was opening the door.

"You should watch that one," she said, rinsing her hands under the running water. "You can't just let the mirage of this city get the best of you, eh—you understand? Amsterdam is smoke and mirrors, smoke and—"

"Yeah, I know, okay? Thanks, sorry, bye."

Outside on the street, there was no sign of Greg. Josh put his arm around Barry and started in the direction of the hostel, pushing through the crowds until breaking onto a quiet side street.

"Are you all right, man? Should I take you to the hospital?"

"And sit there all night? No, thank you. I'm fine; I just need a washcloth and a joint." Barry started laughing, real rolls of the stuff pealing out of him. "What the fuck were we doing in there, man! That girl had fucking upper-arm strength! And that red fuckin' bikini!" He was grinning.

Barry might have been having the time of his life, but Josh wasn't feeling too hot: all at once everything rose through him in a tremendous swoosh of sickness. He let go of Barry and barrelled into an alley and began violently throwing up against the wall.

As he hurled out five days of fried food and weed and beer, a window flew open above him, and a cowboy hat popped out, the accompanying head lost in shadow. "You're not for fucking serious!" a Welsh accent shouted down at him from behind the hat.

"Hey, man, fuck off," Barry hollered back at him.

"Bloody Americans, don't know when to stop," Welsh hat said, slamming the window shut.

"We're Canadian, jackass!" Barry yelled.

Josh eventually stopped yakking, and the two of them stumbled back to the hostel, Barry's hand on his bloodied head, Josh's mouth and nose rank with burnt marijuana and vomit, the triangled houses' odd angles throwing wide shadows across the cobblestones.

Back at the hostel, the dorm room was empty. Barry fell into the chair, and Josh got onto his bed, kicking at the unmade sheets that were already bunched up at the bottom. There were jeans everywhere, t-shirts, towels, food containers, the sugary sparkle of marijuana crystals. Barry had duct-taped a rolled-up sock onto the side of his head.

They sat as if underwater until the door swung open. Josh sat up with a start, and Barry turned his head. Greg came into the room, in a white towel, kitbag in hand.

"Look who it is, the exterminator," Barry said.

Greg looked much better. "Sorry dudes, that pot brownie got right on top of me. I majorly freaked out."

"I'm going to get some water," Josh said, pushing past him. He marched down the hall and up the stairs. The kitchen was empty except for the Germans, sitting at the table, playing their cards. The brown-haired girl was at the stove with the tall, lanky one, making grilled cheese sandwiches in two pans. They both had a spatula in one hand and an oven mitt on the other.

"Rough night?" she said to Josh as he filled up his water.

"What? Oh, no, not really ..."

"Would you like a sandwich?" she asked, holding one out on her spatula.

"Yeah, why not?" Josh said. One of their friends at the table pulled back a chair and Josh sat down.

"Where are you guys from?" Josh asked, taking a large bite of the buttery grilled cheese.

"Belgium," one of them said. The whole table rocked with laughter.

"We're all the children of farmers!" another one said. They all laughed again.

Josh ate the rest of his sandwich in silence. When they tried to deal him in, he shook his hand, no, thanks. He got up, said goodnight, and made for the stairs. He felt sick, idiotic, useless, terrified. What did he know about Anne Frank? What did he know about Germany, about Amsterdam, about Israel? What did he know about anything? Smoke and mirrors, smoke and mirrors. Back in the dorm room, Barry and Greg were already asleep, the overhead light still on. Josh had never felt more tired in his entire life, too tired to worry about Barry having a possible concussion, too tired to do anything but turn off the light, get into bed, and ride the last dip of the night into unconsciousness, slide into watery dreams of old buildings with heavy wooden doors.

During the taxi ride to the airport, they watched the city flatten into rolling farmland.

"My parents would have killed me if I had to pay a hospital bill," Barry said, ending the silence.

Josh nodded. Greg coughed. They had yet to speak to each other. Barry had thought it wise to remove the duct tape and bloody sock. He had a large, smooth bump where he had hit the sink.

"How much money do you guys have left?" Josh asked.

"Enough for a suite at a nice beachside hotel," Barry said, putting his arms around his two best friends. "We deserve it."

Searching for Crude

Ricky Rosenfeld didn't want an affair. He didn't want a divorce. He didn't want a car fancier or more expensive than the six he already owned. He was already exceedingly successful, already exceedingly wealthy, with a house in the valley and a cottage with three hundred feet of untrammeled shoreline on the second most prestigious lake in Muskoka. So what was it, then, that Ricky Rosenfeld wanted? What was it that had so completely consumed him that he was willing to blow it all on? It was simple: He wanted to be able to pick up a guitar and play howling music—to perform magic, change lives, melt hearts. To not only master the instrument, but for it to master him.

And it was all because of Crude.

Ricky first experienced Crude Franzen during the cocktail hour of his nephew's wedding. He stood at the bar, Trudy beside him talking tennis with his brother and sister-in-law, his two children—back for the weekend from Montreal, mad at him as usual for some inexplicable reason—off with their cousins, and watched the trio of two guitars and a double bass play gypsy jazz in the corner, ill-fitting pink kippahs plopped on their heads. The rhythm guitarist and the bassist were obviously both accomplished musicians, but it was Crude that had Ricky mesmerized: every note sung right through the bullshit and remained humming in Ricky's chest long after Crude's fingers moved on. It was a barrage of tremendous melodies and three-note rushes of chordal harmony, Crude's emotive face smiling throughout. Ricky was entranced. His children, brothers, family friends, business contacts, even the wedding-day radiance of his nephew's new wife—everything was forgotten. For the first time in his life, Ricky felt unsatisfied with what he had accomplished, what he had made of himself—what did any of it matter in the face of such torrential beauty?

After the doors to the banquet hall had opened and as the musicians were packing up their gear, Ricky went up to speak to Crude. Ricky had regular business dealings with the most powerful people in Toronto, had a standing lunch date with the fourth richest man in Taiwan whenever he was in the country, but approaching Crude lazily coiling his patch chords, the pink kippah sitting like a puffball on his head, Ricky was as nervous as a hormonal teenager.

"Hi, uh. I just wanted to say. I really liked your stuff," he said. "It was very ... eye-opening."

Crude looked up. His eyes downright twinkled. "Why, thank you, kind sir," he said.

Ricky stood there. He had to say something else. "Do you, uh, do you have a business card?"

Crude laughed. "No boss, no card. The name's Crude, though." He stuck out his hand, and Ricky shook it; it was rough, calloused. Warm.

"Oh, well here, take mine," Ricky said, reaching into his suit pocket and handing Crude his card: *Ricky Rosenfeld, CEO, Funding Partner*. He had always been proud of the graphic for Masada Assets and Investing, the unscalable heft of the chunky block letters, but as Crude took it from him he became unsure, thought it looked cheap, disposable. Crude took the small piece of cardstock like it was a custom unknown to him, let it drop into his open guitar case. He stared at Ricky, waiting for him to say something so he could get back to packing up. Ricky was trying to decide if he should lavish this man with praise or just keep it cool, swinging wildly between the two alternatives.

An impasse.

"Yeah," Crude said eventually, drawing the word out. "Hey, I'm playing this Tuesday night at the Socialist's Cousin, downtown, if you want to come check it out."

Ricky blinked. "Oh, yeah, great." He started nodding profusely, as if he were making a long series of decisions. "The Socialist's Cousin, got it." They shook hands, and Ricky went to find his wife in the banquet hall. When he came out again an hour later, unable to focus on his brother's speech, which was droning on and on, tired of the scowl his son, Jonah, hadn't failed all night to exhibit when looking Ricky's way, Crude and his bandmates were gone, two chairs and a glass with half-melted ice and a chewed white straw the only things left from their performance.

Trudy had no interest in going to a bar the night before a tennis match, so two nights after his nephew's wedding, Ricky drove down himself, parked on a side street, and walked three blocks too far before backtracking till he found the place.

Calling the Socialist's Cousin a hole-in-the-wall would be gross hyperbole. With its three tables, four feet of bar with five barstools, and a stage the size of a school desk, it was a hole-in-the-ground at best. A hole-in-the-head more like it, Ricky thought as he entered the bar. He sat down on the only available barstool and ordered a gimlet. A half hour later, the bar packed to the rafters, Crude showed up—and judging by the double bass player who had been sitting on the stage impatiently checking his watch, he was late. He had on a black leather jacket over a faded t-shirt, worn Wranglers, and unlaced boots, an outfit that fit him much better than the dress slacks and black button-down he wore at the wedding. A few days' blond-grey stubble textured his face. He was sans kippah. He sat down on the stage, took his beat-up guitar out of its case, slammed back the shot of whiskey the short, bright-eyed, bald bartender handed him, and started to play. With the first open-chord strum, the raucous bar's noise ceased, all eyes pivoting onto Crude.

Just like at the wedding, Crude's music seemed greater than anything Ricky had ever heard before. It reverberated in his most untouched places, plunged him into an ocean of unknown emotional possibilities. It was bigger than the first time he had sex, with Kat Fischer in the woods at sleepover camp; it was more euphoric than his first million. If anything at all approached what he was feeling now, it would have to be being present the moments his two children, Jonah and Samantha, came into the world, the same too-painful rawness ensconced in sizzling bliss. Ricky wasn't used to being in the same room with someone he didn't feel superior to, and now the muscles in his arms and legs were commanding him to fall to the floor in piety, in obeisance, in ego-demolishing praise. Crude played for ninety minutes, took a short break, and then played another, shorter set. Each time the tip pitcher came around, Ricky gleefully stuffed in handfuls of twenties. By the time Crude played his last song—an impossibly beautiful rendition of "Ramble On" sung in a gravelly baritone—the bar was tighter with bodies than Ricky thought possible, which on any other occasion would deeply rankle. But not tonight. Crude looked up from his guitar, the last notes still humming around him, and the bar erupted with delirious applause.

"Hey, Crude," Ricky called after the musician had put away his guitar and was drinking a pint at the end of the bar. Crude looked at Ricky as if he was trying to determine if this older, well-dressed, silver-haired man was an undercover cop.

"You were at that wedding on the weekend, right?" he said finally, his face relaxing.

"That's right. And I have to say, tonight was even more impressive." A lucrative day at the office paired with the three gimlets had given Ricky the confidence he had found himself without the last time they had spoken. "Let me buy you a drink," he said. Crude smiled. "A round of drinks for everybody!" Ricky yelled. He was cheered and slapped on the back, the beers spreading through the bar as fast as they could be poured.

At the end of the night, the bar having cleared out, Ricky was onto his ninth gimlet and had ended up in a discussion with a man with a small head, short black hair, black eyebrows, a black, trimmed beard, and dark little eyes. The man was going on about something to do with oil, oil and water—too much oil? Not enough water?—though Ricky was finding it hard to pay attention, kept watching the door, waiting for Crude to return from a smoke.

The man, whose name was Stan, thought he had an attentive listener in Ricky, and just kept on going: "Harper and his corporate lackies are too focused on oil. What we should be doing, what our responsibility is as a water-rich country, and, don't kid yourself, we are lousy with the stuff, is donating it to the third world, to the parched, to the drained, to the droughted and famined. That's what we should be building all those gushing pipelines for! The redistribution of water! Liquid life!"

It was hard for Ricky to only pretend to be listening now—Stan was yelling, pounding the table. Ricky's company happened to own majority shares in a number of extraction and refinement operations. Still, as yet another example of how Crude's music had affected him, Ricky kept quiet: What did this elfish person know about oil markets, about trade agreements, about energy needs? About profit margins?

The door opened, and Crude came back in. To Ricky's delight, he beelined straight to their table. "Is Stan trying to indoctrinate you?" he asked, laughing, slapping Stan on the back. "A bunch of us are going over to Troy's place to loosen up, play some guitar, make a night of it. Want to tag along?"

Ricky downed his drink, slammed four hundreds on the bar, and stood up, a little wobbly. He nodded. Yes. He wanted to tag along. Yes. Oh yes. He was going to follow this pied piper anywhere.

Troy—who Ricky had noticed at the bar, his nearly seven-foot frame and large afro framing a triangular face hard to miss—lived near the Socialist's Cousin on the top floor of a three-floor walk-up. It was two large rooms, with a large balcony off the bedroom. The floor-to-ceiling shelves were stacked half with records, half with books organized by size; black-and-white framed photographs of iconic Toronto buildings hung on the walls of the bedroom, and strange little sculptures squatted on the coffee table, on the stovetop, on the dresser, even (as Ricky would soon find out) on the bathtub ledge. For a quick moment, Ricky wondered if this was what Jonah's apartment in the McGill ghetto was like, if his son spent the money he was eternally ungrateful for on music and literature and art like this tall beanstalk of a man. Thinking of Jonah, Ricky filled with the strange hollowness he had first felt when Jonah moved out of the house, which intensified a year later when Samantha followed him, the hollowness that he had filled with work, acquisitions, vehement firings, that he could now swallow down like a bad burp. Troy bent down to open the fridge, pulling out a comical amount of PBR six packs, guitar cases were unclasped, and the dozen or so people who had journeyed from the bar settled into the couches and chairs that formed a rough semicircle around the room.

Some time later and Ricky was once again taking Crude in through bleary eyes, the room at a terrific slant. It was magic. What the man did with his hands, the instrument, his mouth, his body, even his feet and eyes, was magic. The riffs swirled Ricky's drunkenness into paroxysms of joy; the rhythms built ever-changing geometric shapes around his accelerated heart rate. Ricky was too drunk, too entranced, too arrogant, to feel out of place, though some of those present, in particular the brown-skinned woman in a red skirt and jean jacket holding hands with Stan, a splotch of white paint in her black hair, were looking at him as if he didn't belong. By the beginning of the fifth song, a few of the women in attendance had taken their shirts off, their arms raised above them in the light of a half dozen lamps; hell, if Ricky thought it would get Crude to notice him, he would have flushed his own Armani dress shirt down the toilet. The seating arrangement changed. Guitars moved from lap to lap. After the beer ran out, Troy produced three bottles of whiskey, drugs met bloodstreams—the one constant was Crude playing guitar on a low wooden chair in the middle of the room, first rock, then folk, then bluegrass, then, with Troy on double bass, dizzyingly fast jazz, the easy smile never leaving his face.

Near sunrise, Ricky looked down to discover a guitar in his hands. After fumbling through "The Ants Go Marching One by One," Crude cheering him on, he started laying down shaky chords: Em7, Dm, Am7. Neil Young's "Cortez the Killer," a song Ricky had been working on for ten years, whenever, once or twice a month, he would pick up the Martin he kept around the house. Crude obviously knew the tune, because he belted out the lyrics as he noodled softly under Ricky's chords, which after a dozen bars and Crude's fearless singing started to pick up in confidence. After the second chorus, everyone still present screaming out the refrain, Crude started to lay down a solo: slow, quiet at first, picking up its pieces, getting louder, more determined, mining deep holes of melodic ore, and then peaking, bellowing, pronouncing, relentless streamers of beauty pouring out of him. Ricky closed his eyes. It was like he was being taken by Crude, pierced by the tonics of his devastating runs. Ricky was providing a bare-bone base, but it was enough to allow Crude to construct glorious superstructures. The song eventually wound down, Ricky instinctually following Crude's lead, as if they were on the same toboggan and were nearing the dip at the mountain's bottom, slowing, softening, until he was barely strumming at all, melting into the now silent room, coming to rest. The room liquid gold, Ricky's mind shucked open. The look on everybody's face, even Stan's and his girlfriend's, was the last thing Ricky remembered. When he opened his eyes, he was lying on Troy's scratchy bed, still in his suit, brilliant sunlight pouring through the glass balcony doors. He stood up, his joints sore. Stumbling into the other room, he found Troy sitting crosslegged on the floor: he had changed into a white t-shirt and basketball shorts, and he appeared to be gluing beer coasters, which he had a small hoard of on the floor next to him, into complex shapes. Crude, along with everybody else, had vanished.

"Where'd Crude go?" Ricky asked, his voice hoarse.

"He left with Sasha and Autumn," Troy said, not looking up from his work.

"Right. Do you have his number? I was hoping to talk to him about something."

Troy raised his head. "A *phone* number? Nah man, that's not how Crude operates."

"Operates? What do you mean?"

Troy shook his head and went back to his coasters. "Crude lives how Crude lives man."

Ricky's eyes landed on the oven clock. It was 5:45 a.m. He left Troy on the floor, took a cab to his car, drove the awakening streets to his house, ran upstairs, showered, put on a clean suit, and got back into the car. Once at his office—seven thirty sharp, every day, six days a week, since he was twenty-one—he paged his secretary. "Clare, find me Crude Franzen. The guitar player." He sat back in his chair, still high from the night's music. Ricky looked out at his view of the Toronto skyline: it had always given him fortitude before, all that human striving transmogrified into steel and glass, and this morning, the sky blue and clear against the buildings' glinting headstocks, was no exception. What hadn't Ricky accomplished that he had set his mind on? He owned his first company by twenty-five, had cycled through four yachts by thirty-three; through an almost preternatural savvy, through acquisition, through mercilessness, he had turned his business into a multinational corporation. Since he had been sitting at his desk this very morning he had probably made more money than all the patrons of the Socialist's Cousin in a year combined. Whether the playing field was stacked or not, he had always delivered. And this would be no different. Deliver he shall. He was going to learn how to create Crude's magic.

Next Tuesday, and Ricky was back at the Socialist's Cousin. Locating a gigging musician in Toronto was harder than Ricky had assumed. The man didn't seem to have a permanent address, a phone, anything with which to pull him towards Ricky. After four days of looking, his secretary found a booking agent at the North Star Hotel, but she didn't have any contact information for Crude: Crude would call once a month, and the agent would tell him about any upcoming gigs. Ricky even badgered his brother to give him the name and room number of the Caribbean hotel where his nephew and his bride were spending their honeymoon, but he was no help either: the wedding planner had hired the trio, and he just led Ricky back to the North Star booking agent. Another dead end.

So here he was at the SoCo. "Is Crude playing tonight?" he asked the same short, bright-eyed bartender from last week.

"Crude? Oh no. He comes in only a couple of times a year. We wish he played weekly, if only. You wouldn't believe what his guitar does to tips." While he was talking, he had mixed Ricky an unasked-for gimlet, placing it in front of him.

"Why you looking for Crude?" the man next to Ricky asked. He had hair past his shoulders, a goatee, a loose wool sweater, big hands flat on the bar. He was much too large for this place: he looked like a full-grown adult stuffed into a kindergartener's desk-chair.

"I want to hire him," Ricky said, surprising himself.

The giant next to him looked just as surprised. "Hire him? For what?"

"For ... guitar lessons."

The man laughed, took his pint into his meaty paw, drank half of it before putting it down. "Crude's not exactly the lessons type," he said with a slight Quebecois accent, wiping his mouth with the back of his hand. "He would never be able to sit still long enough."

"What Seb here's trying to say," the bartender said, suddenly standing in front of them with another gimlet for Ricky, "is that he'll gladly give you guitar lessons."

Seb laughed deeply. "Now Ivo, don't go spreading rumours. Though sadly, it's true: I've been known to give the occasional lesson, to trade my hard-earned talents for a meager piece of bread."

Ricky looked at Seb's hands. Did they contain the same magic as Crude's? Ricky wasn't usually one to settle for second best. He sipped his drink.

"What's your rate?" he asked.

"Usually fifty an hour, but for you, for you I could do forty."

Ricky blinked. "Seems fair," he said.

They settled on Wednesday evenings at Seb's apartment in the west end, seven o' clock. To close the deal, they drank.

It wasn't until he had finished his third drink and was on his way up from the basement washrooms that he noticed what was different about the bar: there was a series of paintings hanging on what little wall space was available, above the narrow cluster of tables, and on both sides of the basement stairway. Each painting was of a body floating in water, the body itself just an outline, no details or features. Every object in the frame—the body, the water, the sky, and the halo emanating off of each body—was a different solid colour. A green, lithe female body in yellow water, giving off a pink aura, the sky blue; a large red man floating in rosy seas leeching a lavender emission; at the top of the stairs, an androgynous body, rich blue, the water black, the sky grey, sharp yellow daggers pulsing from him/her. A price tag under each canvas said four hundred dollars. The series struck a deep chord within Ricky; he almost started to cry. "Who did these paintings?" he asked Ivo.

"Seema did. She's right over there," he said, motioning to the corner table, where Stan was sitting with the same woman he was with at Troy's the week before. Ricky approached.

"I love your work," he said, his words spilling out before he stopped moving. "I'll take them."

Seema smiled. "Which one?"

"All of them!"

Stan snorted. "Just like the one percent to think they can hoard everything beautiful in this world."

"Stan, shut up," Seema said. She raised an eyebrow at Ricky. "You serious?"

"Why not?" Ricky asked, falling into an empty chair.

"Why not," Seema repeated. Stan continued to stare at Ricky.

"Trudy, my wife, usually takes care of the art, but what can I say? They really caught my attention." Ricky could have gone on: since first hearing Crude's guitar, his appreciation for the littler things—not only art and music, but the sunrise on his way to the office, the potpourri Trudy kept in the main floor powder room, a perfectly cold glass of ice water—had ballooned to looming proportions.

"It's easy for the rich to know what they want," Stan spat. "Seema didn't pour herself into those paintings so you could hit your conspicuous consumption quota for this quarter. Right, buddy?" Stan seemed to be in a bad mood, not at all like the ebullient revolutionary who had spouted off about water rights the week before.

Seema laughed, a full, buttery sound that softened Stan and refocused Ricky's attention. "Don't mind him." She leaned towards Ricky, her hair dangerously close to the tealight burning in the middle of the table. "His new movie isn't going so well," she mock-whispered into his ear.

"Not going well. Ha! That's an understatement." He turned to Ricky, his dark eyes reflective as unrefined oil. "All we wanted to do was ambush the MPPs as they left parliament, question them about their mining abuses up north, but what happens? Boris pisses against one tree, and we get slapped with an injunction. Just like the cops trying to keep the truth at bay!" Talk of Stan's film troubles had roused him, and now that he had started, it didn't appear like he was going to stop.

When Ricky glanced towards Seema, she raised an eyebrow, smiled as if they were secret allies in the barrage of Stan's words.

And so began a new phase of Ricky's life, one not predicated on quarterly reports or overseas stock indices. Guitar lessons with Seb, nights drinking at the SoCo, lending money to his new friends for their various artistic projects, hours spent practising—Ricky's weeks took on new shapes and configurations.

Seb, as it turned out, knew his way around classical, rock, folk, blues, bluegrass, the daunting complexity of jazz, and Ricky was hungry for all of it. And while Seb didn't play at the same heightened level as Crude, it was obvious he had a studied, workmanlike knowledge of the fretboard. Ricky hadn't taken guitar lessons since high school and took to the exercises with determined fervor. Seb insisted on starting off slow, so they went over the basics, worked through rudimentary theory, broke everything down into manageable pieces. Their work quickly showed dividends: after a few weeks, Ricky's understanding of the fretboard had increased dramatically, and he could confidently play more than half of the beginner guitar book they were tackling. Ricky was practising three, four hours a day. At the end of the month, he bought two Yamaha AC3Ms, one for the office and one for home.

That summer he saw improvements nearly daily. The better he got, the more lofty his goals became, the harder he worked, the more confident he became in his coming greatness. The rest of his life—even work—was dialed down to the lowest-possible vibration. Come September, he had doubled up on his weekly lessons, had hired a team of contractors to build a soundproof studio in the basement. Trudy, who was preoccupied herself with the upcoming annual women's tennis tournament at the country club, had okayed the new studio. She was practising almost as intently with Mikhail, her trainer, as Ricky was with Seb; she had placed third last year, and both she and Mikhail, who had played on the professional circuit for a few years— and, as Ricky never failed to remind Trudy, was never able to crack the top fifty—thought she had a good chance of winning gold. It was like the early years of their marriage all over again. They'd pass each other in the hall in the evenings, talk briefly, Trudy with her tennis bag, Ricky with a guitar case, often enough with a new guitar inside it. He bought, in quick succession, a '59 Fender Telecaster, a 1961 Gibson Les Paul with cherry sunburst finish, and a Taylor 710ce Dreadnought with an Engelmann spruce top, mahogany neck, and ebony fretboard. Showing the Telecaster around at the SoCo, Stan scoffed, berating Ricky, "You do know that Leo Fender was the Henry Ford of guitars, don't you?!"

Once the lessons started going for two, three hours, Ricky started taking Seb out for dinner. They would go to restaurants that Seb would never have gone to unless he was hired as the entertainment, and though at first he would protest, pretty soon he was downing the four-hundred dollar bottles of wine Ricky ordered with aplomb. A gentle, long-haired giant in the grey pinstripe suit Ricky bought for him, Seb was game for anything. Seb's girlfriend Shell would sometimes come as well (though she was not as quick to imbibe and ingest everything that Ricky's money could buy), and the night would usually end at the SoCo, where Ricky was treated as a celebrity. He knew it was mostly due to his money, the rounds he continually bought, his unprecedented generosity with the tip jar, but he didn't care. Stan was always there, plotting to overthrow the government in the back corner, Seema coming in from her studio, Troy sitting with Shell and Bianca and Autumn. During those late, foggy nights, Ricky would stay alert for any word on Crude. The man existed in rumours. Some said he had fallen into an alcoholic funk and checked himself into rehab. Stan was sure he was involved in a top-secret recording project in Ottawa. Other times an estranged son in San Francisco was mentioned, twin daughters in Nashville.

As the leaves changed colour and Ricky's guitar collection grew large enough to warrant bringing the contractors back to wall off a section of the great room to ensure air quality, as Ricky's ability to move fluidly between open chords increased, as the speed with which he could play the A minor pentatonic backwards and forwards incrementally improved, the magic of Crude began to recede from the forefront of Ricky's consciousness. Ricky still wanted to dominate the guitar and the room in the same indefinable way, but with his free time—and much of his workday, feet on his desk, guitar in his lap, the city of Toronto cheering him on—devoted entirely to chord progressions, fingerings, and picking technique, with the nights at the SoCo, Crude's absence weighed lightly. When Seb and Ricky started working on some of the easier Beatles songs, Ricky bought a Gretsch G6122, a Rickenbacker 325, and the first of many subsequent basses, a Hofner 500/1.

Standing in a rare guitar collector's basement in farthest
Scarborough, Ricky suddenly remembered the Danelectro he bought
his daughter Samantha a month after her bat mitzvah—she hadn't
spoken to him for a full fifteen days after the party, supposedly
because of how badly he had embarrassed her during his speech, and
to try and patch things up, he bought her the same guitar Beck, her
current fav rock star, played. Where was that guitar now? Maybe she
had it with her in Montreal. He'd have to ask Trudy.

On a blustery day in mid-October, Ricky and Trudy went to the opening
of Seema's first solo exhibit on Queen West. Trudy had yet to meet
Ricky's new friends and had so far shown zero interest; Ricky was both
surprised and nervous when she said she would come to the opening.
As soon as they entered the small gallery, everybody rushed over,
excited to meet Ricky's wife. Ricky made the introductions, introducing
Stan as Seema's boyfriend, though, as far as he could tell, Stan
and Seema were boyfriend and girlfriend in name only—the sexual
promiscuity of the SoCo crowd was truly incestuous. Stan, in particular,
would disappear into the bathroom or Troy's bedroom with someone
new almost every night. The only truly monogamous relationship, as
far as Ricky could surmise, was between Seb and Shell; he had once
heard Autumn refer to the two of them as "the adults."
    Ricky's worry that someone would be rude to Trudy was
unfounded; only Stan said something slightly inappropriate: "So, you're
the one who buys the art, eh?" Trudy, used to dealing with arrogant
men (who, regardless of profession, banker or burger slinger, were
all still arrogant in the same exact way) smiled a friendly smile and
said, "Only if the art's good," which Stan got a real kick out of. Trudy
actually *did* really like Seema's work. The paintings were renditions of
Group of Seven and other iconic Canadian landscape painters' images,
but with some slight, subversive transformations: The ice-cream
mountains of north Superior had a mining shaft sliced through their
core; an autumnal lake scene with all the trees clearcut, one ghostly
jack pine floating over the stumps; the solid browns and greens of the
BC forest disrupted by a pipeline running through the foreground, a
single drop of black oil oozing out of a joint. Ricky and Trudy bought

three of the paintings, one for his office, one for the bedroom, and one for the cottage. Seema kissed him on the cheek after each purchase, Trudy watching from across the room, where she was talking about investment portfolios with Autumn, who, for a flitty hippie, had a pretty sound sense of the market. Stan was in the best mood Ricky had ever seen him in, getting people beer and wine, joking with the yuppies who were milling around the small gallery, making loud pronouncements on the revolutionary potential of fine art.

"Hey, Stan," Ivo yelled, calling him over to where a gaggle of SoCo regulars were congregated, "remember when you tried to shoot that post-apocalyptic war movie during the air show?"

Stan grinned. "Yeah, we never did get the timing right, did we?"

Autumn started to laugh. "What about that time you wanted to set up cameras and televisions in all different parts of the city, have a feed of Rosedale Valley playing at Jane and Finch, Rexdale at Yorkville, Kensington at the Beaches?"

"If I had caught you with a camera in front of my house, I would have skinned you alive!" Ricky said, everybody, even Trudy, bursting into laughter.

"What, do you think capitalism is going to bring down itself?" Stan enthused, enjoying the attention. "Seema! Seema! Seema!" he called once the laughter had eased, moving towards his girlfriend, who was talking with a tall mustachioed man in a three-piece suit.

That night, Ricky and Trudy made love for the first time since the kids were in high school.

Ricky was showing up later for work, eight, eight thirty, still before business hours, but the thrill he used to get from a brilliant outmaneuver, from telling somebody off and slamming down the telephone, had waned. He had begun to delegate tasks to his employees; it was obvious the way the other executives and board members were acting they thought Ricky was moving towards early retirement (and were positively foaming at the mouths for a share of Ricky's clients), but all Ricky cared to do was practise the new chord shapes and progressions, work on the pentatonic and major scales, listen to the Django and Bach CDs Seb recommended, scour the city's guitar stores with Troy and Autumn. After the night of Seema's opening, his relationship with Trudy slid right back into the cordial business partnership they had both become accustomed to, though Trudy was becoming more vocal about her frustration with Ricky's new mindset with each passing day, a vocality that Ricky, having had years of practice, easily ignored.

And throughout it all, like Catholics wait for Jesus, like his liberal brother waited for peace in the Middle East, like a hunger striker waiting not for food, but for justice, he waited for Crude.

At the end of November, Ricky took Seb, Shell, and a dozen other SoCo regulars up to his cottage for a funky and creative weekend of music, art, autumn sun, and debauchery. Ricky mentioned the plan to Trudy, but thankfully she had the quarter finals that weekend and so had to stay home. The night before the scheduled departure, the tension between them came to a head, and they had a blow-out fight. She stormed through the house, adjusting paintings, fluffing pillows, scratching gunk off of doorknobs, Ricky following behind.

"You're never around anymore! It was bad enough when it was eighty-hour work weeks and dinners with your lawyers that kept you away—that I could understand—but this! Gallivanting around with those musicians and artists! Who are you?! Do you know what you would have said about these so-called new friends a year ago? You spend more time with them than you ever did with us! I really don't have the energy for this. I've got a match in two days! Mikhail says I have a chance of beating Sandra Cohen, but I have to stay focused, slept, and balanced. Focused, slept, and balanced!"

"If you can stay on top of Sandra's backhand, he's probably right," Ricky muttered, watching Trudy pick up the guitar books strewn around their bedroom.

"So you want to go to the cottage, you want to go to *our* cottage, and live out your middle-aged bohemian wet dream? Go afucking head, Rick, make my day. Consider it a let. Who needs you downstairs repeating the same five notes over and over again on those idiotic guitars while I'm trying to maintain a decent headspace! You know what, forget the let. This is a fault. A fucking fault!" They were standing at the bedroom door now. Trudy shoved the guitar books into Ricky's hands. "Mikhail says that you're just going through a phase, that it'll pass, that the guitars are some sort of call for help, but I don't know, I think you've just gone psychopathic!" Trudy stepped back into the bedroom and slammed the door. Ricky went downstairs to his guitars. He had to decide which ones to bring up north.

Early the next morning, everybody loaded into three of Ricky's cars, and they drove to the lake. Crude, as usual, was nowhere to be found, though everyone assured Ricky he would be back for the gig-abundant Christmas season. They caravanned up to the cottage, stopping twice for more liquor, once for lunch, and again for fresh steaks at a butcher's outside Gravenhurst. They arrived at the gate to the property in the late afternoon, Ricky keyed in the passcode, the gate opened, and they rolled into the large circular front lot.

"Wow, these are some sweet, sweet digs," Seb said after they piled out of the cars, putting into words what the others could only express with stunned faces. Stan, in particular, looked like he was standing inside the walls of the Kremlin. Pre-revolution. From where they were standing, they could see the mansion-sized main cottage, the bunkhouse that was the size of a regular house, the tennis court, and the basketball court fanned out in a semicircle around them. All the buildings were painted a vibrant royal blue. The main cottage had eight bedrooms, each with en-suite full baths. The bunkhouse had three bedrooms. The triple boathouse that was visible from the dining room's floor-to-ceiling windows and that was built right into the rock had a loft space with four beds.

The first night, Ivo and Phil barbecued the steaks, and they ate at the eighteen-person dining-room table. There was beer, whiskey, gin, rum, gimlets. There was pot, coke, a chorus of uppers and downers. And there was music. Oh, was there music. They set up Ivo's drum kit in the main room, erected a small cityscape of amps. Ricky had brought his two latest acquisitions, a prewar Martin D-45 acoustic and a sea-foam green early nineties Telecaster. "I'm thinking of putting a studio here," he said, framing off a corner of the den with his hands. "Bulletproof glass, soundproofed ceiling, a big roaring fireplace." Music—great, loud, eclectic music, swelling and subsiding, blasting and calmly noodling—was played at every hour of the day and night, everyone coming and going from the dock, the bedrooms, the basketball court, the kitchen. On any part of the property, at any time, there was always a jam or a song-writing session to jump into, a political or philosophical debate to take sides in. Ivo kept a steady rhythm; Stan pontificated. The long weekend naturally spilled out into the week. Ricky's Mazda 3 left on Monday with those who had gigs they couldn't get out of. Seema and Stan, armed with Ricky's credit card, took the Jaguar into town for food, alcohol, supplies. Every afternoon Ricky and Seb went down to the boathouse for his lesson. Ricky was making serious gains: he could now play around in the pentatonic over Seb's two chord vamps, and his rhythm was gaining shape.

On Wednesday afternoon, Ricky, still in his bathrobe, a gimlet in hand, picked his way down the lawn to the dock. Seema was sitting at the end of it with an easel and paint, was working on a canvas. "What d'ya think, Ricky?" she asked, pulling the brush away. It was a life-like rendition of the landscape in front of them: the white-capped lake, the rocky shoreline, the pines, the crowns of maple supple under the blue sky. However, breaking the representational verisimilitude of the painting, wavy dollar-signs, the colour of putrid lettuce, were emanating from the water, rising out of the lake and right off the top edge of the canvas as if they were toxic emissions from a sulphuric swamp. "Haunting," Ricky said, sipping his drink. A strong wind was blowing off the lake. "I'm going to do a whole series of them," she said, "*The Smell of the Wilderness*. Or *Off-Gassing*. I'm not sure." She knelt down to look through her paints, her bum resting on Ricky's shins. He sipped his drink, looked at the unfinished painting, his roiling lake. "Stan thinks you're having a crisis of faith," Seema said, standing and turning to face Ricky, smiling. "That you're waking up to the devastations of capitalism. But I know better." She brought her mouth to Ricky's ear, put her hand on his hip, the wind whipping her dress against him. "You just want to buy us. Suck out what's good and throw away the rest." For some reason, Ricky thought of Crude, the power he wielded over him that for the first time in Ricky's adult life had absolutely nothing to do with material wealth. Seema's hand moved.

That night, after a two-hour psychedelic rock jam, Ricky retired to the bunkhouse with Seema and Stan. The three of them screwed, licked, sucked, and snorted lines to a soundtrack of Prince, Janis Joplin, the Rolling Stones, and, as the sun rose pale and fresh over the mirror-flat lake, Miles Davis and Thelonious Monk. When Ricky woke up in the late afternoon, he was sitting on a throne of pillows, Seema and Stan hidden under blankets, one or both of them going down on him. Ricky leaned off the bed, picked up his '65 archtop, readjusted into the pillows, and started running through his fingerpicking exercises. Bass-note strum, bass-note strum, bass-note strum, bass-note strum, the bunkie alive with golden light, the guitar strings flashing like diamonds, everybody working away.

Thursday night, they had a raging bonfire, singing songs, roasting meat and vegan marshmallows, howling at the moon. Troy cut a fistful of his hair off and, screaming "This is no longer a part of me," tossed it into the flames, which were almost as tall as him and licked the lower branches of the white pines. Ricky, with Seb's backing, played "Here Comes the Sun" for the first time in public. Eventually, the sun actually did come.

On Friday, they went home.

When Ricky would look back at this part of his life, that week at the cottage would be the undisputed zenith, when mastery of the guitar, plugging right into the foaming hurricane, seemed most attainable. As soon as they got back, things started to fall apart. Ricky's guitar playing hit a wall. He just couldn't get past the linearity of the pentatonic. His fingers would not hold the rhythm he could hear and feel in his head; his timing remained rudimentary and inconsistent. Not that Seb had given up: they worked through book after book, technique after technique. Seb patiently took Ricky through a riff ten, twenty, fifty times, until eventually Ricky would throw down his guitar in disgust with a "Fuck it, let's eat." The more fed up he got with his progress, the more extravagant the dinners, the longer cured the crates of whiskey, the more rare and expensive the guitar, the more seed money to the group members' various projects.

Shortly after returning from the cottage, Ricky made official his leave from his company, letting his ungrateful VPs fight it out for the top spot. He practised less and less, spent more and more of his time hunting out and buying rare guitars. He now owned thirty-two Stratocasters, nineteen Telecasters, a ridiculously rare Nocaster that he and Seb had to drive down to Cleveland to pick up, twenty-one Les Pauls, an arsenal of Taylors, Martins, Yamahas, and Ibanezes. For a week, he bought every Danelectro he could find in the GTA. His most recent acquisition was a twelve-thousand-dollar customshop Gibson SG, a "straightforward rock 'n roll weapon," in the words of the Burlington guitar clerk who sold it to him, and he was in talks with a British man he had found on a rare guitar forum who claimed he had John Lennon's 1962 sonic-blue Strat that had been stolen in 1968, and, though priceless, would sell it to Ricky for three hundred thousand pounds.

At the SoCo the night Ricky returned from Burlington with the Gibson, Troy and Ivo's new bluegrass project played a couple of sets, Ivo on banjo, Troy on guitar. At around midnight, Ricky at a table with Seema, Seb, and Autumn, Stan stalked in, his foul mood beating off of him as if it were being run through a delay pedal.

"What's wrong, Stan the man?" Ricky asked. The two of them had developed a seamless rapport, Stan digging into Ricky for his money and upper-class pretensions, Ricky goading Stan with right-wing pronouncements.

Stan flopped into a chair. "I got rejected from the Anarchist Art Network Executive Committee. Again." He was talking to Seema, staring at her with his small eyes. "They say my projects aren't 'feasible' enough. Feasible! As if revolution is supposed to be something you can do in your bathrobe!"

"Oh, poor Stanislav," Seema said soothingly.

"That's not all. They accused me of not reading *Capital*!"

"You haven't read *Capital*."

"Well, no, not all of it," Stan said, dejected, near tears. "My activism is of more of an experiential nature."

Seema put her arm around him. "Who needs those guys anyways? Fuck 'em!"

"Fuck 'em!" everybody echoed.

"More of an experiential nature," Stan said quietly to himself.

Troy came up to the table, his arms and face shiny with sweat. "Great set, T!"

"Since when could you roll like that? Are you secretly from deepest Tennessee?" Autumn joked, putting on a heavy Southern accent.

"Thank you, thank you," Troy said, bending almost perpendicular at the hip. "Hey, don't forget that any used guitar strings, paint brushes, stretchers, pickups, anything from your work that you're going to throw out, I want it."

"How could we forget, sugar?" Autumn drawled in her new accent. "It is positively *all* you speak of these days!"

"What about my heart, Troy? I'm about ready to scrap that fucking little organ!"

"Whoa, Stan, easy," Troy said, putting his hands up in mock-defence. "What, did Seema finally realize that she can do way better and kick you and your theory chapbooks to the curb?!"

Stan's face twisted itself into a mask of apoplectic rage, his short black hair bristling. "Great, good, fuck!" He jumped up and stormed out of the bar.

Troy smirked. "What? What did I say?"

"Don't worry, he's just having a bad day. It's the low point of his creative cycle. He'll bounce back," Seema said, but Ricky noticed her eyes lingering at the door.

Mid-December, a time of year Ricky would usually spend at corporate Christmas parties, making up for his general absence with exceedingly lavish Hanukkah gifts for Jonah and Samantha, Trudy left him. She said it was because she had fallen in love with Mikhail. "Did you even notice that I won the tournament?" she asked him the night she left. "Or were you too busy buying guitars, gallivanting with those leeching musicians? What happened to you, Ricky? What happened to the focused, ruthless man I used to know?"

"What happened to me?" Ricky screamed. "Nothing! What happened to you, Trudy?! What happened to you?!"

Trudy smiled like she was talking to a young child, a misbehaving puppy. "Mikhail says you've gone crazy," she said quietly, "that the money and the power finally corrupted you. He saw it constantly in

Russia after the Soviets fell. I know what really happened though. Your mind snapped, somewhere back there. Something you snorted at that ridiculous dump you call a bar. Socialist's Cousin! What a joke! More like Capitalist's Rich, Creepy Uncle!" Trudy took a breath. She had to speak rationally, even in the face of such irrationality. "We've lived two separate lives for a long time now, ever since the kids moved out, even earlier." Ricky shook his head in defiance and stormed out of the house.

Slamming back gimlets at the SoCo, he raged against Mikhail to Seb, to Ivo, to Stan, to anybody who would listen, swerving from anger to deep regret to deeper anger. "That Stalinist bastard. We were so in love when we got married. She's not getting my guitars, my amps. There's no way. If she lays her hands on even a single neck, I'll sue her."

Trudy would get the house, of course, the cottage, most of the cars. The kids sided with Trudy. Surprise, surprise. Jonah even mailed back his Hanukkah gift—a very large cheque—unopened. A first. "Your mother left me," he said to Samantha when he finally managed to get her on the phone.

"From what I hear, you checked out a long time ago," Samantha said, her voice cold, distant. "She told me all about it. What's with all the guitars?"

"Your mother just doesn't understand what I'm doing. I'm going to change the world through my music."

"Dad. Are you really so far gone that you can't see how ridiculous you are acting?"

"What ever happened to that Danelectro I bought you?" Ricky asked loudly, almost barking. "I need it back."

"That piece of junk? I think Michael has it."

"Michael? Your boyfriend?"

"Dad. We broke up six years ago." Samantha laughed, cutting a deep gash into Ricky's heart. "You are too rich. You really are."

"Find me that Danelectro," Ricky screamed, slamming down the phone.

But, worst of all by far, his friends had been wrong: the holiday season was in full swing, and Crude hadn't reappeared. "He's never been gone this long before," Troy said whenever Ricky brought it up. Since Trudy left him, Crude had begun occupying more and more of Ricky's focus, until it was all he thought of, listless days at the bar, sleepless nights with his guitars, his lessons forgotten, practice a thing of the past, meals of canned tuna and crackers.

Crude would show up any day now. He had to. The faint melodic noodling at the back of Ricky's soul would, at any moment, burst into flame.

Crude would fix everything, make it all worthwhile.

Crude would save him.

A few days after New Year's, Ricky showed up at the SoCo with a present for Seb. Ricky's reception at the bar had noticeably diminished in recent weeks. He was fast becoming just another SoCo regular, a silver-haired man with crazed eyes and a sad story. Even Stan—who had yet to recover from the funk he had fallen into—had lost interest in the fallen CEO, had started spending all his time with his new friends, tattooed men who wore sunglasses even in the dark cave of the SoCo; the three of them were always hunched together at the back table talking in low voices. The only person who Ricky still got solace from was Seb: his guitar teacher, his confidante, his adviser, his friend. Seb would always be there for Ricky.

"And that's why I got you a little something," he said as he ushered Seb outside, everyone else following behind them into the chilly January afternoon. Parked at the curb was a brand new candy-yellow F-Type Jaguar convertible, the roof down, a matching yellow Fender Jaguar guitar sitting in the passenger seat. Black leather, custom tuning knobs, top-of-the-line Pioneer sound system, the hubcaps and strings gleaming in the bright winter sun.

"Whoa, Rick, I can't accept this," Seb said, backing up, shaking his hands, palms out.

"Don't be ridiculous, big guy, of course you can! I bought one for myself too, got a sweet deal."

"Whoa, Rick," he said again, dropping his hands.

"It's very generous of you," Shell said, tentatively. She glanced at the car and then back at Ricky, her eyes finally settling on Seb, who looked like he had gone into a trance, his breath coming out in slow rolls. She didn't know if Seb should take the car or refuse. She had been getting more nervous about Ricky's insinuation into Seb's life with every new gift, meal, guitar. And now this. What was he playing at? What would people like her and Seb want with a car like that? Shell had her bike; Seb had his rusty hatchback for out-of-town gigs. They were content. At least, they used to be content: Shell had watched with increasing worry as Ricky's money had slowly but surely made its mark on Seb. Look at him! He used to care for nothing else but a good PA system, a well-played show—and now this! The guitar, all right, fine, but a *Jaguar*? The insurance alone would probably be as much as their rent. And what did he mean when he said he got one for himself too— was he referring to the car or the guitar? Such gluttonous behaviour. Shell and Seb usually let each other explore and develop without interference, but this thing with this man was getting out of hand. He had just become too, too *involved* in Seb's life. She was going to have to say something. She tried to catch Seb's eye, but he was already on the other side of the street, standing with Ricky at the matching toys, bare arms crossed against the winter cold.

Stan came out of the alley, his two new friends hanging back, their sunglasses metallic mirrors. The smell of marijuana curled off of them; Stan was shivering violently. He glanced at the car, but seemed too preoccupied to care. "Hey, Rick, old buddy, can I borrow the Denali for the night?" Stan twitched nervously, his friends looking on expectantly.

"Yeah, sure, whatever," Ricky said, watching Seb reverentially run his hands along the Jaguar. He handed Stan the keys. Stan took them quickly, and the three of them vanished.

Eventually they went back inside and started to drink. Seb brought his new guitar with him.

The night of the Jaguars was the same night Crude reappeared. He came into the bar a little after eleven, guitar case in hand. His leather jacket sported a few new tears, he was rocking a thick, full beard, and, as the door shut on the icy wind that momentarily rushed in, the bar went silent. Ricky, already quite inebriated, was struck dumb. "Crude," Ivo shouted from behind the bar. "My man! You here to play?"

Crude cracked a devastating grin. "Why else?"

It was like a night from the halcyon days of last summer. Crude played a raging set. Ricky opened his wallet. The booze flowed freely. Everyone finally gave in to the holiday spirit. Somehow Crude had only gotten better with absence. Ricky had known it all along: Crude was the real thing—a musician without equal, a craftsman of the highest order, peerless. A half year of anticipation and here he was, blowing Ricky's memories out of orbit. Seb sat in with Crude for a set, and though his workmanlike solos were accomplished, even fiery, when he traded off with Crude, it was like a precocious child's painting compared to an Old Master's. During a brief pause in the music, when Ricky went downstairs to relieve his bladder, he found Autumn hugging the toilet in one of the two stalls, the door fully open. "Hey, Autumn, you okay? Want me to call you a cab?" Autumn shook her head, resumed vomiting into the bowl. "Must. Fuck. Crude," she cried out between heaves. Ricky watched her for a minute, then slipped into the other stall; he didn't want to miss anything upstairs. Autumn came back up eventually, switched from tequila to beer, and an hour later they closed out the bar, piled into Seb's new Jag, and crawled the four blocks to Troy's place, the frozen air diamonds on their faces. They were all there: Ricky, Seb, Seema, Jacques, Phil, Troy, Autumn, Bianca, Sasha, Marlee. Crude. Ivo showed up after he had finished mopping the bar. (Shell had gone home shortly after Crude arrived, saying she had been struck with poetic inspiration; Stan hadn't been seen since he borrowed the Denali.) Troy broke out the whiskey. Ricky dropped a gram of cocaine on the table. Phil rolled a series of joints of varying sizes. Someone lit some candles. Troy's new statue, a mass of brushes, broken easels, coiled guitar strings, and fractured guitar necks, sat in a corner of the room. Crude jammed with whoever had a guitar.

By early morning the alcohol, drugs, music, and pre-dawn glow had turned Troy's apartment into a space station orbiting a distant moon. Ricky had spent the last hour watching Crude play by himself: he had been running through an endless stream of mounting arpeggios before imperceptibly modulating into sizzling single note runs—he was playing faster than Ricky thought possible, screaming through an incredible amount of notes, each one ringing crystal clear. Ricky had no idea that time could be broken down into such minuscule units. But now Crude had stopped, was sitting on the edge of his chair, using his guitar to steady himself, his chin resting on the headstock. Ricky took a breath and went over to him.

"How do you do it, Crude?" he blurted.

Crude laughed. His eyes were bloodshot, and Ricky noticed for the first time how tired he looked, how old. His face was craggly; his hands shook.

"What can I tell you, Barney? It's something I've always had. It's a language, and I speak it, and people like listening to me speak it. It's always been like that. I picked up my first guitar when I was five, and from then on I couldn't get away from it. What does it mean? It means I've never had to try, to focus, to really work at anything, to be responsible. The music has always just been there. Sometimes I feel like it's a great fathomless ocean, thousands of kilograms of pressure, and I'm just a tiny little porthole keeping it at bay. It's all I can do not to let it drown me, crush me into paste. So you like it, so you are enthralled. Isn't everybody? What's it worth, Barney? What has it brought me? I have a daughter I never see—did you know that? I'm a fucking alcoholic. No matter how hard I try and get away, it always catches up with me. That's it. That's everything. No joy, this," he said, lifting the guitar, bringing it down hard onto the floor. "Not anymore. Not for a long time."

"I miss my kids, too," Ricky said, the words triggering a tidal wave of emotion, slamming into him. He held his breath so he wouldn't burst into tears, he and Crude both swaying, eyes locked. The wave pulled back, washed everything away, leaving only anger. Red hot, drunken anger. Ricky's famous anger, resurgent.

He blinked.

"Don't give me that bullshit!" he yelled. "Do you know how long I've waited for you?! How long we've all been waiting? How much do you want? How much will it cost for you to show me how to do it?!" Ricky had taken out his wallet, was throwing hundreds at Crude's feet. "How much?! How much?!"

Crude stared, his eyes empty. Finally, he smiled placatingly.

"How much will it cost? It's simple, buddy. Show me how to turn it off for an evening, an afternoon, ten fucking minutes of peace, and it's yours, Cortez. It's all yours."

Crude laughed, two sharp ha's, and jumped up, tossing his guitar onto the couch. He walked over to the increasingly wasted Autumn and started making out with her, pulling Bianca in with his free hand. The three of them stood up, like a newborn creature unsure of its legs, and moved as a single wobbling mass towards the bedroom, but tripped halfway there and fell out the open front door. One of the girls screamed. Ricky carefully picked his way towards the door, images of Jonah and Samantha as toddlers, as teenagers, at their bar and bat mitzvahs flashing through his head. With difficulty, he stepped over Troy, passed out beside the couch. He went out onto the landing and looked down. They had slid down half the flight of stairs, were lying in a pile of arms and legs. Ricky watched as Autumn emerged from the jumble and peeled her shirt off. Crude buried his face in her chest. Ricky couldn't be sure, but it sounded like he was crying. Ricky blinked. Crude was really howling now. Golden morning light was filtering through the door at the bottom of the stairs. Ricky blinked again. What was he doing here? Who were these people? Why wasn't he at his desk, the city of Toronto laid out before him, conducting the flow of global capital, eating those who were too slow and too weak, building empires, doing what he was great at?

Ricky was opening his mouth to say something to Crude, when from outside came the rising sound of screeching tires that peaked in a terrific, echoing crash. Ricky walked back into the apartment. Seb was coming in from the balcony, the others rushing behind him. Troy was already at the small window that looked out on the street, his face up against the glass. "An SUV slammed into Seb's Jag," Troy called out, not moving from the window. "It looks like it's your Denali, Rick." Ricky was standing in the middle of the apartment, obliterated, disillusioned, so, so tired. "The Denali?" Seema asked. "Oh my God, Stan!" She turned to Ricky. "This is all your fault!" she screamed. Ricky opened his mouth to respond, but before he could, there was a commotion out back. "Freeze!" someone called out. "Don't move! Shit, they're jumping the fences. Stop! Police!" Seb, Troy, Seema, and everybody else bolted towards the balcony; Ricky, as if in a dream, went out the front door barefoot and walked down the stairs. Crude and the girls had vanished, though Autumn's blue shirt was still lying on the steps. Ricky pushed open the door and walked out onto the street. His Denali had caved in the Jaguar, like a bowling ball dropped onto a birthday cake. The carnage the large SUV had done driving the wrong way on the one-way street was apparent: fences smashed, cars dented, the thick reek of burning rubber. A cop car was parked haphazardly in the middle of the street, on top of what, for a slow instant, Ricky thought was the spewed silver and gold guts of the Jaguar, but turned out to be thousands and thousands of toonies, the two-tone coins strewn all over the road, sidewalk, and lawns, as well as the footstep and passenger seat of the Denali, the door of which was hanging open at a horribly unnatural angle. The money glittered, a lake of silver. Two more cruisers pulled up, officers nimbly jumping out. "Sir, please stand back. There are armed bank robbers in the vicinity. Please go back into your house." Ricky nodded slightly, started walking up the street, ignoring the shouting and the gunshots, his feet bleeding from the broken glass, starting to burn with cold. Once on the main street, he flagged a taxi and got in.

As they drove through the empty streets, the city slowly awakening, Ricky took stock of his holdings, an old habit that he had not indulged in for some time. No house, no wife. One hundred and seventy-three guitars, ranging from a few hundred dollars to a few hundred thousand, in an CCTV-monitored storage space in the city's east end (where, lately, he had been sleeping on an army surplus camping bed), all carefully catalogued. Half of his stock portfolio, minus the monthly payments to Trudy. Four and a half million dollars in an off-shore account that nobody, not even his team of accountants, knew about. Another million in bonds. A few hundred thousand and change here and there. Forty-five acres and a small cabin in the Californian mountains, bought during the last financial crisis in his mother's name. Trudy had no idea about that one either. Jonah and Samantha. That afternoon in the bunkhouse, when the music was in reach. Crude playing his guitar, tunnelling right into the centre of the world, hauling out his gold, sharing it, keeping none for himself. Ricky was not

Crude; that was clear now. For the first time since he met him, Ricky understood that he didn't want to be Crude. He wanted to consume him, to take his unrefined magic and keep it locked in a safe.

Ricky felt like he had woken up from a long, fitful sleep. He smiled to himself as they pulled up in front of the high-rise whose entire forty-fifth floor belonged to him, the glass walls catching bright slugs of early morning light. He knew what he had to do. He had to call his children. But first, he had to reclaim his empire. Ricky began to feel the old excitement rushing back. He paid the taxi driver with a crumpled fifty he found in his back pocket. His wallet was gone. Add it to the loss column.

He got out of the cab, walked barefoot into the lobby, trailing blood on the gleaming tiles.

He was home.

Ninety-Nine

As soon as I heard the sex of the baby, I knew what it meant. It meant a decision. It meant confrontation. It meant a staring contest with tradition. Needless to say, once I had started thinking about it, I couldn't stop; I was stuck, at a loss, transfixed. And Rob, well it would've been easier if Rob felt strongly one way or another. If at no other time, this was when some strong male guidance was needed, but whenever I brought it up he said the same thing: "You know that in the end we're going to go through with it, right, so why worry so much? Eh, Orly? Is it really worth the parental shit storm?"

"Yeah, yeah," I countered the last time we talked about it. I was sitting on the loveseat, my feet on the ottoman, my belly a planet; Rob, as usual, was at his computer. "Yeah, yeah," I said, "but doesn't it just seem like something we wouldn't do? Isn't it just so not us?"

It amazes me how much Rob still surprises me. I would have put money down that he would hold a very strong opinion on the matter, but he has seemingly given up before the fight has even begun. A part of me says maybe Rob's right, why push against something so huge, so benign, the whole weight of Jewish history imploring us just to get on with it? But it's not easy like that for me. There's something real, something powerful, impelling me to resist.

Alone in the kitchen, I sit in the blue wash of the computer. I open a browser.

I will read. I will research. I will become an expert on the covenant, on the medical debate, on the five-thousand-year history of the act, generation after generation, ceremony after ceremony, marker of difference after marker of difference. I will let the anonymous internet purveyors of opinion and vitriol fight it out for me. The antisemites. The fanatics. The even-keeled—a rare breed in the comment sections, I know, but perhaps exactly what I need. I imagine the moment of realization, the answer crystallizing, the path becoming clear, the doubt evaporating.

I type in the word that suddenly so much hinges on.

A single, stupid word.

"You know why you're so hung up on this?" Rob says, rustling the newspaper. I'm drinking from a gallon of orange juice. I have a client meeting in half an hour, and I'm still not dressed. I started working as a wedding planner in my second year of university, and I've been doing it ever since. Planning a wedding is an opportunity for the fiancées to dry-run all the tensions and arguments and reconciliations that will get them through fifty years of marriage, and it's my job to absorb it all, take the brunt of a half year of stress over the bouquets, the colour schemes, the late-night freakouts over the seating list, to absorb it and to transform it and then, finally, to steer them through the magical night itself, make the dream on my clipboard a reality. To say I'm looking forward to the impending time off would be a gross understatement. Rob lowers the paper and looks me in the eye. "You know why, don't you? Marni."

I tilt my head back and chug the thick liquid, juice spilling out of my mouth and onto my shirt.

"You know that, right? That it's Marni?"

His new book is on the history of Esperanto. The idealistic dream and humbling failure of a self-made language. I want to yell, "Who gives a fuck about Esperanto?"

"This is all your fault," I say instead. "You and your patriarchy."

Rob gets up and does his little dance, elbows in at the stomach, fists and head bobbing to some private rhythm. It gets me every time; I almost barf orange juice.

"Marni and her beliefs," he says, stooping down to kiss my round stomach.

Marni and I could be a case study for how inconceivably different two girls could become, two girls who from the ages of five to nineteen were so similar. Best friends from the moment we compared lunchboxes on the first day of kindergarten. From then on: the same haircuts, the same posters, the same summer camps, the same plans.

It amazes me now how after spending a whole day at school together (and most likely a good chunk of the evening) we could talk on the phone for another two, three hours, every single night, our mothers knocking on our doors, telling us to go to bed, Marni calling back from the basement on her father's business line after getting yelled at for being too loud. (Rob and I don't talk nearly as much: our conversations are open, incredible, but they last for minutes, moments.)

In grade eight, we called two boys we knew had crushes on us and made out with them in Marni's room, she and her boy on the bed, me and my boy on the floor. We ate grilled cheese after, watched cartoons, delighted in our naughtiness.

Our first boys. Our first cigarettes. Our first vodka shots. Our first hangovers. We shared books, clothes, bands, university classes, a winter and half a spring of veganism.

The summer between second and third year spent at my parents' cottage while they gallivanted across Europe, a constant stream of friends and parties and drugs. We dropped acid by the lake, talked about our futures, irrevocably entwined, our children calling us aunt, our neighbouring houses in Kensington Market, in San Francisco, in the 5th arrondissement, our lives as free-loving professors of cultural studies (this was the summer I met Rob; we wouldn't date for years still, though he made out with Marni on the floating dock, a fact I didn't tire of pointing out during our first years together).

Then ... then what? Then something changed. That December we both went on Birthright, a free ten days in Israel too good to pass up, even if up until then Israel had meant very little to us and we had barely given a thought to it. And though we both drank rivers of vodka and slept with one or two boys on our trip, as well as a soldier each, being on that bus plummeting through the desert started something in Marni. When we got back to Toronto, she took one of those six-week classes at LaBriute where they pay *you* to sit and listen about how special it is to have a Jewish soul, and then she took another, and by the spring she was wearing skirts and not using the phone on Saturdays. Too much LSD this summer, I joked at first, but as her absence from my life became real, I quickly stopped. She took a leave of absence from school, went to Israel to study in Jerusalem. Calls in the middle of the night to tell me how important it is to be a traditional Jewish woman. How all those guys we've slept with, how it's all right, as long as we now see the error of our ways.

It's a phase, I said, to my other girlfriends, to myself. A phase. She'll come back to me.

The last wedding before my self-imposed mat leave. I imagine myself spending the day in bed, waiting for the moment when my life changes irrevocably. I imagine Rob feeding me birdlike from his open mouth. If I suggested it, he'd probably do it. My crazy historian. The wedding's at a reception hall downtown, near the water. A pretty, petite Chinese woman marrying a hulking Jewish man with curly copper hair. They're both doctors. The wedding party is almost entirely doctors. The bride is wearing a simple white dress, an elegant black sash around her stomach. A mermaid to my humpback whale. I cry during the ceremony, standing at the back of the chapel, clipboard in hand.

The party goes well. Almost all of the speeches, anecdotes, jokes, and promises have to do with the hospital, the operating room. I watch as the alcohol and music work their magic on the guests, the transformation from stiff and formal to loose and sweaty. The usual wash and pull of a wedding. There's a bit of a scene when the security guard, a large, mustachioed man, grabs the microphone from the bride's brother and accuses everybody present of conspiring to steal his pen, which someone had borrowed to sign the guestbook and never returned. His most favourite pen. Around midnight, I grab the bride by the arm and march her into the bridal suite, push her into the bathroom. I lift her dress. "Sit," I say. "Pee," I say. (Even after so many years, Rob still doesn't believe that someone can forget this most basic of bodily functions, but trust me, I've seen what happens when brides are left to their own devices on the best night of their lives.)

The bathroom is so small that there is barely room for the three of us. Her face slackens with relief. Her hand finds itself on my stomach. I'm still holding her dress. She looks up at me with her big brown eyes.

"Is it a boy or a girl?" she asks.

"A boy," I say.

We cry. For different reasons, but it doesn't matter.

Marni had phoned me five weeks before my own wedding. Rob had just finished his first book then, and I was still learning to fear the long-distance ring.

"Hey, Marn. How's New York?" I remembered too late that she goes by Miriam now, but she didn't correct me.

"It's great, Orly. We're actually leaving for a while. Smuli got a contract to teach Talmud in Hebron; we're going in the fall. We spoke with our rabbi, and I don't think we're going to be able to come to your wedding. We're worried about you, Orls. We're worried about your children. You know that if you don't get married in an Orthodox shul, their souls won't be Jewish, right? Is that fair to them? Don't do it for yourselves, Orls, if that's how you want to think about it. Do it for them."

I was winded. Wounded.

"Don't call me Orls." Silence, the need to retract. I forced a laugh. "That was a long time ago, wasn't it?" I said, trying to sound light, fluffy.

"Yes, it was. Listen, Orly. Smuli wants to send you some literature. He's worried about you. He knows how much you meant to me growing up. He likes you. Rob too, though his politics are misguided. It's not too late to change your mind, you know. If not for you, for your future children. It's what HaShem wants."

I didn't know what to say, so I said nothing. I didn't know the person on the other end of the line. I gave Marni my mailing address. The conversation broke down. Hanging up, I wished we weren't getting married by a rabbi at all, even the guitar-playing lesbian one we found after months of searching. "Why couldn't you have been a Christian," I yelled at Rob after telling him about the phone call, wrestling him to the kitchen floor, "or a Hindu?"

"Imagine if I was Muslim," Rob said, flipping me over, tickling my armpits. "Marni's head would have popped off!" I was laughing from the tickling, tears streaming down my face. Rob has had close friends find Orthodox Judaism too, but for him it's different. They can still laugh and watch sports. Rob is so comfortable in his beliefs, in himself, that he just shrugs off their attempts to convert him, to guilt him.

But not me. Not with Marni. With Marni I feel torn, angry, small.

I know that whatever I do will be in relation to her. Either in opposition or in compromise.

I can't help it. I want to oppose.

"How about some pickles and ice cream?" Rob says. He's wearing an apron, slicing eggplant with a butcher's knife, the large bamboo cutting board filling with the thick disks. For weeks he's been trying to entice me with the strangest combinations he can think of. Waffles and mayonnaise. Herring pizza. Baked bean popsicles. I've been a disappointing pregnant woman though, craving nothing more than cheeseburgers, Nutella on toast, mounds and mounds of bacon. The vegetarian teenager inside me is appalled.

"What are we going to do, Rob? I can't go through with it. Why should we make decisions for him?"

Rob cuts the bulging purple fruit into perfect circles, light flinging off the rectangular blade.

"Salt," he says. "We need lots of salt."

I stand at the bay window in my bedroom, watching the street. I can hear Rob moving around the kitchen below me, whistling as he unloads the dishwasher, puts on water for tea. How can anybody know what to do in this world, let alone with their children? Their speechless, helpless children? I can't even decide for myself. What it's about. What's at stake. Religion? Tradition? The parents? Am I taking out anger at an old friend on my child? Am I that callous? Or does Marni just allow me to see who I really am? The outdatedness and hypocrisy of it all? Maybe after the birth it'll be clearer.

Eight days. Eight days of wholeness before we deal you your first loss. Why? Because we're your parents, and we say so.

I have no idea why.

Marni must have children by now, I think. The thought floors me. I'm flooded with resentment, with the familiar betrayal, and in a sudden moment of clarity, I know that Rob is right, that we will go through with it. Even the thought of bringing it up to my mom, to my dad, stops my breath. I know it's inevitable. We will mutilate our son. And then the moment is gone. It is not inevitable. My parents will get over it; everything will be as it should.

I pad downstairs, grab hold of Rob as he stands at the sink, clasp my hands around his torso, my belly pushing against his back. "Maybe it's time for that herring pizza," I say. Rob turns, his eyes sparkling.

"Fucking Miriam," I say into his shoulder.

The phone rang long distance sometime between Rosh Hashanah and Yom Kippur. It was Marni, calling to apologize for any wrongs she may have done to me in the past year. Rob and I had just moved into our first apartment together and were spending most of our time making love in all the different rooms, amid unpacked boxes and stacks of unshelved books. Rob hadn't yet finished his coursework; the first book was still a twinkle in his eye.

"Don't be silly, Marn. What could you have done? We've barely spoken all year," I said, laughing nervously.

"It's not funny, Orly. This is a time of pensive thought and reflection, a time to make right. HaShem has set apart these days for us to take stock."

Even though I had only met Smuli twice before, I could easily hear his voice, his cadence, behind Orly's words. They had met in Israel a year before and had been married for six months. Their wedding was in New York, in the basement of a shul. A portable wall on the dance floor separated the men from the women. I spent most of the reception sitting in my chair, watching Rob get drunk with all the black-hatted, big-bearded men on the other side of the room. He had them in stitches. ("What were you saying that was so funny?" I asked on our way back to our hotel. Rob laughed. "I was telling old Yiddish jokes," he said.) Smuli's speech was about not bowing to false idols, and for examples he gave television, secular learning, and the pursuit of money. How could I help thinking he was talking about Rob and me? Marni hadn't asked me to help with the wedding, or to even be a bridesmaid.

I thought about bringing this up now, on the phone, but decided not to. Would Marni really apologize for something she probably didn't even know she did?

All fall, the year after my wedding—my low-key, tasteful, fun wedding—I expected to hear the long-distance ring, Marni calling to apologize, to say our friendship was more important to her than what some rabbi says. Nobody but banks I don't have accounts at, cruise-ship horns announcing my big prize.

I stand by the window, thinking of Marni, of our lost friendship. Even after so much time, I still feel severed. Halved. Sometimes I am stupefied with guilt. I think of the little boy being synthesized from pieces of me, the movement of my body, the smells and curves of my memories. Will Rob's eyes, his intelligence, his certainty, make it into the mix? I think of Abraham, progenitor of so much trouble, doing it to himself at the age of ninety-nine, more than old enough to know what you want. Who you are. I think of my parents, my father stern and lecturing, my mother crying inconsolably. I fill with exhaustion, with numbness, with resignation. I will blink first. I picture me and Marni as teenagers, trying on each other's clothes in her bedroom, laughing for minutes at a time, melting over our latest rock-star crush, his poster on the wall, gorgeous, talented, and unattainable, pondering late into the night what our forbidden offspring would look like.

Movies

My father dropped me off at the back of the movie theatre's enormous parking lot at seven thirty, a half hour before I was supposed to meet Bruce and Marco. "Give 'em hell," he said as he drove away. I started walking towards the massive cineplex, an outsized cement box painted dark green, which, for some reason, the corporate execs had given a forest motif: three sprawling fake treetops were bolted to the roof, and beavers, moose, bears, and birds were painted onto the sides of the building, as incongruous as could be with the asphalt, highways, high-rises, and strip malls that surrounded it. There must have been five, six hundred teenagers congregating on the wide cement steps, spilling into the theatre's atrium and onto the road—the theatre, open for just over a year, was a giant flame, and we, the single-minded moths, were compelled to its bright, dangerous glory from all corners of Toronto's northern suburban sprawl. We would come on Friday nights, Saturday nights, Tuesday nights; we would loiter, flirt, get high, and, as long as we bought food, drank soft drinks, fed quarters into the stiff metal mouths of the arcade machines, and paid thirteen dollars a ticket for the latest blockbuster, management seemed content to let us take over the theatre at the expense of young families and the elderly, who quickly learned on which nights to steer clear.

I found Marco in the arcade. He was playing *Death Fighter IX*, his swatch of so-blond-it's-white hair giving him a few inches on the machine. I sat down on the air hockey table and watched him: he'd put in his two quarters, let the computer kill him, and then put in another two quarters and do it again. "Why are you doing that?" I finally asked, throwing the air hockey striker at him.

"It's more realistic this way," he said, not turning around.

"Whatever, let's go find Bruce."

Outside of the arcade, the cineplex was thronging with teenagers. Some of them I knew by name, from my high school or other nights at the theatre. Some of them I knew only as faces. Others I had never seen before but felt like I'd known since kindergarten. Bruce was waiting for us by the far left doors, calmly watching two people make out in the hollow made by the cineplex walls and the row of cement-framed movie posters. We bumped fists; I flashed Bruce and Marco the tape case that contained the four-gram joint I had carefully rolled that afternoon in my basement bathroom. It was the biggest joint I had ever produced; it took me four tries, half a pack of papers.

"Where should we go?" Bruce asked.

"I don't know; the parking lot is sketch now. Tom and those guys got busted last weekend."

"Follow me," Bruce said.

We pushed through the crowds and skirted the cineplex. There was a narrow back parking lot and then a large field. We started through the tall grass, heading towards the skeleton of an abandoned building, the lights of the two highways streaming by behind it. About halfway there, I felt a tingling on the back of my neck: we were being followed. And I was pretty sure it wasn't by the lone security guard the theatre had hired to try and keep us in order. I tried to ignore it, not looking back. We entered the building. It wasn't abandoned after all, but was in the process of being rebuilt. There were skids of bricks, undersized tractors, the muddy footprints of work boots. I followed with my eyes the support beams that stretched from the cement floor all the way up to the open roof and darkening sky. Exposed like this, the building seemed incredibly fragile, only staying up because we chose to collectively believe it would. I pushed against a small section of drywall, surprised that the whole thing didn't come toppling down on top of us.

"You know that the theatre used to be a slaughterhouse, right?" Bruce said, smacking a pallet of bricks with his hand. "They'd kill a thousand plus heads of cattle a day. It was the biggest killing floor in southern Ontario. This building is where they would store the carcasses. They're turning it into a high-rise or some shit."

"You're fucking with us, right?" Marco said, looking around wide eyed. It's funny: already, at sixteen, I didn't trust most people, thought everything they said, even the most banal chitchat, was a lie. Except Bruce. For some reason, I took Bruce at his word. He didn't have any of that false pretense that everybody else around me had, wasn't constantly wanting, desiring, plotting. He was utterly free of social compromise, which was probably why he was one of the only people in my high school I could stand (or who could stand me). And Marco, well, Marco was just Marco.

"Of course not," Bruce said, "look, you can see right over there the ramp they used to bring the bodies in on and—"

"Yo, shut up," I said. We had turned a corner, and I saw the two guys who were following us—I recognized them right away: they were hanging out near us when I showed Bruce the joint back at the theatre, a tall guy and a fat guy, both in baggy jeans and Timberlands. They were trailing us, keeping back a calculated distance. "Let's get out of here," I said, not wanting to confirm their realness by telling Bruce about them.

"You know what? I think I can smell it now," Marco said as we climbed out an unframed window. I didn't smell anything, but I was still happy to be out of there; Bruce's words were conjuring ghosts. We were behind the supposed ex-slaughterhouse now, the highways in front of us, the new highway dark and imposing above the rundown old one. We stopped at the top of a ditch that fell fifteen or so metres before rising again to the highway barrier.

"So, pull out the joint!" Bruce had to yell to be heard over the traffic.

The two guys who had been following us joined our circle. The tall, lanky one had a red baseball cap and forearm tattoos, a long scar on his right temple; the short, fat one had a shaved head, a faint blond mustache, and was wearing an enormous white t-shirt, was working on a bag of sunflower seeds. They both sparked with unmistakable menace.

"Yo bros, what saying?" the one in the red hat said, the apparent friendliness in his greeting soaked with arrogance, spiked with threat. "You flashed us that spliffie back at the theatre; we figured we'd see if we could join in on the sesh." He was hammered enough to be swaying, his eyes cloudy white pools.

"Fuck that, we want the whole thing!" the bigger guy bellowed, all pretense of friendliness gone. No one spoke. Marco's fear wafted over to me like a cool breeze, gently stoking my own terror into a roaring bonfire. I looked up: the new highway was a fast-moving river of brilliant, sparkling machines, the old highway a rumbling assembly line of compromised mufflers and oily exhaust.

"We'd be happy to pass it around," Bruce said, cracking the tension, putting out his short, thick-fingered hand. Red Hat made like he was going to shake, but pulled back his other arm and punched Bruce hard in the face instead. Bruce absorbed the shock, shook it off, and tackled Red Hat. They tumbled down the hill, rolling through the grass, punching, grabbing, swearing, digging into each other. I stood there with Marco and Sunflower Seeds, watching them roll down the ditch, the cars and trucks roaring above us. My lungs were filling with cement.

Sunflower looked at me. "Should we fight?" he asked casually, spitting a mouthful of shells down the hill.

I turned away. Marco had vanished. Bruce and Red Hat had landed at the bottom of the ditch. Bruce was sitting cross-legged, and Red Hat's head was sort of lying in Bruce's lap. They were still punching each other, Red Hat uppercutting Bruce's chin, Bruce working Red Hat's face and arms.

Sunflower was watching too, munching loudly. He looked at me, shrugged. "We should fight," he said, dropping his bag of seeds into the grass.

I was going to crap my pants, vomit, disintegrate. I'm surprised the fear wasn't enough to stop my heart. I put my hand in my pocket and made a fist around the pen I had in there. If he hit me, I would try to pop him in the eye. It was the only way I stood a chance.

Sunflower rolled his shoulders, cracked his knuckles, lolled his melon-sized head. He put his fists up, squared his feet, and smiled. I tightened my grip.

"Hey, hey, it's cool. They're done," Marco called out, materializing from the shadows. He pointed towards the bottom of the ditch. Red Hat and Bruce were slowly walking up the steep incline, muddy and bloody, their arms around each other. We stood dumbly watching as they crested the hill.

"Good fight," Red Hat said.

"Good fight," Bruce concurred. They clasped hands and hugged.

"What are you waiting for? Light up the doo-bay!" Sunflower enthused, suddenly celebratory, slapping me on the back. I winced, took the joint out of the case. My hands still shaking, I lit it with my Zippo. I took my time with it, puffing gently, turning it in my fingers, working the flame, listening to the paper crackle. I eventually passed it to Red Hat, who was standing on my left, its nickel-sized cherry burning round and bright, like the sun, like a planet on fire.

Red Hat took an enormous, drawn-out drag. "What school you troublefuckers from?" he asked, taking short, sucking inhales to force the smoke deeper into his lungs. Bruce answered. The joint went from hand to hand. Red Hat produced a plastic water bottle of whiskey, a patch of fuzzy white where the label used to be, and started it around. I watched Red Hat and Sunflower through shifting perspectives as the alcohol and the weed worked their chemical changes.

"I laced the joint with PCP," I said after the whiskey was done and the spliff had gone around the circle four or five times, now nothing but a stubby little roach.

My announcement was met with stunned silence. I was staring at Red Hat when I said it, and for a glorious instant I saw his toughness evaporate, like a drop of water on burning steel, and he looked like a scared child. Only for an instant, and he was back, a foaming sea of confidence.

"Fuck, yeah," he said, turning the brim of his hat to the side. "Fuck yeah! Haven't gotten wet in a while!"

Sunflower chuckled slowly, his eyes moving from the highways to the sky to the ground and back up again. It looked like Marco had eaten something bad and was going to be sick. Bruce, who had the uncanny ability to always appear untouched by a session, no matter how much we smoked, drank, or ate, took a final drag on the roach and heeled it into the dirt. The wind brought in the cool night air. The highways blurred into a single burning conduit of liquid gold. The five of us walked through the long grass back to the theatre, diamond-sharp stars coming down all around us, cutting deep gashes into the night sky, lighting up the cineplex's fake treetops.

After eating at the painfully bright food court (Bruce and Marco greasy, dull-coloured burgers, myself sugar-sweet vegetarian pizza, cola that burned my insides syrupy-clean), the three of us snuck into a half-full theatre and watched some random movie—I don't even remember which one. There were some big explosions, some impressive set pieces, some glossy seduction; some witty one-liners. Some buff white man saving the day. Even then, I knew it was total bullshit. Hundreds of millions of dollars wasted to entertain stoned and horny teenage pretenders. I was much too high to pay any real attention, though; I kept seeing meat hooks swinging from the ceiling, twitching cow bodies floating in the darkness of the theatre's high corners. The audience's laughter mutated into cattle screams, the backs of their heads floating between me and the terrible screen, sprouting sad animal eyes, mute, alive, knowing.

"Do you smell that?" I whispered into Bruce's face. He was eating from an extra-large bag of popcorn with his mouth, drinking it, his eyes fault-lined with red, the buttery bruises on his face coming to vibrant life in front of me. "The death, do you smell it?" I said again, louder.

Bruce's eyes widened, and he burst out laughing. I turned to Marco. He was splayed across two chairs, his legs thrown over the next row, his eyes closed, his shock of white hair catching the light of the projector. It looked like he was dreaming peacefully.

Later, past midnight, Bruce and Marco long gone, I would stand awkwardly near the arcade, waiting for my father to show up, the employees shutting down the concession stands, mopping the floor, giving each other high fives—but at that moment, Bruce, Marco, and I surrounded by apparitions, I had never felt more alone.

A/V

Fall

After rolling the road cases out of the truck, through the loading bay, up a skinny elevator, through an endless industrial kitchen of stainless-steel tables, mixers, and closet-sized ovens—milling cooks eyeing us suspiciously as we wheel past—down a long hallway of dirty carpet and peeling walls, and into the event space, we get to work. It takes the four of us a half dozen round trips from the loading bay to the banquet hall to unload the truck. Once the thirty-odd cases are arranged in the middle of the room, we spend the next four hours opening, rolling, placing, powering, setting up, plugging in, locking, adjusting, taping down, booting up, testing. There are two 7x10 rear-projection screens (the projector lenses costing more than a year's rent), four subwoofers with tops, two additional speakers, the entire room draped in plush black, uplit with alternating blue and purple par cans. The stage is washed in the bright spotlight of two Lekos. Gabe shows up just as we are finishing, Jatinder and I going around cleaning up, taping the speaker cables to their stands. As usual, he has us rearrange everything, eating up another two hours. Finally, we roll the last of the empty road cases behind the drape line. The room looks good, though considering tonight's the last night of the film festival and this is the eighteenth room I've set up in ten days, I probably can't tell a decent setup from a total disaster.

"Shit, we gotta go," Jatinder says, looking at his watch. "We gotta get to the Breakwater."

"You guys haven't set up the Breakwater yet?" Gabe yells at us, his phone muted in his cupped palm. "What the fuck are you waiting for?!"

Jatinder jiggles his keys, and we leave the banquet hall, make our way to the truck.

"How much sleep you get last night?" I ask, as we sit in the cab waiting for the loading bay door to open, the truck rumbling underneath us.

"I don't know. An hour. Two. I went over to Rachel's for a drink after the teardown."

"I forgot to tell you—Jackie showed up at my door this morning."

"Fuck," Jatinder says, putting the truck into gear and driving up the ramp and into blinding downtown sunlight. "Maybe I didn't sleep at all."

"She's back from the coast. First time in five years. She says she's planning on staying in Toronto for a while. I gave her a key." We're stopped at a traffic snarl, the high-rises of the financial district glinting above us, the spire of the CN Tower visible through a ruler-wide opening in the buildings, overseeing the hustle and motion of the city.

"I don't think I've had a decent night's sleep since the summer ended." .

"What're you talking about, JT? We haven't had a decent night's sleep since high school ended." We double-park at a Timmy's, run inside. "Gabe would be so pissed if he found out we stopped to eat," I say when we're back in the truck, scarfing our sandwiches.

"So Jackie's back, eh?" Jatinder says, looking out the window at the downtown blur, grimacing as he sips his coffee, his voice heavy with suggestion.

We meet up with Jerry, Maximilian, and the other truck at the Breakwater. They've unloaded half of the truck without us, are leaning against the loading bay wall smoking cigarettes; "Boys boys boys," Maximilian yells in his confident swagger, taking a final drag on his smoke. "You're late! What, did Gabe have you jack him off one at a time?" We slap hands, bump fists, heel out cigarettes, put on gloves, start rolling out the remaining road cases. The Breakwater is newer and chicer than the Kingtrooper, all clean white moldings, shiny blond hardwood floors, and sparkling reclaimed chandeliers. Even working at breakneck speed, we cut it pretty close—Jatinder is still tamping down the cable lines with black duct tape as the guests start arriving. I jog out to the truck, change into my suit, inhale a cigarette, and hurry around the building to the front entrance, through the lobby and into the banquet hall, stationing myself beside Maximilian, who's already

DJing, black and gold headphones over his ears. Jerry takes the rental truck back to the warehouse. Jatinder disappears with the other truck. Maximilian is on sound; I am on lights. I dial in the appropriate runs, sweeps, washes, and colours, highlight the producers, agents, and directors as they shmooze, get liquored up, and make their multimillion-dollar deals. As far as I can tell, there are no famous actors present, though Jatinder saw Bill Maher smoking a joint with some waiters in the basement of the Bearclaw Bistro the other night. During dinner I raise the lights, sit down, try not to fall asleep.

The party peaks around ten thirty, then plummets steeply. Everybody has been drinking and celebrating and networking for twelve nights, is looking forward to going back to NY or LA, recharging before the next orgy of distribution deals, glamour, and money. So by eleven thirty, only a few stragglers are left in the room. Jatinder appears beside us at front of house, watching the remaining guests. I glance at him: he's no longer wearing black pants and a black button-down, but blue jeans and a Pink Floyd t-shirt with a rip over the stomach that he's had since grade eight. He smells like sex. We wait until the last person leaves before we start the strike. If Maximilian weren't here, we'd be here all night: he talks nonstop, veering from sports to the newest A/V equipment to describing in minute detail a shocking variety of sexual encounters, but he does the work of three people, and we're out of here just before one in the morning. "A/V, A/V, A/V, am I right, my brothers?" he shouts as he hoists the road cases into the truck, his biceps bulging footballs. "You guys know what A/V really stands for, don't you? Anal-Vaginal. Anal-Vaginal! Every man has a choice, a ha ha ha ha. Pick your poison!" That's Maximilian for you: built like a soldier, shockingly good looking, magnetic, motormouthed, filthy, he and Jatinder the only regular non-Jewish workers in Gabe's stable of DJs, techs, and A/V specialists. He doesn't stop talking until he is literally driving away in his Beamer. Jatinder and I only hit one red light on the race to the Kingtrooper. Gabe's there, in his let's-make-some-new-clients pinstripe, mousse in his hair, shmoozing with some tuxedoed men with strong chins, tanned faces, tired-but-still-hungry eyes. We hang back until Gabe gives us the nod. We fan out into the room, start powering off, unplugging, disconnecting. The Chairs Chairs Chairs guys show up, start collapsing the tables, rolling them out—as usual, besides a nod here and there, we ignore each other. Gabe yells at Jatinder for his jeans and t-shirt; if anybody else showed up to a strike dressed like that, he would be reamed out and fired on the spot, but Jatinder, of course, gets a pass. We take down and pack the lights in their road cases, zip the speakers into their bags, coil cables, dismantle trusses, unlatch and drop the screens, unsnap, fold, dismantle, and put away the frames. As soon as Gabe finishes packing up the computers and mixers at front of house, he takes off, and I go to the bathroom and splash cold water on my face, watch myself in the mirror. I laugh out loud when I notice I forgot to change out of my suit. There's a long black stain on the pants, oil or grease from one of the road cases. Back in the banquet hall, the road cases are huddled in the middle of the room, shut and latched, and we start rolling them to the truck: through the staff hallway, the kitchen piled with dirty dishes and pans and glasses, one lone worker mopping the floor, down the elevator two cases at a time, another hallway, the cavernous loading bay, up the ramp and into the truck. We hoist cases on top of each other, fit everything together like a three-dimensional jigsaw puzzle. As I ratchet-strap the whole load secure, Jatinder runs back to do a dummy check. I light two cigarettes, lean against the truck, wait for Jatinder.

We leave the hotel at four thirty, get to Gabe's warehouse in Toronto's north end just before five, the streets empty, the traffic lights changing only for us. Jerry is there with the other truck, asleep on a four-foot road case, waiting for us, an unopened sixty of Jack Daniel's nuzzled in his arm. We unload, roll everything into its proper place under the warehouse's buzzing fluorescent lights. Jerry opens the Jack, we stand in the chilly warehouse passing it around, smoke a joint, celebrate the last event of the festival, joke about how we used to end every night like this, how we've become old men. We linger in the circle for longer than we intended to. Finally: lights, alarm, doors. Jatinder gives me a lift home in his Kia Rio, which he bought in grade twelve and, thanks to loving maintenance and oil changes, has had for 350,000 kilometres.

"How long have we been doing this for?" he asks me as we cruise through the city. Jatinder's sex smell has defused, making room for the mixture of sweat, grease, metal, whiskey, and weed that exudes off of both of us. There's still no traffic, but we're nearing the end of that sweet spot where you can get from the top of the city to downtown in fifteen minutes. As we get on the Allen, the CN Tower blinks in the distance, a lighthouse that we are being pulled towards.

"I don't know man, since high school." My eyes are closing, sleep swallowing me whole.

"Fifteen years, Mark. Fifteen years! Aren't you tired of working freelance, of being at the mercy of Gabe's poor scheduling, his bad moods, his rants? Let's start our own company. I have enough contacts, we could buy some old equipment from Olga. I've been saving up; we can do this right. Corporate events, weddings, the odd bar mitzvah—who else knows the industry like we do? It's time we become our own bosses, break out into the world. C'mon man, you and me. Like always." I'm listening to him through a dense ocean of sleep, my head nodding with the car's motion. I'm startled awake at the first full stop since we left the warehouse. We're outside my building. Jatinder is looking at me with bright eyes. My oldest friend. "C'mon man. What'dya say?"

"It's late Jatinder. I don't know."

"Think about it. Think about it!" he calls, driving away.

I open the door to my apartment, freeze when I see Jackie sleeping on the couch, my heart almost stopping, until I remember I had given her a key that morning. Almost twenty-four hours ago. I eat two bowls of cereal as the kitchen fills with full, headachey sunlight. I wake Jackie up, follow her into my bedroom, a blanket around her shoulders, her black hair loose, down to her bum. Tomorrow's my first day off in what feels like years, though Gabe could always call with a last-minute load-in. I collapse onto the bed, still in my suit.

"I can't believe you only have one fork," Jackie says sleepily, slipping into the bathroom.

"I'll get another one tomorrow," I say into the pillow. I fall asleep before Jackie gets back, don't open my eyes again until the day's sunlight is already gone.

I sit up in bed. I'm groggy, hungover, sore. Fifteen years, I say to myself, staring at Jackie's suitcase and political-button-laden knapsack leaning against my dresser, a pair of her jeans crumpled by the door. I listen for sounds of her in the apartment, don't hear any. Fifteen years. I drift back into darkness.

Winter

Jatinder and I both started doing A/V back in the tenth grade. Started in the bar mitzvah circuit, learned the ropes, delighted in the late hours, the physicality, the camaraderie, the money—more than we could have made working at the food court or selling weed. Much, much more. Even though Ben Goldstein himself DJed my bar mitzvah, sweaty and fat and loud and booked two years in advance, it was Jatinder who first started third manning for him. Jatinder and his sister Kavita were the only brown people at our high school, though we'd been jokingly calling him an honorary Jew ever since he came over for his first Hanukkah when we were nine years old and lit the candles himself. He had been to as many bar and bat mitzvahs as any of us, and Goldstein quickly discovered that parents appreciated the colour of his skin, making them feel good about the oodles of money they were spending to celebrate their sons' and daughters' transition into Jewish adulthood. Jatinder—with the same ease he attracted girls and won sporting events—cultivated for himself the precise mixture of confidence, suaveness, and magnetism that was needed for Goldstein to invite you into his inner circle. By the time I third manned my first party, Jatinder had already graduated to DJ. I wasn't as smooth as Jatinder, I couldn't get an entire banquet hall of horny thirteen-year-olds, middle-aged Jews, and old-world grandparents sweating it out to "Macarena" like he could, but I was a good worker and learned fast, and within weeks I was working every Saturday night.

Our teenage lives revolved around Goldstein's warehouse. We spent our weekends there, dated the dancers, made our money throwing extravagant parties for the city's middle-class Jewish population. We learned how to light and drape a room, how to set up and manage basic sound, how to mix and DJ and MC, how to say yes to every request from the audience but to play none of them, how to flirt with the mother of the bar mitzvah child just enough to get a cash tip at the end of the night. Goldstein acted like a king, and we treated him like one. (Don't ask me how a fat, sweaty, balding Jewish man was able to monopolize the entire bar mitzvah circuit in a city of 200,000 Jews, because I wouldn't be able to tell you.) Goldstein had a fleet of trucks, an enormous warehouse, a stable of DJs, a roster of dancers, an entire bureaucracy to put together the four or five weekly celebrations of the Jewish coming-of-age. I loved being a part of it, to belong to the nightly rhythm of swagger, music, shmooze, work, and drugs. After a few years we barely noticed the children.

When Goldstein retired, at the ripe old age of forty-seven, his vast DJ empire was divided among his top lieutenants: Brian started FreeFall Entertainment, Rick and Petrov founded Be Good Productions, and Olga, Goldstein's warehouse manager, an indeterminately-aged Russian woman most of us were terrified of, bought seventy percent of his gear and started renting it out to the newly formed companies. Word is that Goldstein still gets a cut of every dollar Brian, Rick, and Petrov make. Who knows. Gabe took over Goldstein's fledgling non-bar mitzvah business: the corporate parties, the weddings, the conferences. And Goldstein, Goldstein bought a mountain in Colorado, built a ski chalet, called his protégés once a week, ruled in absentia. After the shake-up and reforming, the whole business changed, and Jatinder and I became freelancers. We worked for all three of the new companies, our rate for each four-hour call higher than most, but by then we were the most experienced, the most trustworthy techs, truck drivers, schleppers, and DJs. Most of us my age who started in high school eventually moved on: university, travel, careers, family. But not us. We're still here, still living the life, still doing lights, sound, visuals. A few years back, as the staff at Be Good and FreeFall kept getting younger and the bar mitzvahs became more and more extravagant, we started working almost exclusively for Gabe. What started as a way to make quick, insane money to buy weed and McDonald's, has, without my noticing, become my life.

And until Jatinder blindsided me with the idea of starting our own company, I had barely given it a second thought.

In past years, there would be a brief lull between the film fest and the start of the corporate season, but not this year. Even though the rest of the world is sunk in an economic depression, it hasn't seemed to have had much effect on the event budgets for the banks, law firms, and hedgefunds of Toronto. After barely three days off—most of which I spent with Jackie in bed—Jatinder and I are back to working fifteen-hour days. In my teens and early twenties, I could easily go four days without sleep, surviving on coffee, cigarettes, gyros, McDonald's daily Meal Deals, the adrenaline of physical work. Now, somewhere around the thirty-eighth hour, I lose sensation in my feet, couldn't care less if it was a ten-foot, thirty-foot, or fifty-foot cable I just dropped in the fifty-foot bin, lose faith in the entirety of civilization. I know I should start saying no to calls, but I just keep accepting, keep starting my days at the warehouse and ending them at sunrise. It's the only way I know how to be. The money pours in. Jatinder asks me every few nights if I've given any thought to his proposal, and I keep making excuses.

Almost every afternoon, Jackie and I meet at the apartment, have sex and eat Portuguese chicken from the place across the alley, get to know each other again.

When Jackie was twenty-one, she quit dancing for Goldstein, travelled in Europe for a winter, and moved to Vancouver the summer before she started at UBC. It was there, at the other end of the country, where she had what she calls her "political awakening," going to protests, writing papers about free-trade coffee and Indigenous rights and the ethics of deforestation. After getting her degree, she worked at a series of not-for-profits and NGOs, mostly environment-focused, spent two years at a company that invested in renewable energy in third-world countries. About a year ago, she started getting tired of the coast, of Vancouver, of her over-earnest, over-eager, Keen-sandal wearing social group. She quit her job, took two weeks to drive across the country, staying with activist friends in Edmonton, Saskatoon, Winnipeg, Thunder Bay. And now here she is, at my place, telling me all about it. Listening to her stories, I'm impressed, intimidated. It's not hard for me to picture her at these organizations as she tells me about them: solving problems, writing passionately worded grant applications, friends with everybody in the office but not holding back when someone is not pulling their weight, all with the same devotion and energy she brings to every aspect of her life. And it's not like I would call myself apolitical exactly, but it's not something that propels me through the day like it does for Jackie, that fills me with purpose, with mission.

After a few days recuperating from her travels at my place, Jackie started handing out resumes, trying to get a foothold in the activist scene here in Toronto. She was finding it harder than she thought. "I had no idea how cliquey everything is in Toronto," she told me one afternoon. We were eating our roasted chicken on my couch. I watched Jackie eat, her pointy nose twitching as she chewed. I thought of how Jackie was when we first started hooking up: one of Goldstein's dancers, wore black and red t-shirts and leggings as she danced on the raised platform in front of the DJ, stomping and clapping and stepping and whipping her hair from side to side along with the two or three other dancers, all dressed identically. We dated for three years, from seventeen until twenty; it was the longest relationship I've been in, and when she showed up in September I felt a mixture of excitement, fear, doubt, and sexual arousal that has shifted percentages but stayed basically the same since. "I knew Toronto was more commerce oriented, more go go go," she said, chewing her chicken thoughtfully, "which was one of the reasons I *wanted* to come back ... but I had no idea how hard it would be to break in."

"Maybe you should start dancing again," I said.

"Mark!" Jackie's eyes flashed. She put a hand through her hair. We scrambled up from the table and rushed to the bedroom.

Now, it's halfway through November and Jackie has cut back on her resume campaign, has turned her attention to my apartment, cleaning, organizing, unsubtly dropping hints about what I need to buy, upgrade, throw out. When I come home from a gig, I can't help but see my living space as if through her eyes, and it isn't pretty: the lack of chairs, the wooden toilet seat that, if it weren't for a rusty nail, would be in two discrete pieces, the half-dead potted tree blocking the unplugged television. The kitchen is the most distressing to Jackie, what she can't get over—not only do I only have one fork, but I also have one knife and one bowl, though I do have two plates, a big and a small pan, a good-sized pot. Not that I cook with it much. One day while I was at work, Jackie cleared off half of my dresser, and now four seeds are sprouting in envelopes of wet paper towel. They are labelled in Jackie's square, clear hand: Douglas Fir, California Redwood, Ponderosa Pine, Lodgepole. "I thought I'd bring some of the coast back with me," she said, pulling me onto the bed.

I come home from a teardown to find Jackie sitting on my bed in a pair of my boxer shorts, painting her nails a pastel pink.

"I thought you weren't going to be home till late," she says, blowing on her nails. I sit down on the floor.

"We finished early, for once. After the bride barfed all over the groom's father, everyone cleared out pretty quick. Jatinder and Jerry went up to the warehouse."

Jackie laughs. "Welcome to the family!" She finishes her last nail, closes the polish bottle. "All these weddings, must be fun," she says.

"It's all right," I say.

"Remember all those bar and bat mitzvahs we worked together? It seems like another life."

"Not for me," I say, with more edge than intended.

"Oh yeah?" Jackie asks, raising an eyebrow. "I thought it was all weddings, weddings, weddings. When's the last time you did one?"

"A bar mitzvah? A few years ago. I really try to avoid them. I just meant that after your two hundredth party, they all seem to melt together. You should see what's at these bar mitzvahs now, Jackie. Thousand-dollar dance floor emblems, lasers, truss arches of lights you wouldn't see at a Jay-Z concert. The last party I did there was a fifteen-minute video of celebrities and sports stars talking about the kid. The video ended with the bar mitzvah boy sitting on a throne—I kid you not, a throne—thanking everybody for celebrating with him. I almost threw up."

"Jeez," Jackie says. "I remember when a speaker or two, a disco ball, a couple of dancers was more than enough." We sit silently for a minute, thinking of the old days. Eventually Jackie gets off the bed and joins me on the floor, putting her head on my shoulder. Her skin smells like my Irish Spring body wash, her hair like my Pantene, all mixed with the chemical stink of the nail polish; it's incredibly arousing.

"Our kids will have low-key, tasteful bat mitzvahs, and instead of gifts, we'll ask everybody to give donations to an NGO," she says, snuggling into me.

"Kids?" I say, falling asleep. "No kids," I mumble.

Jackie coos into my ear, her hand on my leg. I wake up slightly. Why is Jackie talking about kids? And with me? Jackie and I hadn't talked about what was going on between us, but I thought we were both on the same page: she was tired of the men on the coast—who, from how she told it, were barely able to sit still long enough for a real date let alone a relationship—and had come out to Toronto to get away from it and just landed at my door. We were having a fun time, but nothing serious. Not a relationship. Not *children*. Jackie's hand becomes more insistent, and my thoughts get pulled downwards.

I turn my mouth to hers.

Thomas is back. I arrive at the warehouse on a freezing early-December morning with a tray of steaming coffee, and there's his beat-up Tercel, the backseat crammed with broken tom drums and bent cymbals. And there he is inside the warehouse, standing by the open truck with Jatinder. Thomas started in the industry at the same time as Jatinder and me, did A/V off and on for years—though, as he never tired of telling anybody who would listen, his real aspiration was to be a screenwriter. From the first week I'd met him, he would always have a prospective writing contract, his script would be about to be picked up, he was dialoguing with a famous director, though nothing ever came from any of it. A few years ago, he just took off, bought a plane ticket to Paris, and a week later was gone. "If I'm going to succeed as a writer, I have to go all in," he explained to me. Thomas looks the same: short, with a big chest and powerful arms and a complicated face—a beard of a thousand individual hairs, old acne scars, a copse of beauty marks under his left eye. I take him in, the coffees still in my hands. Thomas was always a handful: always talking, always plotting, always going on about film trivia and critical theory ephemera. Maybe he's mellowed out in his time abroad.

"Back from expat paradise?" Gabe yells from the doorway of his office. "So, big shot, where's the multimillion-dollar studio deal?"

Thomas smiles from ear-to-ear. "On the way, big guy, on the way," he calls out happily.

Later, at the event space, Thomas tells us about his latest script. We're standing at the cable road case. I had been watching Jatinder talking with the client in the corner, their heads bent, hoping Gabe didn't notice. I'd been catching Jatinder talking up clients all month: at the Berkowitz and Dershowitz law firm holiday party, the end-of-quarter bank extravaganzas. He'd throw a meaningful glance my way, and I'd know what he was doing: shoring up potential clients. Everybody loves Jatinder, it's true, and though Gabe heavily applied the shmooze when he was talking with a client, it wasn't hard to catch him in a moment of verbal abuse with one of his crew. Jatinder shakes hands with the client and comes to join me and Thomas. I see Gabe shut his phone and start walking towards us. I bend down and start grabbing cable. Thomas starts explaining his script to Jatinder from the beginning: "It's set in a dystopic future where it's discovered that watching porn cures cancer, right? And not just a glance, but hours of porn a day! Enough for serious psychological damage. It's called *Impure Thoughts about the Houseguest*. It's a laugh riot, but also a biting social satire. It's actually pretending to be a film noir detective movie, a film noir sci-fi detective mashup, but underneath all the postmodern fun is a deep criticism of all of our cultural mores."

I stifle a laugh at how Thomas overpronounces *mores*. More-EHS.

"Yo Thomas, less talk, more work!" Gabe shouts.

Thomas leans in to where Jatinder and I are standing. "I've gotten some serious interest from some major studios. Can't say anything about it yet, confidentiality and everything." I notice for the first time that Thomas may in fact be affecting a slight—and, needless to say, poor—French accent.

"NOW!" Gabe roars.

"Yes boss, right away, boss," Thomas responds, grabbing an armful of cables and heading off.

"Same old Thomas," Jatinder whispers in my ear.

The truth is, there's no way I want to start my own company. Working for people like Goldstein and Gabe is one thing, but to *become* one of them? For some reason, I can't stomach the thought of it. Owning an A/V company terrifies me. I hate the corporations, the waste of weddings, the industries that exist solely to make money off of people's love. I hadn't realized how critical I was of the world I was a part of until Jatinder started me thinking on it. But what could I do instead? I know nothing but A/V, how to drive anything with an engine, the feel of a truck loaded with gear gliding through midnight Toronto streets, the CN Tower coming in and out of view. I can't help feeling that I've started thinking about what I want from my life ten years too late.

Between all the corporate events this winter is a wedding or two; it's at such a wedding, at Beth Sinai, that I see the statue. I'm heading back to the banquet hall from the washroom, my work gloves in my hand, when it grabs my attention. I've been through this foyer countless times—not just as a worker, but as a guest at long-ago bat mitzvahs, the weddings of second cousins once removed, once even a bris and a funeral the same week—but today something draws me to it. The statue's on a lacquered wood pedestal, eye level, and is made of rough clay. From far away it would look like a skinny, pitted volcano, but when you approach it, you realize that it is actually made up of bodies, limbs flaying, indistinct faces melting, arms and legs climbing on top of each other. The body at the top of the cone is the most recognizably human, their hand raised up as if grasping for something to pull itself up on, their face a hollow mask, their sex indeterminate; underneath the reaching figure, the bodies become more messy, until at the bottom it is just a rippling block of barely discernible human matter. A plaque gives the artist's name and says, "For the Six Million Who Perished in the Shoah and for All of Us Who Live On in Their Name. Never Again." I continue staring at it. My mind does a quick shuffle through all the shuls I've worked or partied at over the years: all of them have display cases of Judaica, plaques with donors, founders, and presidents; there's the colourfully tiled fountain at the Sephardic synagogue at Bathurst and Steeles, a gift from the king of Morocco; sometimes there's a small exhibition on some aspect of Jewish history, usually the Holocaust or Israel—but nowhere have I seen something as arresting, as dark, as this statue. It opens up deep reverberating bass notes from a subwoofer I didn't know was inside me. The door to the banquet hall swings open, and I tear my eyes away. Gabe's standing in the doorway with his new too-short haircut, on the phone, giving me a meaningful look. I slip my hands into my gloves and join him.

I'm distracted for the rest of the setup. I haven't thought about the Holocaust for years, but as I strap lights onto the top of trusses, run par cans along the back wall, everything I had read, learned, or seen rushes into consciousness. A dark lake of emotion sloshing right behind my mouth, spilling into my nostrils, stinging the back of my eyes.

That night, I tell Jackie about it. We're in my bedroom. I'm sitting on the floor, Jackie is sitting on my bed, her legs crossed, pensively smoking a cigarette.

"My grandparents were survivors," she says, after I describe the statue to her, my unexpected response.

"What? I had no idea."

"I think about the Holocaust pretty much all the time," Jackie says, watching me as she does so.

"Really? How come?"

Jackie laughs. "How come? It's the defining moment of the twentieth century. That we are capable of doing that. What's stopping us from doing it again? I don't know, I guess I like keeping myself aware of the abyss we all exist on top of."

"What do you mean what we are capable of doing? Didn't they do it to us?"

Jackie smiles. "We are humans before we are Jews, Mark," she says, putting out her cigarette in the bedside ashtray. "Come over here," she says, her tone different, patting the bed. I get up, sit down next to her. "Have you seen *Schindler's List*?" she asks.

"Not really."

"I have it on my computer." She's already opening her laptop. "In high school, I would watch it, like, once a week, easy."

I cozy up to her, she presses play, and a new phase of our relationship—of my life—starts with a girl in a red coat.

Company party for the city's Sweet Ride Spin and Run franchises. A casino-themed party for Treadsoft Ltd. The annual blowout celebration for Massada Assets Inc. The interchangeable, instantly forgettable affairs held by every major bank with a Toronto headquarters. Jackie and I watch *The Pianist*. *Life is Beautiful*. *The Nuremberg Trials*. End-of-year parties at the Kingtrooper, the Breakwater, the Hyatt, the Westin. Ricky Rosenfeld hires me to DJ a private function at his Rosedale mansion. I've known Ricky since I was the pointman for his son's bar mitzvah, ten years ago (back when I did such things), and every now and then he pays me large sums of money to DJ his private events. (I wouldn't want to imagine Gabe's reaction if he found out I was working for Ricky on the side.) Jackie and I watch *Anne Frank*; we watch *Anne Frank: The Whole Story*; we watch *The Attic: The Hiding of Anne Frank*. Anne Frank Goes to the Beach. Anne Frank: The Director's Cut. Anne Frank Unplugged. Wherever we are in the city, I glance up to look for the CN Tower: driving up Strachan from the highway, leaving the warehouse, through the netting of streetcar wires at College and Bathurst, the new warehouse-turned-event-space at the waterfront, the roof of the Kingtrooper. New Year's Eve party in the penthouse of the Breakwater, all day setup, I DJ with Jatinder, Jackie partying with her new friends from Tamp and Pour, the cafe she's been hanging out at, we both get home around 5:00 a.m., fall asleep in each other's arms. Up at noon for the teardown. New Year's Day. We stand around eating pizza. "I didn't think I'd miss A/V so much while I was gone," Thomas says, his mouth full of cheese and pepperoni. "I love it! Especially the weddings! My God! Every day I go to work is the best day of somebody's life." Maximilian nods exaggeratedly: "Yeah man, I love this job too, 'cause during the father-daughter dance, I can go jack off in the washroom!" He stuffs an entire slice into his mouth and walks off. "Man, does he take nothing seriously?" Thomas asks. Like most of our conversations, we end up talking about how far A/V has come in the past two decades. "Pretty soon, it'll go a hundred percent wireless," Thomas says.

"And that's when we'll be obsolete," Jatinder says, everybody laughing.

"I'm never going to be obsolete," Maximilian roars, coming towards us, his arms laden with par cans, which he lets drop into a road case. "Wireless or not, somebody's going to have to turn these fucking things on!"

Back at the warehouse, late afternoon and already dark out, Gabe gives each of us a bottle of wine for a successful corporate season. He looks calm, relaxed, his hair three weeks out from his last haircut, a little disheveled. This is the most complacent Gabe will be all year, before the three to five weeks of relative quiet, before the spring, before the weddings, before it all starts over again.

"Happy New Year's, boys," he says.

A few days after New Year's, I drive Jatinder and Rachel to the airport. They're taking advantage of the January to mid-February A/V lull with a trip to an all-inclusive in Cuba.

"You sure you don't want to borrow the car while we're gone?" Jatinder asks as I merge onto the 427. A week ago, Jatinder got rid of his old Kia Rio and bought a brand new Honda SUV. I push on the gas and zip into the passing lane.

"I've got Jackie's if I need a car for anything."

"Fair enough." Jatinder watches the city pass outside the window. I know what's coming next. "Listen, dude, enough's enough. We don't need to work for Gabe anymore. Let's break out."

I check my blindspot, merge. "I'll think about it," I say noncommittally.

"Do it, Mark!" Rachel says enthusiastically. I glance at Rachel in the rear view. Tall, cropped blond hair, her clothes and attitude always giving off an effortless, unassuming hipness, she had run a successful online clothing store since high school, designing (and for the first few years actually making by hand) the clothes, but suddenly decided she wanted to go to law school, scored in the ninety-ninth percentile on the LSATs, and is now in her second year at U of T. I've known her almost as long as I've known Jatinder; she's like a sister. "What have you got to be afraid of?" she asks. I nod in response.

"When I get back, you'll have made up your mind?" Jatinder asks.

"Yeah, when you get back, I'll have made up my mind." I'm pulling up to the passenger drop off.

"Good, 'cause if not, I'm going to find somebody else."

I laugh. "Who? Maximilian? Thomas?"

Jatinder joins my laughter, slaps me on the back, and a few minutes later he and Rachel are rolling their way through the sliding glass doors of the airport.

On the drive back downtown, a light snow dusting the highway, I think seriously about Jatinder's offer. I have to admit, the idea of starting a company with Jatinder is becoming more and more attractive. He's promised me he'll deal with the client end of things, the sweet talking and gig booking, leaving me in charge of the warehouse, the trucks, the events themselves. And after all of these Holocaust movies I've been watching with Jackie, I feel like it's time I make something of my life. I've been thinking a lot about Mengele, about the line into Auschwitz, the selection: To death or to work, to poison gas or to postponed death. Which way would the cruel doctor have sent me? Would I have been one of the twenty percent who was sent towards work, towards a chance of survival, tattooed, branded, pitted? And, most frightening to me, which way would I want to go? Isn't it my duty to select the path towards work, towards life, to do all I can, to make the most out of what I've been dealt? It might be impossible to exist in the world without being tainted by it, but does that mean I shouldn't try?

Rachel's right: What do I have to be afraid of? What do I have to lose? I won't say anything yet, though; I want to be absolutely sure. I have a few quiet winter weeks to think it through. At the bottom of the city the 427 splits; I stay to the left, city bound. I hit standstill traffic on the Gardiner, look out the window. I can just make out the spire of the CN Tower, its bright lights declaring its presence even in this opaque weather.

Spring

Once the jobs start coming again, I'm tossed right back into the rhythm of things. Jackie, having yet to find a job, started taking a few shifts a week at the Tamp and Pour, comes home in the evening exhausted, jittery from the bottomless coffee, smelling like espresso beans and patchouli. Not being involved in the betterment of the world is getting her down; I catch her more than once Facebook-stalking photo albums of old friends playing with their kids at the park, holding newborn babies, smiling broadly on a family tromp through an old-growth forest newly saved from the loggers' blades.

I barely moved for three weeks during the quiet season, got flabby and limp. "If I didn't do A/V, I think I'd die from inertia," I say to Jackie. We're in bed eating ice cream, watching the final installment of *Holocaust*, which Jackie took out from the public library. For a TV miniseries, it's pretty fucking dark: all of the main characters dead except Rudi, the show ending with him playing soccer with the orphaned Jewish children, about to sneak them into the still-gestating state of Israel.

"If you didn't do A/V, you'd die from an aortic infarction," Jackie, who goes for a sixty-five minute run every morning, says.

I still haven't decided about the company with Jatinder, keep swinging between wanting to do it and not wanting to do it. *Holocaust* is not helping. The miniseries is the most complete narrative Jackie and I have watched so far about the genocide: the rise of the Nazi party, the vilification of the Jews, the killing of the mentally ill, the ghettoization, the burning synagogues and mass murders, Babi Yar, the concentration camps—it's all there. How Germany collapsed into such abject horror is beyond me. How did it happen? What I do know, what I can't stop thinking about, what I don't even mention to Jackie, my tour guide through the Holocaust filmography, is that if we woke up tomorrow and decided to kill six million people, it would be much, much easier than it was fifty years ago. Our ability to kill has only grown, advanced. Progressed. I'm starting to think, irrationally I'm sure, that this very fact is reason enough to say no to Jatinder. How can I commit to making a living off of celebrations, religious and corporate, in the face of so much death, of such recent horrific history? We've done nothing to fix the problems of the world.

Then again, maybe celebration is all we have.

It's the busiest spring I can remember. I'm working indiscriminately, doing weddings all over southern Ontario. On a sunny Thursday in the middle of May, Jatinder and I set up a wedding, a corporate event, and a school dance. We set up the dance first, are out of there before noon; the wedding's at Temple Israel: we store the road cases in the synagogue's small library, as we always do, race back to the warehouse to load the truck with a dozen four-foot cases of drape, fight our way back to the east-end event space. The event is for a bottled water company called MindPure, and we have to turn the second-floor loft into a multi-roomed show floor, using only pipe and drape. The event is the next day, which is a good thing because we're there until well after midnight, Gabe having us redo everything two full times. Finally satisfied, Jatinder and I jump into the truck, Thomas following in his car; we grab fish fillets from McDonald's, get to Temple Israel to tear down at two in the morning.

The Mexican night watchman greets us at the loading gate. He's very unhappy that we're only just arriving. "You done in twenty?" he asks. Thomas laughs. "Naw, no way man." Jatinder looks at me. "Let's do this fast so we can get out of here. You and Thomas bring in the road cases, I'll start unplugging everything." We walk across the tiled foyer and into the library. We don't bother turning the lights on, just strong-arm as many road cases as we can and roll them across the tiles and into the ballroom. When I go back for the last case, I happen to glance at the books. Though it's a pretty substantial library, I can only make out two shelves in the darkness: one shelf contains books about Israel, the other one books about the Holocaust. A vertical metre stick of light from the foyer is falling on two of the books. I lean in, squinting. The two titles are *The Holocaust and the Western World: What the Six Million Died For* and, right next to it, *Holocaust: The End of the Project of Humanity*. I stare at the two titles, my hand reaching towards *What the Six Million Died For*, veering at the last second and pulling *The End of the Project of Humanity* from the shelf. The hardcover book audibly creaks when I open it, making me wonder if I'm the first to do so. I read a paragraph from the middle of the page I've turned to: "This is it, then, isn't it? The Holocaust, the systematic, technological, organized, calculated murder of millions isn't an aberration, no, isn't an abomination on an otherwise idyllic journey, no, oh no—the Holocaust is the apogee of progress, the telos of dividing everyone and everything into categories, this world we've built for ourselves taken to its logical extremes. Looked at cleanly, with clear eyes, its message is abundantly clear: we, as a society, as a species, need to take a step back, look around, and think of where we want to fit into this place called the world. We need to stop using this event to justify borders and slaughterhouses; we need to accept what we should've known all along: something is very, very wrong with the house we've erected on this green earth." Something shifts in the library, a noise, the air, the light—whatever it is, I am good and spooked, my mind a tangled patch cord.

I put the book back on the shelf, grab the last road case, and roll it out into the banquet hall.

Two days later, Maximilian is picking me up in front of my apartment at 4:30 a.m. It's technically Saturday morning, even though Friday night's darkness hasn't dissipated yet. When Maximilian first asked if I would do a wedding with him in the outskirts of Kitchener, I refused, but when he offered me five-hundred dollars for the day, I relented. Thankfully, I ended up having Friday off, spent it mostly in bed playing videogames, thinking about the Holocaust, falling asleep before Jackie got home from the cafe.

Now here I am, waiting for Maximilian. When his Beamer pulls up, I run out from under the awning, through the light rain and into the car, throwing my suit and gig bag into the backseat. We barrel to the top of the city, pick up the truck at the rental agency, head to Gabe's, load the gear in the blue predawn, stop at Olga's for the high-end laser lights, grab coffee and breakfast sandwiches, and slide onto the highway, the sunrise pink and messy in the rear-view.

What happened in that library threw me for a loop. To see the titles of those two books immediately after ingesting so many movies about the Holocaust, to read those pointed words in the midst of my crisis. A gift from the A/V gods, Thomas would say. As much as I don't want to, everything I've seen and felt in the past few weeks is forcing me to agree with the passage I read: counter to the message underlining all of the Hollywood depictions of the Holocaust, didn't the fact of the death camps put the lie to the human project of civilization? Isn't the happy ending of *Schindler's List* ridiculous? It's like *Hamlet* ending with a wedding! And *Holocaust*, Rudi going to Israel, as if that undoes what happened to his entire family! The horror of what happened in those camps and those shuls and those pits might be inherently unknowable, but a happy ending? A happy ending is absurd. (It's the happy endings that draw Jackie to these movies, I'm sure; they validate her conviction that the world is improvable, something I'm seriously starting to doubt.) To say I'm not used to such dark thoughts would be an understatement; I have no idea how to process them, am walking around in a fog, bickering with Jackie, not fitting into the world in my low-key, usual way.

"What's wrong, buddy? You've been off lately," Maximilian calls out.

Sitting beside Maximilian's large, uncomplicated confidence in a rumbling truck cab streaming on the highway, an enormous lake to our left, I take his opening. I unload on him. "Ha ha, I don't know, man. I've been watching a lot of Holocaust movies, I guess. It's giving me real trouble with, with everything we've done as a species. To each other. To the world. I don't know. It's so fucking confusing. I'm sick inside a McDonald's. I can't go on my Facebook, where it's all *Israel Israel Israel*. Do you have any idea how many nuclear bombs are ready to go off at the touch of a button?! The oppression and poverty the world over! And we just ignore it. We're all skimming across a terrifying abyss of violence and pain." I'm surprised at the words spewing out of my mouth, but I can't stop. "It's like, it's just a matter of perspective, you know, like those cubes you'd draw in elementary school by making two connected squares? We're taught to see the good side of society, of technology, of politics, but if you just flip the perspective, you see the true unutterable horror behind the lights and the drape. How do we square such a contradiction?"

Maximilian looks at me, both of his muscled hands huge on the wheel. His eyes are like I've never seen them before, deep fluid tunnels. I've suddenly become ridiculously nervous. Maximilian breathes out, calm, collected. "Yeah, the world's the diarrhea of some sadistic rapist. Of *course* it is. Do you have any idea what my parents went through in Soviet Hungary? But buck up, Mark, there's nothing to do about it. Sounds like you're having a third-life crisis. It happens to all of us." He looks at me, smiling wickedly. "You need to get laid, my friend. This is what happens when your baby-juice backs up, you start seeing the world for what it really is."

I laugh, unsure. Should I tell him about all the sex I'm having with Jackie? It's more than I've ever had before, and the truth is it's not making me feel better, it's making me feel worse. I just don't have Maximilian's blaze-ahead, take-no-prisoners virility. I shake myself out of my thoughts. Maximilian is still talking.

"I'm sure there'll be someone there for you tonight, Marcus. A nice, farm-raised girl. Yeah, the place will be rife with farmers' daughters. Maybe we can even find some twins! And wait until I reveal tonight's door prize! Oh Marky Mark, we're in for one hell of a night!"

We pull into the country club around ten thirty, leave the truck in the near-empty lot. It's a cool, dewy morning, heavy white clouds racing against a blue sky. I follow Maximilian around as he looks for someone on staff to talk to. The wedding is going to be in a big white event tent set up adjacent to the club house. I shoot the shit with the talkative electrician, an older man with a lined face and yellow teeth, who is running around making sure the hook-ups inside the tent are working. "Too much power and the whole place will short out," he says, laughing. "Words to live by," I say, laughing too. The clouds melt into the sky, turning it grey. We unload the truck through a side door into the tent, start setting up. Two trusses with skirts, Colorados along the wall, the DJ table framed in black tech surround. One of the country-club staff members, a bubbly girl with blond highlights who introduced herself as Becky, walks in with a platter of burgers, a mound of golden fries. "On the house, sweethearts!" Later, I catch her staring at Maximilian's muscles as he singlehandedly hoists a four-foot road case over his head.

We work steadily. The caterers arrive around two, start setting up large barbecues, workstations, coolers of meat and shrimp. When we're finished the setup, I take a dirty, plunging nap in the truck, the windows open to the breeze. A train rushes past on the other side of the field, startling me awake; I watch the unending line of cars, shipping crates, oil and gas tankers rumble by. Maximilian joins me as I'm finishing a cigarette. I hand him one without being asked. "The door prize," Maximilian says solemnly, pulling a ziplock of mushrooms out of his cargo pants pocket. I watch the bag of wrinkled drugs as he waves it in front of my face. I haven't shroomed since high school, but I take the stems and caps as Maximilian hands them to me one at a time, put them in my mouth, chew, swallow. They're not as bad as I remember, though I light a second cigarette to get rid of the squishy, bitter texture. We change into our suits. I have yet to dry clean mine since I got it stained last fall, the oily streak still across the trouser legs.

The parking lot starts to fill up with revellers, women in high heels and up-dos, men in suits. I try not to think about the fungal poison working its way towards my brain, focus on the lights as the bride and groom are introduced, the dancing starts, the alcohol flows. The groom is big, blond, rosy cheeked, with the chest and arms of a quarterback, the affability and social skills of a provincial politician. The speeches start. "First off, I want to thank the big guy up there," the groom says, pointing to heaven with a fat finger. "He's talking about you," Maximilian whispers into my ear. "I think he's talking about Biggie Smalls," I whisper back, making Max guffaw. I work the lights, watch the party. Observing a wedding is so second nature it barely registers as experience; I've become more than a little jaded towards these celebrations, but still, there's always something worth noticing. The gorgeous woman in the form-fitting black dress. A massive mountain man, with a thick grey beard and a suit that could double as sheets for a king-sized bed, bending down to talk to a four-year-old girl with blond ringlets and a pink party dress. In the giant's shadow, the child's face turns into a mask of fear. I go to the bar every twenty minutes for a rum and Coke for Maximilian, a ginger ale for me. I can't tell if the mushrooms have kicked in or not, but am beginning to feel like I'm moving under water. Becky comes over whenever she has a minute from the dinner service to flirt with Maximilian, her cheeks flushed, her cleavage dark and mysterious in the low lights, Maximilian sending her into paroxysms of laughter. I'm enjoying the burgeoning sexual tension. Every movement and action is drenched in meaning, in premonition, in pulsing dread.

At some point, I step outside into the cold night. The sun is long set. The wind whips across the field; I can see a dull glow that must be Kitchener, its feeble lights nothing to the night's spreading power. I light a cigarette, stare at the field, the oak tree at the other end shuddering in the wind, a million leaves shaking as one, which I can feel as a strange tickling in my head. It wouldn't be hard to imagine a death camp here, I say to myself, the thought appearing fully formed, with teeth. The train tracks already built, all they would need is a barracks or two, a shower room, the crematorium. The bearded mountain man would be a capo, the electrician a sunken-eyed prisoner who buried bodies, cleaned out the ovens. The groom a blustery guard, smiling and joking as he leads us into the killing showers. Why not?

Why not?

I turn my face into the wind, toss the half-smoked cigarette, sneak back into the party. I'm watching too many Holocaust movies.

A half hour later, the power blows as I'm sitting at the DJ table working through a heaping plate of shrimp (I needed something without a central nervous system). Maximilian looks at me with harried eyes; he's had a dozen drinks easy, ate two stems for every one of mine, yet seems as sober as a tree. I drop my plate and run onto the dance floor, everything in my field of vision coloured shrimp-pink. The bartender had plugged in a lamp, and it was just enough to blow the fuse. I unplug the lamp, find the fuse box, reset the fuse; there's an audible sigh as the lights and music come roaring back to life. At twelve thirty, I see the groom sloppily hand Maximilian three new-looking hundred dollar bills, and we keep the party going until ten minutes after two. We strike in an hour, Maximilian doing most of the work. The wind has died. Becky's changed out of her work clothes, into sweats and a white tank top, asks if we can give her a ride back to Toronto, she's visiting her mom in the city tomorrow. "You're driving," Maximilian says, tossing me the keys. We drive home, not bothering to change out of our suits, Becky and Maximilian making out in the backseat as I focus on the road, Maximilian's trance music blasting through the stereo. The highways are deserted except for the convoys of tractor trailers, full of consumer goods, factory-made chocolate bars, animals on the way to slaughter. The highways are steel-and-cement veins pumping along to an accelerated heart rate. It is not the truck that is moving, but the world. My mind is a narrow tunnel, and the tunnel is the road. The sun rises as we pass Oakville, the CN Tower aflame, a lone sentinel over a city of vertically stacked road cases. We stop for pancakes, Maximilian deliberately counting out six hundred and fifty dollars on the Formica tabletop and sliding it over to me. Only now do I detect a difference in Maximilian, an altered state, his eyes turned metallic mirrors, his words-per-minute slightly decreased. He offers to handle the gear and the truck tomorrow; as they drive away from my building, Becky gives a whoop of joy out the open windows, Maximilian echoing with a yell of his own, both of them now howling in unfiltered unison. I get into my apartment just after nine, get into bed beside Jackie. The bed is warm, Jackie's weight and presence comforting, and I plunge into a wide, bracing lake of sleep.

My alarm starts going at noon. I grab my phone: I completely forgot I told Gabe I'd do a wedding for him. I groan long and loud into my pillow. There's not even time for a shower. At least I don't have to go to the warehouse. On the way up to the shul, my thoughts are dark, the hallucinated southern Ontario concentration camp I had laughed off last night not so easily vanquished, sitting in my gut, leaching its toxins, taking the place of the long-gone mushrooms. I work through it, my body knowing how to set up a party even with my mind's absence.

When I get home in the late afternoon, there are a half dozen blue cereal bowls sitting on the table. It's not much, but it's enough to tip me over the edge.

"What's with the bowls?" I say to Jackie, whom I find in the bedroom.

Jackie looks up at me. "I thought it was time you grew up a little."

"Well, thanks, but no thanks."

Jackie stands up, walks towards me. I can smell the coffee on her breath. She's alert, electric, emanating sexual heat.

"Mark. Let's make babies together."

I cough, my insides twisting. "What?" So here it is.

"I want babies. I want babies with you, Mark."

"... Jackie."

"What? Why not? We have a good thing going, don't we? I didn't think I'd want kids either, trust me—*trust* me—but last year in Vancouver something changed. Creating another human life, raising a thoughtful, compassionate, empathetic human being from scratch:

how could someone live their beliefs in any more profound a way? I let it sit there, in my gut, as I took stock of my surroundings for what felt like the first time in years. I looked around me, and nobody I knew out there seemed like the person I'd want to father my children. That's when I started thinking about you, Mark, about our relationship, about how caring and thoughtful you are, how dedicated. So I quit, packed up, made my illustrious return to Toronto."

The look I give her must be borderline deranged. The idea of someone like Jackie moving cities for someone like me is flabbergasting. Jackie ignores my face, puts her hand on my arm.

"We're good people, Mark; we're the good guys. Let's make babies together."

"Are we? Are we good people?" I'm yelling. I take a step back. "What do we do that's so good? I spend my days and nights helping the rich feel good about themselves. You said it yourself, didn't you? How we're all skimming across a deep lake of shit? Why deliver anybody into that? Huh?"

"That's why we have to do it! Look the darkness right in the face and say no! Say, 'I will not back down!'" Jackie's crying, her skin goosebumped.

"Jackie. I could have told you right when you knocked on my door that I didn't want kids. And after everything you've shown me, especially not now." Though, if I did want kids (I can't help thinking), it would be with her. Jackie shakes herself out of her tears, stares daggers at me.

"Oh Mark, feeling *so* sorry for yourself. There are people in the world who are *actually* suffering, you know. Get out of yourself for half a minute and be grateful for what you have. What you could have had!"

Jackie grabs her bag and leaves the apartment. I slump onto the couch, stare into space. Six hours later, I drive myself to the teardown in Jackie's car. I'm early. The party is still in full swing, strapping men in tuxes smoking on the pavement, swaying women sitting on the stairs, heels in hand. Usually I would hang back until it was more cleared out, but I'm feeling reckless.

"Hey Mark, is that you, man?" someone calls out as I'm walking through the party-goers. I turn around. It's Larry Newman. The last time I found myself on his Facebook page, Newman had recently finished his residency at Mount Sinai, was still with Sonia Hillberg, his high-school girlfriend. He looks me up and down. I can already tell that his arrogance and ego have not diminished since the last time I saw him. "What, you still doing A/V? Still DJing bar mitzvahs? I don't believe it! Ha ha. You'll be doing my kids' soon enough. Ha ha. I'm kidding, buddy, I'm kidding."

I try not to scowl. "I don't do bar mitzvahs much these days," I say. "Whose wedding is this?"

"Did you not go to university or anything?" he asks, narrowing his eyes.

"Nope," I say as upbeatly as possible.

"Who, this?" Larry says, nodding with his head to the building behind him. "Julie Bronfman's."

I remember Julie. I wonder who she's marrying, though I don't ask. Everyone is pairing off, reproducing, continuing the species without a second thought. Meanwhile, I've become one long second thought. I get away from Larry as quickly as possible. The ballroom is a war zone: toppled chairs, destroyed tables, spilled beer and wine, broken glasses, confetti. Someone's poured what looks like ginger ale into the cavity of one of the subwoofers. I start yanking out the lights, coiling cable, ripping the drape to the floor. Jatinder and Thomas will fold it whenever they decide to show up.

Everything collapses around me.

Summer

Without anyone asking it to, life comes roaring back to Toronto. Suddenly the streets are full of laughter and flip-flops and skin. Everything's drenched in sex. Jackie has officially given up on the job search, spends her days at the Tamp and Pour, on either side of the counter, growing bored, growing morose. When she's at home, she's on Facebook, looking at pictures of the coast. Her trees have budded, though. She's moved them to four clay pots, each one a different colour: grey, blue, green, skull white.

The summer thus far. Maximilian's shotgun wedding to Becky was in early July. Becky looked ravishing in her wedding dress, her four-month pregnancy giving her the faintest pudge, Maximilian beaming with the cleanest, proudest joy I've ever seen. Jatinder and I drove down to Niagara Falls to set up an international mining conference. Since the winter, Jatinder's cooled down on the new company front: he and Rachel got engaged in April; they're busy putting together a massive Indian-Jewish wedding week, are looking at houses. Jatinder's been distracted, distant, only talks about money, mortgages, interest rates, student loans. Not the usual Jatinder. At the mining conference, we were comped a falls-view room, got hammered on tequila, slept with the balcony doors open to the roar of the falls. At first I found the noise comforting, something real, something tangible, but then I remembered that we even have a switch to turn off the roar, that even something as magnificent as Niagara Falls has been demoted into a false front. Jerry takes two weeks off to follow the rock band Grizzly around the States; Gabe makes vicious fun of him the entire time he is gone, calling him a dirty hippie, a lousy worker, a lost millennial, on and on. It's his favourite topic. A middle of the night traffic jam on the road outside of Nottawasaga Resort, ten minutes of steady cars before an opening for us to slip into (back at the warehouse, Thomas informed us it was the night shift at the Ford plant letting out; his father worked there in the eighties. Two different worlds crossing in the night). Dropping off some gear at Olga's, she takes me aside and asks if I want to become warehouse manager for her. "We need someone of your competence and intelligence. You're not like the others. No bullshit."

For some reason, I don't say no right away.

And looming over everything, the Holocaust. I've been having a recurring dream where I'm doing A/V for a Nazi concentration camp. I'm working alone, in my soiled suit, rushing to finish before the first trainload of prisoners arrives. I position speakers in the platz, drape the barracks, run around in a frenzy looking for someone who knows which outlets are on which circuits, but none of the guards have mouths and ignore me anyway. I uplight the chimneys, stage-deck the arrival platforms. It's going to be a big night. Sometimes the CN Tower is there, a sleek guard tower rising above the camp, throwing brilliant white light along the perimeter; sometimes it's not. When the first cattle cars arrive, I'm still not finished. There's still so much to do. I balloon with panic and—pop!—wake up. The first few times I had it, I was a mess the whole day, drove the truck jerkily, smashed road cases into walls, got reamed out by Gabe, but it's amazing how quickly you can get used to something, no matter how fucked up.

It's way easier than I thought it would be: going through an existential crisis—or whatever this is—but continuing my role as a working member of society, going through the motions. How many of us are completely disengaged yet keep going on?

Things are winding down with Jackie. Ever since our blowout babies argument she's been putting distance between us, in the careful, purposeful way she does everything. More time at the Tamp and Pour, more talk of going back to Vancouver. "I'm thinking that I was wrong about the coast. There's just more opportunity out there for someone like me," she says. She looks quickly at me, turns away. "Work opportunities, I mean."

What can I say? The summer rolls on, a season of extremes. I'm working full tilt or I'm not leaving my bedroom. Jackie and I fight about the broken toilet seat and have tectonic sex, or we talk in clipped pleasantries, sleep at opposite edges of the bed. We're quickly devolving from lovers to roommates to roommates-who-hate-each-other. My recurring nightmare continues its bleed into the waking world. Everything I touch at work is burning hot. My bed is ice cold.

Somehow, even with the rot I feel in my stomach every time I see the CN Tower, my equilibrium holds until late August. It all unravels at the load-in for Gabe's biggest event of the year, the TreadSoft annual shareholders gala. Gabe started doing it the second year of G & G Entertainment's existence; I have no idea how he managed to get a tender that big as such a small company (though I wouldn't be surprised if Ben Goldstein called in a couple of favours), but he's held onto it for all he's worth. Everybody's on it. I'm not particularly looking forward to the event. Gabe usually has at least three tantrums. Historically, the load-in could be ten, twelve hours of work, which is almost three-hundred dollars, and since staying at home doesn't seem like an appealing alternative, I arrive at the warehouse at 6:30 a.m.

Jatinder is standing at the loading doors, smoking a cigarette. We nod at each other. I can see Gabe, Jerry (recently back from the States, sunburned and hemp necklaced), and a couple of the new guys Gabe poached from FreeFall standing around Thomas near the truss wall.

"What's going on in there? Thomas holding court?"

"Ha ha. Pretty much. He's finished *Impure Thoughts about the Houseguest*. He's boring Gabe with all the deets, as if Gabe gives a shit."

"Maybe this will finally be his big break," I say. For some reason, Thomas has been on my mind a lot lately. Out of all of us in Gabe's employ, he's the only one with some kind of outside ambition. To make movies. And yes, his ambition makes him incredibly annoying, but, like Jackie, he truly believes that what he does can have an effect on the world, whereas I'm beginning to think more and more that nothing I do can stop the march of destruction.

"Speaking of breaks," Jatinder says, "I've been really stressing out lately, man. This wedding, the house, it's really pulling on our savings. And Rachel didn't get an articling job for next year. There are too many law students, not enough firms. We don't know what we're going to do."

I've never seen Jatinder like this before. I say something innocuous, slap him on the shoulder, go into the warehouse. On my way towards the bathroom, I overhear Thomas use the phrase "revolutionize cinema." By the time I join them, I can see Gabe's face has hardened.

"All right, enough with your fucking script," he says, the anger in his voice heating up. "You're annoying, Jerry is a fucking hippie high on acid with mud on his dick, and look who it is, Mark. What's wrong with you lately, eh? You're acting like somebody's blackmailing you. Don't tell me, don't tell me, I don't fucking want to know. Okay boys, let's load up!"

We have to fit an impossible amount of gear into the two trucks; almost all of Gabe's equipment is coming with us. Jatinder and I stay in the truck, place the road cases Jerry and the new kids roll up the ramp for us. We stack all the four-foot cases at the back, three high, the wheels locking into the grooves on the tops of the cases. We load the two-footers next, Jatinder helping one of the new kids pull the heavy base cases up the ramp. By the time I close and latch the truck gate, I'm sweating, my muscles loose. The sun is a few inches into the sky and the industrial backlot is full of light. Jatinder pulls Gabe's truck out of the bay, I back the rental in, and we quickly fill it up with a dozen trusses, the six screen cases, and other odds and ends. Gabe is getting frantic now, is pacing back and forth in the warehouse.

"Jerry, why don't you and the newbies head down now, we'll meet up with you," Jatinder says, reacting to Gabe's dismay. The three of them leave in the fully loaded truck, Jatinder and Gabe hurriedly go over the packing order, and Jatinder and I jump in the rental. We have to go two industrial parks over to pick up the rental gear from Olga's.

"What's coming with us from Olga's?" I ask as we idle in the Tim Horton's drive-through. Once we're out of Gabe's overbearing presence, the urgency mellows out.

Jatinder grabs the order form. "Some extra trusses, some poles for the Lekos, and the staging."

"Goody."

Once we're at Olga's, I drive around back, position the truck, wait while Jatinder gets out, opens the truck door, and gets back in, and back up to the loading dock, the truck's reverse warning beeping repetitively. I'm a half-foot off, so I switch into drive, pull forward, adjust, switch back into reverse, and bring it home. We unbuckle, squeeze through the door into the bed. "Shit." Unlike Gabe's loading bay, Olga's ramp slants down, so full-sized tractor-trailer beds will line up with the warehouse. In the rental, we're a good three feet below the lip of the warehouse door. Which would normally be fine, but the staging's going to be a real headache.

Jatinder bangs on the door with his open palm. I hope Olga's not here; I haven't given her an answer about her job offer yet (nor have I told Jatinder about it). A moment later it rolls up, and we're eye-level with the massive kneecaps of Maximilian.

"Ah, shitbeards," he says, beaming, "you're half an hour late."

"Yeah, fuck you too," I say, climbing into the warehouse, slapping hands with him. I can't help it: seeing Maximilian gives me a boost. Our gear is lined up neatly behind him, ready to go.

"Looks like we're going to have to handbomb these turdrags," Maximilian says, pounding the staging braces with his open hand.

First, the three of us have to take all the staging out of the deck carts. Then, very carefully, very dangerously, we have to get the deck carts into the truck, then we have to bring in the staging one deck at a time and load it back into place. Each deck easily weighs a hundred and fifty pounds. If Maximilian weren't here, I probably would quit on the spot. The man is a beast. As he works, he talks non-stop, telling us about the night he had.

"It started with us going for drinks with Randal and his girl, Clarissa. Do you know Randal? Black guy, DJs for Be Good? Yeah, anyways, doesn't fucking matter. We started at Sneaky Dick's, had a couple pitchers, moved on to the Horseshoe-In-Your-Ass, broke into the whiskey. We were pounding. Not sure if we were still there or already at the water when Becky handed out the X. She didn't do any, being preggers and all. Whoa, easy, Marcus, easy, don't want to pull your cock-muscle just to make sure Gabe's happy. Anyways, where was I? Yeah, yeah. We were at the water, blitzed out of our gourds, the X coming on like a slowed-down jizz-blast, the moon just this beautiful fuckin' tit hanging over the lake, turning it all silver-like, ya know? Can you see it, JT? Somehow or other, we start talking about breaking into Ontario Place. I had done it once or twice the summer before, and at the moment, in that place, the X blasting through us, it seemed like the only thing to do. So we did. We walked right up to the gate. I was all prepared to jump over the fence, but just for shit's sake, I tried the lock, one of those heavy-duty mother fuckers. But, get this. The thing wasn't even *locked*. I pulled it off, unwound the chain, and we were in. We had the whole place to ourselves. It was amazing. We walked through the weather silos, all those exhibits in permanent darkness. We sat at the top of the slides, tossed a glow-in-the-dark Frisbee in the cafeteria. Becky and I went down on each other and fucked on the roof in the moonlight, just like a good hubby and wifey. Anyways. What? Yeah, all that stuff's coming with. Anyways, on our way out, we ended up in some warehouse behind the offices, and, you know, just for the hell of it, I started opening doors. I'm telling you, the whole place was unlocked. We found a room full of brand-new life jackets, a room full of skids of candy bars and chips, and, get this, a room full, FULL, of A/V equipment. There must have been a few hundred grand worth of stuff in there. I was really fucking cracked-out at this point, but I swear on my morning erection, I saw at least a half dozen Sanyo lenses, digital mixers, turntables, cases of lights and speakers. All there for the taking. Fuck. Yeah, so, on the way out, literally feet from the exit, we bump into two security guards. The sun is coming up; I'm seeing triple at this point. But Becky, Becky that awesome fucking Frigidaire, went off on this story about how we were at a yacht party and were trying to get to the road to get a cab home. 'Which dock slip?' The guard asked. 'Forty-five,' Beck said. 'What were their last names?' He asked. Here we go, we're fucked now, I thought. 'Hmm. I don't know,' Becky said. 'We went with friends, never got the last name.' Well, she had them there. The guards escorted us to the gate and told us to have a good night. We laughed all the way through breakfast."

By the time Maximilian is finished with his story, we have loaded all of the gear into the truck. We couldn't fit another piece of equipment in there if the survival of our species depended on it. I am sweating, breathing hard, my arms already sore. When Maximilian got to the part about the room with the A/V equipment, I happened to be looking at Jatinder. His eyes went large, exactly like they had earlier at the warehouse, and I don't think it was just because of the piece of staging he was pulling into the truck. Now, as I take my gloves off and am wishing I had grabbed a water bottle from Gabe's, Jatinder, as he straps down the load, asks if Maximilian thinks those rooms would still be unlocked, even after the guards had caught them.

"Are you kidding, brother? Of course. No doubt. Becky had those lightweights wrapped around her dirty little finger."

"Interesting ..."

"You coming to the load-in?" I ask, interrupting, hoping to speed things along.

"What? Oh yeah, just have to handle a few more pickups here, then you guys are stuck with me."

On the drive downtown, I tell Jatinder that Jackie left.

"Shit, man. When?"

"A few days ago. Back to the coast. She couldn't get anything going on the job front, and she felt it was too hard to get involved in the progressive community here. In Toronto."

"Shit, man. Sorry. Looked like you guys had a good thing going."

We drive in silence.

"Dude, Rachel's pregnant," Jatinder says eventually.

"What? Great! I didn't even know you were trying."

"We weren't, not exactly. Anyways, like I was saying earlier, with the wedding and the house and the new car and everything, the money I had for starting our own company has become sort of, well, spoken for. I think we're going to have to put our plan on hold."

"Oh, cool."

"Not that I have any idea how I'm going to make enough money to keep us afloat! At least until Rachel finds an articling job. Shit, imagine our own company, Mark? The stability, the freedom, the guaranteed income!"

I don't say anything.

At the event space, there are almost a dozen of us working. There's plenty to do, and we all try to do it while avoiding Gabe. I spend three hours doing the staging with Jatinder and Thomas, work on the lights with Jerry for a while, set up the screens and TVs throughout the room, jump onto the drapes. Maximilian shows up around three, gets to work without having to be told what needs doing; the man may have a big mouth, but he has a preternatural understanding of event spaces. I overhear him and Jatinder talking about stealing that A/V equipment from Ontario Place. It sounds like they're joking, but I can't tell; Jatinder still has that weird tone in his voice. I'm working way too fast, haven't eaten or drunk anything except for that coffee.

"Hey Gabe, how 'bout ordering a pizza or three?" I call from the top of the ladder, where I'm adjusting a Leko.

"How about you stop fucking around and get some work done?" Gabe shoots back.

The room slowly comes together. Chairs Chairs Chairs shows up midafternoon, starts rolling in the tables and chairs. I have to admit, the space looks good. Gabe and Jerry are already testing the sound, the screens and TVs running through the slideshow of TreadSoft advertising, showing all the things we take for granted that TreadSoft is involved in making in some way: cars, the internet, grocery stores, plastics, metal, gas. Gabe asks Thomas to speak into the podium mic

121 A/V

while they do the sound test, adjust the levels throughout the room. Thomas scampers up onto the stage. "Is everybody in? Is everybody in?" he intones in a deep, slow baritone. "Is. Everybody. In?"

"Just speak normally. Tell us about your screenplay," Gabe shouts from the front-of-house. Either Thomas doesn't hear, or he ignores him. "All things flow according to the whim of the great sea goddess," he continues, "and who was I to defy her? Everything was Skittles, Skittles, Skittles."

I'm still up on the ladder when whatever it is that's been wanting to give this whole year finally gives. Jackie leaving, my Holocaust nightmare, Gabe yelling at Thomas as he continues to rant into the microphone, the images on the screens in front of me of smiling workers in clean white factories under the caption *TreadSoft: Making Your Life As Easy As Possible*, all coalesce, and I snap. "If art is not human, then what's so great about being human?" Thomas says, as I slowly climb down the ladder, worried that if I go too fast, I'll have an aneurysm and drop dead. The last thing I hear him say, Jerry, now just playing around, having turned the echo way up, is, "If literature is an axe to break the frozen seas within us, then there isn't much time left, is there? Is there? Is there?"

I go outside to smoke a cigarette. New thoughts are raging through me. Once the trains carried millions of people to their deaths, how could anybody, without a severe act of self-mutilation, board a train again? How can any of us take showers? Use a computer? Bake muffins in an oven? And it's not like what the Nazis did was all that novel. We transport slaves in ships, we murder and steal—we ethnically cleansed our way across the continent for fuck's sake!—we buy our iPhones and sweatshirts knowing full well where they came from. We burn entire Carthages to the ground over and over, sometimes with different reasoning, sometimes with no reasoning at all. Hope, progress, comfort, all of it lies. Anne Frank was wrong. Anne Frank couldn't have been more wrong. What was I doing helping these warlords celebrate their year-end dividends?

Before, before the war maybe—but probably way, way before that—you had to actually *do* bad to be bad, but now, the way we have things set up, we can live as passive a life as possible, yet remain entirely complicit. You don't have to kill, you don't have to beat or abuse or oppress (though there's still *plenty* of that), you just have to go to a grocery store, use your phone, not speak up. Isn't that the defining nature of the present? Carthage eternally burning, over there, allowing some of us to be the most comfortable, ignorant lifeforms ever evolved. And the lies! The lies! That the Holocaust isn't us at our best, our most creative and industrious and efficient. That the Holocaust is an aberration, not the norm, that all we need to know about our species isn't given to us time and time again!

Suddenly, in a burst of cold recognition, it's clear to me. I must renounce what little power I have. The power to amplify, to light, to frame. How can it be any other way?

I light another cigarette. Take a breath. I glance up. The sun is about to set.

The summer can't be over soon enough.

Fall

Somehow it's September again, which means film festival. The city fills with movie stars, directors, producers, executives, entourages, fans. The streets around the Bell Lightbox are closed to cars, streetcars. The restaurants get booked. And in hotel penthouses, event spaces, and restaurants, the industry celebrates itself.

I can't believe a whole year has passed already. Hard to believe it's only been two weeks since Jackie left. Since the night of the TreadSoft load-in, when I decided once and for all to get out of A/V. As soon as I knew that I had to get out, things became easier. I work, I drink my protein shakes, I sleep, I shower, I wait for the right moment to bow out. The year Jackie lived with me is like a barely remembered dream. Jatinder and Maximilian still talk about robbing Ontario Place, though it's hard to tell how serious they're being (a few days ago, they asked if I wanted to "get in on it" with them; I laughed, said grand larceny isn't really my specialty). My apartment has fallen back into disrepair. Jackie's four trees died. I don't dare touch their corpses.

The first night of the festival, Gabe hires us for another massive gala. Ricardo Ricardo's annual hobnob with the rich and famous; FreeFall had always done it, but Gabe managed to poach it from them.

It's going to be massive.

When I get to the warehouse, Thomas is overeager about something. He is positively bouncing around the warehouse. He bounces right up to me: "Did you hear who's going to be there tonight?" he asks. "Matilda Coen," he says, not waiting for an answer. I look at him dumbly. "The *hottest* producer in LA right now. If she likes your project, it's a go. I *have* to get *Impure Thoughts about the Houseguest* into her hands. I have to! This is my big chance."

"If you so much as acknowledge Matilda Coen's presence, I will kill you," Gabe says, materialized behind us. So early in the morning and things already so tense.

We load the trucks, pile onto the highway.

"Dude, we did it," Jatinder says to me as we're driving downtown. "We came up to the warehouse last night, took Gabe's truck, went downtown, and lifted all that A/V equipment. It was fucking intense. We piled it into Maximilian's basement. And since Ontario Place is shut down, it's a victimless crime! Isn't it wild?! It's more than enough to start our own outfit. The company is back on, brother! Maximilian is down. What about you?"

I look at Jatinder. He seems to be back to normal. His old, affable self. (I ignore the voice in my head that's saying, see, if even someone like Jatinder can be pushed to such extremes, easy-going, innocent Jatinder.) I fill with relief before I even say anything. "You know what man, I'm actually okay. I'm going to take a break from A/V for a while."

Jatinder nods. "I had a feeling you were wanting out. What are you going to do? Go back to school? Travel?"

"Nothing. I'm going to do nothing. I'm out. I'm done. I'm telling Gabe tonight."

"So what are you going to do for money?"

"I have a pretty good savings account. I've been putting ten percent away since I was a teenager. I'll be fine for a couple of years."

"Well, we'll miss you."

At the event, I see Thomas speaking to a woman with thick-framed black glasses and a frilly teal skirt, her face frowning skeptically. She's getting noticeably flustered, but he seems to not be getting the signals; if anything, he's talking faster, more animatedly, his hands gesticulating as if they had a will of their own. I decide to step in, putting down the cables I was running from one of the TVs to the front-of-house. As I pull him away, I see Gabe staring at us, his whole being a pulsing frown.

To his credit, Gabe waits until we are back at the warehouse before he reams us out. But ream us out he does.

"Do you really think Matilda Coen gives a flying turdfuck about your script? What is wrong with you? I don't hire you to harass and cajole our clients, our clients' guests! Do you know why I hire you? To hang the fucking lights! To plug in the fucking speakers! To haul ass and stay quiet and when the party is over, to fucking pack up and do it all again tomorrow!" We're standing outside the backdoor, next to the truck. The sun is newly risen. Thomas is crying.

Typical, to scream at us for something Thomas did. Overeager Thomas. Though it's not Thomas's fault. It's Gabe's. Fuck him and his CN Tower logic.

"Hey, Gabe man, calm down," I say. Gabe turns to me. His eyes are volcanic.

"Calm down? Why the titballs should I calm down? Thomas's behaviour is going to bankrupt this company! And what's been wrong with you the past six months? You're acting like your family died in a car accident! Your work has been slacking! You've been acting like a little shit!"

I can't help but smile as Gabe unloads on me. I look at Thomas, who is still sniffling, at Jatinder, who is looking away, avoiding eye contact, trying to keep a straight face, back at Gabe. The world is fresh and bright, the rough concrete of the warehouse solid, exact.

This is it.

"What do I have to do with any of this?" I say, as quietly as I can. "This isn't me. Fuck this, man, I'm done." I start walking away. Gabe is screaming: "If you walk away now, Mark, that's it. You're done in this town! Do you hear? Done! You've burned your bridges! You've burned your bridges!"

I can hear Jatinder laughing, and I start to laugh too. It takes me an hour to walk to the subway.

I'm not out quite yet. I still have a few DJing gigs booked. I might be planning on dropping out of society, on drifting unseen and untethered till I see a way out of our collective nightmare, but I'm not yet quite so monstrous or unaware that I would cancel a well-paying gig.

I DJ Ricky Rosenfeld's retirement party in the revolving restaurant at the top of the CN Tower. The speeches are full of dirty jokes, disparagement of the poor, glorification of the mighty. But unlike the past twelve months, I don't feel implicated in any of it. Not anymore. I have knowingly, self-reflectively dropped out. In the face of what we've done to each other, it's the only viable option. I'm already outside of their reach. I have seen past their designs to a deeper, uglier truth, and I have embraced it. I smile to myself, fade in the next song.

The whole city swings by. I glance at it from time to time. I've been in most of those hotels, waited for elevators in most of those skyscraper loading bays, three road cases in my outstretched arms. The condos blocking the waterfront, all of those striving lives piled on top of each other, purposefully ignorant of the great, bottomless wound that sustains them. I look further out, can barely determine the shapes of the suburbs before we swing back around to the lake. We swing around again. Suburbs. Lake. Suburbs. Lake. Suburbs. Lake. For no reason at all, I put on the strobe, slowing everything down, forcing the party's invisible seams to rise to the surface. We continue spinning, the city there. Not there. There. Not there. There.

Not there.

Chasing the Tonic

1. Beginnings

Mordechai Tradewsky was staying at the West Porch Saloon and Hotel in Red Hook, South Dakota when he dropped dead of a heart attack in the spring of 1911. Mr. and Mrs. Childs, the hotel's proprietors, had carried the Jewish musician into the saloon and laid him out on the bar, covering him in his bed sheet. They stood over the corpse in the dark barroom, chairs stacked on tables, floor left in the half-swept state it was in when Mrs. Childs had heard the crash from upstairs. They were at a loss as to what to do.

"I'm going to send for Mr. Klein," Mr. Childs said eventually, dawn starting its slow glow outside the windows. An hour later, Mr. Klein had joined the Childses in contemplating the body.

"And he had no identification on him?"

"No sir, nothing but his violin. He had passed through two or three times before, drew a crowd every time, always left a generous gratuity."

"It sure was a wild night last night," Mrs. Childs added, laughing nervously. "Perhaps it was too much for him."

Mr. Klein stared at the body, wondering what his story was. Mr. Klein himself had only been resident in Red Hook for a year and a half and was part of one of only two established Jewish families—the Hillbergs ran the laundry on the other side of town, and they avoided each other as much as possible.

"Well, since we can't send him home," he said, "I suppose we'll just have to bury him here."

Mr. Klein took it upon himself to travel to the surrounding towns to get the ten Jewish men required for the funeral. He also donated the capital needed to purchase a half acre of the local cemetery, and

Mordechai Tradewsky became the first Jew to be buried in Red Hook. For many years to come, as the Jewish community in Red Hook grew to a small but respectable size—and as Mr. Klein's prosperity grew along with it—Mordechai's violin sat on an end table in his sitting room, and Mr. Klein would often be prompted to tell the story of the mysterious fiddle player to his guests.

While at the time of Mordechai's death, Mr. Klein had only been located in Red Hook for eighteen months, he had been in America for almost fifteen years. He had landed on Ellis Island in 1896 and had spent ten years in Manhattan before striking west with his wife, his kids, and his small fortune. In Red Hook he found everything he wanted: the open spaces, the business opportunities, a populace not infected with antisemitism. He planned on staying. Due to Mordechai Tradewsky's untimely expiration, the fiddle player's time in America was a much briefer affair: He had arrived on American shores only two years before his last night of whiskey and music in Red Hook, and he died wearing the same pants he crossed the Atlantic in. Mordechai had docked, along with his wife and three young daughters, in Galveston, Texas in the summer of 1909, along with a boatload of other Jews from the Russian Pale. From Galveston, they rode the Mississippi and then the Missouri up to the twin cities, where they moved into two small rooms off of Washington Avenue, surviving off whatever tailoring and seamstressing work they could find. When Mordechai's wife, Esther (who, while never approving of her husband's weeks-long escapades, led around by the *meshugana* head of his fiddle, privately acknowledged that it was this very same restless nature that made her love him), did not receive word from her husband for six months, she gathered all the money she could to purchase a death certificate. With the help of the local B'nai B'rith, she bought a tiny headstone, and Mordechai Tradewsky became the first Jew to be buried twice in the United States of America.

Within the year, Esther, her meager savings dwindling, had moved herself and her daughters from Minneapolis to New York City, where her sister was living and where she could support herself as a seamstress. Sharing a flat in the Bronx with her sister and brother-in-law, she raised her three daughters, a bittersweet brew of anger and loneliness rising in her throat whenever she heard a violin. Her youngest, Rose, was the first to get married, to a second-generation union leader named Adam, and together they moved to Camden, New Jersey. Fifty years later, Ruth, the eldest of Rose and Adam's thirteen grandchildren (and Mordechai's first great-granddaughter), met and fell in love with Nate Drucker, a Canadian, while studying English literature at SUNY Albany. She moved with him back to Toronto, where over a period of eight years they had four children. Three boys—Drew, Brian, and Rick—and a girl. Jane.

Jane, born in 1982, grew up under the powerful influence of her three older brothers. Their unforced coolness, love of the sixties and seventies, and devotion to live improvisational music compounded in their little sister. At the age of three, Jane could easily differentiate, after a five-second snippet, between Jimi Hendrix, the Who, the Allman Brothers, Quicksilver, the Beatles, Jefferson Airplane, and, her favourite, the Grateful Dead. By the time she was five, she could tell you, within a few months, what the date was of any given Dead tape, picked at random from the band's more than two decades of near constant touring, a feat her brothers never stopped bragging about at the shows they took her to. Those concerts with her brothers were the best part of Jane's first summers: sitting on Drew's shoulders as they bobbed through the crowds, dancing in her white skirt and flower headband with the other hippie children, sleeping on Rick's lap as they drove back over the border and to home. After her first live experience of the Dead, June 30, 1987, at the Kingswood Music Theatre in Toronto—her earliest memory, which, thanks to Drew's tape of the show, was also one of the first shows she knew off by heart, beginning to end (one of the first, but far, far from the last)—she accompanied her brothers to every show within a five-hour drive. Rochester, July 2, 1987; Detroit, April 4, 1988; both the Hamilton double-headers at Copps Coliseum in '90 and '92; Deer Creek, Indiana, July 19 to 21, 1994. Jane was her brothers' mascot, their prodigy, their archives, and, on more than one occasion, the catalyst for one of the brothers meeting a new girlfriend. Jane loved every minute of it, committed entire decades of setlists to memory as easily as other kids her age accumulated *Saved by the Bell* plot lines and baseball stats. During those early years, she thought all of America was a swirling world of tie-dye and food and shirtless, long-haired men with dinner-plate pupils and their carefree, beautiful women, a place of music and laughter and dancing connected by a sprawling spiderweb of highway, only a security guard in a hut at the border keeping the joyful madness at bay.

Everybody has their gifts, and this was Jane's. For her bat mitzvah, her brothers bought her a beat-up van. After a week of fighting with their mom and dad—one of countless music-related fights Jane would win as much through stubbornness as through tirades sprinkled with *beauty*, with *authentic*, with *transcendent*—the van sat in the driveway waiting for the three years until Jane could get her licence. Even before she could drive it, she would spend whole fall, winter, and spring days in there, with her walkman and tapes, putting to memory the best jams, the sweetest segues, entire multinight runs of unequalled musical expression, developing her mastery of the vulgate, everything outside the van windows the domain of the vulgar. Jane quickly fell in love with the van: its age, its 150,000 kilometres, its scuffed and torn deep-purple interior, even the licence plate: ARKS 066. It was the ultimate tour vehicle. Most days after school, she would end up in there, would fall asleep full of its promise, dreaming of summertime— ah, summertime, when, her friends at sleepover camp singing songs and waterskiing, Jane would be on summer tour, singing songs and expanding her mind, a part of something unique and exciting and genuine and fun, fun, fun.

Those fights with her parents, though. They were legendary. She and her mom would run through the house yelling.

"Your grandparents didn't work their entire lives so you could drive around America listening to the same music over and over again!"

"Mom, you don't get it. You just don't get it! How can I ever explain it to you *if you don't just get it!*"

"This is all your brothers' fault! I should've been more strict with them!"

"You were plenty strict, Ma," Drew would say, munching on an apple in the doorway. (That was his usual amount of contribution to Jane's wars with her mother, to Jane's pre-teen mind as good as betrayal.) Usually Nate, Jane's father, would eventually step in.

"Now Ruth, at least she's with Drew, Brian, and Rick. At least she's getting some worldly experience, right? We had plenty of interesting experiences in our youth, didn't we?"

"Yeah! So there!" Jane would yell before stomping out to the van. She'd lock the doors, light incense, clamp on her headphones, put on her favourite tape, stare at the poster of Jerry Garcia's smiling, beatific face as his improvised guitar melodies calmed and soothed, till the tape side would end, and Jane would go back into the house, cuddle into her mother in front of the television, Drew smirking when he went to the fridge and saw the two women of the house apparently once again best friends.

Jerry's death in 1995 was thirteen-year-old Jane's first experience with mortality, and, along with her brothers, she took it hard. The night of his death, they piled into Jane's van, and Drew drove the four of them up to Red Pine Park, the highest point in their northern Toronto suburb of Thornhill, where they spent the early August night watching the tall buildings of Toronto, many kilometres away, shimmer in the summer haze, listening to their favourite tapes on the car stereo, and passing around joints until they couldn't get up. Jane, tremendously stoned for the first time and unable to put her stormy thoughts into words, couldn't understand what her life would be like without the Grateful Dead. Without the smooth, ropey beauty of Jerry's guitar.

That night, Jane threw up for hours, her mom on the floor with her in the bathroom thinking she had the stomach flu, *there there*-ing her daughter, who, she was sure, would now finally move on from her strange fascination with that repetitive holdover band from the sixties. However, even though she wouldn't smoke pot again until she was well into her twenties, the six hours curled around the toilet bowl did nothing to discourage Jane from devoting herself to the music, from becoming a certified tour kid. It didn't take long before Jane turned her voracious musical hunger towards Phish. Phish was like the Dead but unlike the Dead; they were like nothing she had ever heard before. They were weird and surprising and melodic and frenzied, with unexpected torrents of real beauty. Trey Anastasio's guitar playing was burning hot, able to stoke the world into paroxysms of cathartic release. By the time she saw her first show, Niagara Falls, December 7, 1995, she knew all the songs and impressed the fans sitting next to her with her knowledge of the band's musical history.

Over the next four years, she saw them dozens of times, mostly with Rick and Brian. Drew stayed loyal to the Dead, was unable to make the transition to the four-piece from Vermont. Jane's room was a shrine of posters, officially released CDs, shelf upon shelf of bootlegged tapes, setlists written out in her small meticulous hand, with a closet of peasant skirts, hemp pants, and Baja sweaters, a bureau of tour shirts, new and old, faded tie-dye and Jerry bears and Phish logos. A drawer in her desk, which was once neon green but was now covered in fan-made stickers, held envelopes, stamps, and the blank tapes she would mail out weekly to the various taping trees she belonged to. At school, Jane's musical abilities often translated into perfect math tests, but her lack of attendance and incomplete homework meant bad grades. She spent most of the school day hanging out in the pit behind the school with the other "hippies," smoking cigarettes, listening to jams, falling in love with one dreadheaded boy after another, any outsider with a disdain for authority and an outsized attachment to music, whether metal or punk or classic rock or hip hop or even, briefly in grade twelve, jazz. In her final year, deciding to cut her mother a little slack in their ongoing struggle, Jane applied the scantest amount of attention to her schoolwork and ended up graduating with a B+ average.

Once she turned eighteen, the battles with her mother officially ended. She could no longer keep Jane from venturing farther than the Great Lakes states. In late December, she drove down to Florida with her best friend Vanessa, Drew, his girlfriend Tracy, and Tracy's sister Danika for the 1999 New Year's festival at Big Cypress Indian Reservation. After the seventy-two hours of music and sunrises, a community of eighty thousand bringing in the new millennium together, she thought of almost nothing else. What could anyone want more in life than revelling in being alive through a six-hour set of twenty-minute jams and deep grooves broadcasted straight from the group mind? By the time the band left the stage early New Year's Day to a recording of "Here Comes the Sun," Jane, Vanessa, and Danika were hugging each other, crying, forever best friends, forever changed.

Jane did Phish's entire 2000 summer tour with Vanessa and Danika, eighteen shows. They slept in the back of Jane's van, sold veggie fajitas for gas money, took turns at the wheel as they ate through highways and crisscrossed state lines. The band's hiatus the following year came just in time for Jane, to the much-expressed relief of her parents, to enroll in university, but by the time the band got back together in the winter of 2003, her two and a half semesters of being a university student were already far behind her. Though she enjoyed the political culture and the parties, Jane saw pretty fast that she wasn't cut out for school, for university hall lectures, for paper writing. Jane was cut out for deep, sustained musical appreciation. Her parents were just going to have to live with that fact. She had been waiting tables and living in a house in Kensington Market with six roommates for two years, saving money and waiting for the inevitable announcement of Phish's reunion. And once it came, she didn't miss a single show of '03 and early '04, and neither did Vanessa (Danika came along for all of '03, but when she moved to Vancouver for grad school, her touring days looked to be behind her), her life a fantastic rush of interstates and venues and boys and musical epiphanies, long stretches in the fall and winter spent in Toronto recuperating and checking daily for the announcement of the next tour.

And then, completely out of nowhere, in the middle of summer tour, the band broke up. Disbanded. Collapsed the small but entire world they were the bedrock of. The band—particularly Trey, the guitarist and driving force behind the group—insisted it was final, that they would never play another show again. Phish was done. Finished. Jane was devastated, tossed out of orbit: she was so angry, so full of betrayal, that she jumped off of tour, had the guys she was riding with at the time drop her off at a bus station in Maryland. This was much worse than Jerry's death, she thought bitterly, sitting on the hood of her van in Red Pine Park, watching the sun set over Toronto. Did

Trey not realize how many people depended on him and the band for spiritual sustenance? For spiritual, emotional, sexual, communal, even financial, sustenance?

There were other bands to follow, of course, but what Phish had—the explosive creative genius of the four of them together on stage—was one of a kind. What was she supposed to devote her life to now? Her brothers had all moved on: all three got married within a year of each other, and they had careers now, houses in the suburbs, talk of children. Brian and Rick had started a home renovation company; Drew was a lawyer at a Bay Street firm. Without Jane noticing, they had turned into adults. Jane knew she wasn't ready for anything like that; the very phrase *settling down* made her twitch with anxiety. She needed to move. But it was probably time to at least take a break from the scene for a while. Why should she let Trey dictate her happiness? Why should she predicate her sense of self on a band? Yeah. She would jump into the van and just drive. She would explore the continent. Even with all the touring she had done, the hours on the highway, the motels, the gas stations, the venues, and the campgrounds, she had never just explored, at her own pace, following the roads and what came to her. She knew nothing of America outside of the insular world of tour. She decided to find out.

Three days later, Jane and Vanessa were waiting in a long line of cars to cross the Peace Bridge into Buffalo, the van loaded with their luggage, Vanessa's guitar, two tents, sleeping bags, coolers, and five milk crates of tapes.

Jane and Vanessa were living in a cabin somewhere between Big Sur and San Francisco, working in the vast garden during the day and having mountainous bonfires at night. They had left Toronto nine months ago, had spent two months in the east before picking their way west, and now they were living with Chase and Gavin, young organic farmers they had met in the Sonoran desert. They had arrived in June, already two months ago. Vanessa moved into Chase's room a few days after they arrived; Jane continued alternating between her tent and the cabin floor.

"I feel like I could stay here forever," Jane said, laughing, to Vanessa. It was their day off from the garden, and, as usual, they were spending it walking the crashing Northern California shoreline.

"Oh hon, so do I!"

Jane stopped to watch a big wave crash white and gold at their feet. Walking with Vanessa at the edge of the continent, Jane felt herself opening with possibilities, like the rehearsed part of a song making way for the freeing beauty of improvisation. Vanessa stooped down and picked up a pair of perfect shells lying side by side on the rocks. She held one under Jane's neck and one under her own. "Necklaces," she said, giggling. Vanessa, brown haired and green eyed, a wardrobe of faded Levi's and big sweaters, her best friend. She hadn't said anything, but Jane knew, in that way that lifelong friends know things, that Vanessa and Chase were in love, and Jane couldn't be happier.

Two nights later, three male hitchhikers from San Diego showed up at the house, which wasn't particularly unusual, except that these were tour kids. Jane knew instantly: the corduroy pants with multicoloured patches piped up the sides, the glass mushrooms floating in amber teardrops tied around their necks with pieces of hemp, the *Steal Your Face* patches on their rucksacks and mandolin cases. Three separate forests of dreadlocks, the musk of marijuana, sweat, and teatree oil. Seeing them, Jane felt a bittersweet pang of recognition, like seeing someone from your childhood neighbourhood in a bazaar halfway around the world.

At the bonfire after dinner—where Jane established her tour credentials, the meal taken over by talk of classic Dead shows, monumental Phish runs—the three boys mentioned that they were on their way to Berkeley to see a jam band called Grizzly.

"Grizzly? Who are they?" Jane asked.

"What do you mean *who are they*?" Remil, by far the cutest of the newcomers, exclaimed, his indistinct yet thoroughly American accent twanging up and down. "They're taking the scene by storm, that's who they are!"

"I guess I stopped paying attention when Phish broke up. Are they any good?"

"Are they any *good*? Girl, they are the sauciest band to come our way since Jerry died!"

Remil was short and stocky, with huge brown dreadlocks framing a big, expressive face. He was the indeterminate age of someone who had spent their life on tour—he could've been a weathered twenty-four or a joyful thirty-eight. And judging by the blistery burn marks on his fingers, he was a glass blower, a hunch Jane would soon confirm, most of his rucksack taken up with his nipple-foam cases of one-hitters, pipes, and bubblers. Just looking at him, Jane realized how much she missed the lot, the music, the nightly journey into the unknown.

"Well, that settles it," she said, already filling with the familiar rush, realizing that she had made her mind up as soon as she saw Remil in the garden, feeling more than the usual attraction to the intense boy with the kind eyes. "What do you say, Van? Is it time to move on?"

"I don't know, hon," Vanessa said. "I promised Chase I'd help out at the farmers' market till the end of the month. You go though. We'll meet up after, go visit Danika in BC like we planned."

Jane looked at her best friend, cuddled under a blanket with Chase, beautiful in the firelight. Two days ago, she had no intention of parting with her, but something inside her had reawakened, and she knew she was going to let it take her where it would.

She had to pack.

UC Berkeley's Greek Theatre was unlike any amphitheatre Jane had ever been to. A hundred years old and modelled on the theatres of ancient Athens, it already held a place of honour in the annals of jam-band history: the Dead had played there a total of twenty-nine times, two early shows in the late sixties and then, starting in the eighties, a three-show run every year of that decade. At Remil's urging, Jane described these shows as they drove up the coast, their two vanmates asleep in the backseat: "Well, there's October '69, Phil's bass high in the mix, Jerry's guitar surging and weaving. And then there's July 13, 1984—it was Friday the thirteenth, the moon was full, it was the first show of perhaps their best run at the theatre. Oh my God, I can't believe I've never been there before! And, of course, the last show they played there, August 19, 1989. The end of an era. And did you know that Phish played there too? Only once though, the last show of their '93 summer tour. Imagine it, imagine being there, coming off of a tour of a hundred shows, and to end there, at a venue straight out of the birth of Western civilization!"

"Damn, girl!" Remil exclaimed. "Am I ever lucky to have found you!"

Jane blushed, surprising herself. She curled her body around the steering wheel, leaned into the road.

Remil insisted that they not listen to any Grizzly on the three-hour drive to Berkeley. That way, Jane could go into the show fresh, without any preconceptions. A virgin. Instead, they listened to Phish and the Dead.

"What show is *this*?" Remil asked, ten minutes after Jane had popped a new tape in.

"May 8, 1977. My brother Drew's most treasured tape." Just hearing Jerry's guitar come across the grainy divide of the worn tape filled Jane with her childhood, her adoration for Drew and her other brothers.

Remil's eyes got wide with intrigue. "I knew it. You know this show doesn't actually exist, right?"

Jane laughed, changed lanes. "What do you mean?"

"The entire show was a mind-control experiment put on by the CIA. They wanted to see if they could plant false memories into their enemies—ya know, Vietnam and all—and so who better to try it out on than the hippies? So, ya know, they got all these heads together, connected wires to their foreheads and genitals and shit, and *implanted* memories of the show. Anybody who claims they were there was actually part of a freakin' experiment! There's no record of the show anywhere; no bandmates recall it—it's basically indisputable: the government's pulled a fast one on us, oh yeah, believe it. They've successfully brainwashed thousands of people. Who knows what they're capable of now."

"You're so full of shit!" Jane shouted.

"No, I swear! It's true! It's true!"

"What about this tape, then, huh, mister? Where did all this music come from? Trust me, there isn't another show like it."

Remil raised his eyebrows, his face almost breaking apart with excitement. "That's just it. That's just it. Where *did* it come from?" He rolled down the window, stuck his head out. "Fuck you, CIA! Fuck you, government! You ain't gettin' inside my head!"

Jane refocused on the road, though she couldn't help smiling.

They drove on. A stretch of factories, smoke stacks, and parking lots sparked a discussion of the destruction of the earth, Remil's claim that "It's nothing a hundred million rinses through the hydrological cycle won't fix." When they got pulled over by a police cruiser just outside of Santa Cruz, Remil switched, to Jane's astonishment, into a polite, obsequious citizen, full of apology and deference; after waving them on with only a warning to slow down, the Remil Jane was familiar with rushed back in a curse-word-laden rant against the thought police of Babylon, Jane laughing along. Who was this brimming, dreadlocked boy who had stumbled into her life?

By the time they had entered the Bay Area and were driving through downtown Berkeley towards the university's campus, Jane felt like she knew Remil intimately, and not only because they couldn't keep their hands off each other (or their clothes on the second they were alone). He was full of theories, pronouncements, rants against the government, the police, the UN, the big corporations, anybody who had any power. He didn't believe in the nation-state, in governments, in the army, in owning land. He kept saying that Babylon was erected on false promises and land theft and that its days were numbered. What *did* he believe in? The open road, music, the night sky, that, as he put it more than once, "Music and dancing and the redistribution of wealth can change the world." He actually said that! Jane felt like she had finally met someone who had a handle on twenty-first-century life: like him, all she had to do was discard the bad parts, dig into the good parts, try and be a good person. She felt determined to do so with everything she had.

They parked, easily scored tickets, waited in a long line that snaked right through campus to get into the venue, talked politics with a man with a sharp, intelligent face wearing a red-and-gold jester's hat. Jane felt like she was home after a long absence. The

Greek Theatre was a deep, small bowl situated halfway up the rising Berkeley campus. When Grizzly took the stage and, without any preamble, leapt into a raging funked-out groove that seemed to have actualized out of the air, Jane was blown away. She closed her eyes and imagined the improvised chords and drumbeats and piano washes and bass lines filling the curved cement steps and narrow lawn of the amphitheatre, detaching it from the campus, all of it lifting off into the night, trailing falling clumps of dirt and root as it drifted across the bay and out to sea.

Grizzly, while right out of the Dead-Phish current, was unlike any band Jane had ever heard. Their sound was raw, fresh, the jams driving relentlessly towards their crescendoing peaks before falling into folk-tinged valleys. By the fifth song, Jane had a sense of how to listen to them, the particular twists and changes that made their jams unique. There was a deep, playful intelligence behind the music, but also a driving, fierce musicality. Jane couldn't remember dancing like this before. She closed her eyes again and was a little girl being passed back and forth by her brothers at a Dead show, floating above the crowds as lighters lit up the night, willing the band back on stage for the encore. Word quickly spread that Janice, the lead guitarist, tall and lanky with hands that dwarfed the neck of the guitar, had a nasty cold. Sure enough, when they came back on for the encore, the band played funky background music as Janice, head tilted back, shoulder-length hair waterfalling towards the stage, poured an entire bottle of honey into his open mouth. Jane screamed encouragement along with everybody else in the horseshoe of the amphitheatre.

Jane didn't know the names of any of the songs, not yet, but she felt new, alive, the show rolling around her brain, burning to be examined, dissected, opened up to have its magic shucked out. The scene was so much smaller and cleaner than a Phish show. There didn't seem to be any hangers-on, no one there just for the drugs and the party and the mistaken promise of free sex, everyone there simply for the music. Jane was wearing a light summer dress and had lost her sandals somewhere in the crowd. The keys player had her mesmerized. The bass player—who was, to Jane's delight, female—rocked out some serious rhythms. Janice's fingers burned with electricity. The drummer had not stopped smoking—both cigarettes and on the drums—since taking the stage.

After the show and a lacklustre after-show party in downtown Berkeley with DJ Chris Kuroda, after wading through the rave-like scene of their hotel's lobby, after being in the elevator with Remil for an electric rising moment interrupted when a very large man—obviously a fan, his enormous white t-shirt drenched in sweat, his cheeks red and his eyes popping—got on at the fifth floor and asked, in a tone of heartbreaking intimacy, "Are you guys just getting back?" after all that, but before stumbling off at the tenth floor and trying to determine which hallway led to the room they were sharing with six other people, Jane knew she was hooked. She couldn't wait to learn the names and histories of the band members, revel in their mythology, memorize the shape and movement of their songs, the organic transformations, the hinted-at melodies, the repetitions, a guitar line calling back a piano-led jam from three summers before, to be full of the knowledge that history is being made as you dance and welcome each new song with raised arms and ecstatic yelling, to soak in the musical wonder, the serious, heated discussions, to be re-immersed once again in the constant driving towards release, towards freedom, towards zenith after zenith, towards what everyone who had tasted it and understood called by a single word: tour.

"So, Remil," she said, sliding into bed with him, none of the other roommates back from the celebrations yet, the hotel room theirs, "where's the next show?"

Grizzly had formed in the late nineties in Missoula, Montana, the outcome of the simultaneous demise of two local bands, Takver/Shevek and the Resting Bitch Faces. Takver/Shevek, which had been made up of graduate students in the creative writing program at the university—and whose songs were of a decidedly literary nature, with titles like "Dubliners" and "Anna Sees Vronsky for the First Time"—split ways when the lead singer finished his degree and went off to write his first novel in the wilds of LA. Janice House, the rhythm guitarist, and Paul McClasky, the bassist, decided to start a new band. As it happened, Paul's sister Cody's punk band the Resting Bitch Faces had just disbanded as well. So Janice took the lead, Paul jumped onto the drums, Cody stayed on bass, and Janice's roommate from undergrad, the indomitable Steve Gruen, filled out the rhythm section, playing keys, and, after a few years, horns as well. Steve joined the band after a late-night phone call from Janice, now the stuff of legend, and soon relocated from Tampa to Missoula. The four of them moved into a big house near the university and happily found themselves spending all of their waking hours practising and writing music. Though everyone except Cody was a fan of the Dead and Phish, it was undoubtedly Steve who pushed the band into the improvisational rock direction, showing up in Missoula with three suitcases containing his collection of recorded shows. When they weren't practising, jamming, or writing their highly allusive lyrics, they were listening to these tapes—there was Phish and the Dead, but also the Allman Brothers, moe., Widespread Panic, and the String Cheese Incident, each tape with a new chord change, tempo upswing, or sparkling melody to try their hands at. And they tried their hands at all of it. According to rumour, the first song the band learned together, before Steve had even unpacked, was Phish's "Divided Sky." And with that, Grizzly was born. They were together for five months before their first gig, at the Waterin' Hole Pub in downtown Missoula. The show was a complete disaster, forever after to be referred to as Watergate amongst fans.

Remil told this potted history of the band to Jane, its fine points already polished to a high sheen, as they drove up the coast. When Jane and Remil caught up to the band in Berkeley, Grizzly was reaching the final stages of a steady ascent to the top of the jam-band world, the throne of which had been vacant since Phish broke up. They had spent almost six years gaining experience and followers in the college towns of the Midwest, honing their ability to lock in and play as one eight-limbed mind, and the show at the Greek found them halfway through their second West Coast tour. After leaving Berkeley and spending three large, crashing nights camping in the coastal redwoods, Jane and Remil met up with the tour for a string of indoor shows in Eugene, Portland, and Seattle before driving east to the Gorge Amphitheatre to catch them open for all three nights of the Dave Matthews Band's annual September run. With these shows, Grizzly's biggest so far, the tour would come to a close.

In Berkeley, Jane traded Phish tapes for as many Grizzly shows as she could find and devoured them on the drive. Such energy captured in the analog warmth of the tapes. Her favourite song so far was "Paper," a three-part jam vehicle of epic proportions. As the third part of the song was nearing its impossible peak, they were high up on a cliff-hugging road on the scenic route from Eugene to Portland, mountains to their right, ocean to their left, Janice's guitar climbing the rise with them. "This, right here, Jane, this is the best part of the jam—listen to what Cody does to the melody!" Remil turned up the stereo and a dread brushed against Jane's arm, a dry paintbrush on tingling canvas.

When the tape side ended, Remil said, "Let me put a show on for you," and took a tape out of his bag and popped it in. From the first seconds of static, Jane knew it was Dead. Early '79. They both let the music absorb them, riding the dips and rises of the road.

"I didn't think you had any tapes on you," Jane said eventually, laughing.

"I only travel with one. January 15, 1979. The night I was conceived."

"No way!"

"Way. My parents had met the show before, and they found a corner and got, it, on."

Jane laughed. Remil was a true tour kid: without a doubt, some of Jerry's guitar, Bobby's rhythm, Phil's bass, must have slipped into the brand new zygote.

"So what's *your* story, Janey? Where are you from?"

"Me? No story really. I'm from Toronto; you know that. My parents are actually from the States, but they've lived in Canada for years and years now. Just a middle-class Jewish girl in love with live music."

"A middle-class Jewish girl built for musical satori."

"Ha ha. A middle-class Jewish girl without any marketable skills or a university education."

"A middle-class Jewish girl with a terrific ass!"

"A middle-class Jewish girl who's about to kick *your* ass," Jane said, laughing, smacking Remil in the arm.

"Please, madam, please," Remil said, his hands up in surrender. "I kid. I kid."

Once they pulled into the venue and found shakedown—the rows of shops, food vendors, and tents the focal point of the lot scene—it was a non-stop barrage of reunions and introductions and hugs. Remil knew everybody in the scene, and they all knew him. When they walked the lot together, Jane felt like a queen, a shakedown queen. At the shows where Remil decided to sell his pipes, Jane would help him, both of them walking around with their cases open. *Heady handblown glass! Heady handblown glass! Toke your nug in heady handblown glass!* Remil gave a fair number of pipes away, but he got plenty of food and drugs in return. Jane had never felt more plugged into the scene, a working member of the give and take of the shakedown. Everybody looking out for each other, sharing with each other, helping each other (and, yes, making money for fuel and food and tickets too). And Remil. He fit perfectly in his body, was utterly present wherever he was, whether on lot, in the van, dancing at a show, in the tent. In bed. Shoeless, wearing a red t-shirt, patchwork pants—his feet and calves covered in mud—and the hemp anklet Jane made for him during the drive from Berkeley to Eugene, an energetic, spontaneous koala bear. He was her energetic, strange little koala bear. And the compliments he got on his hair! It never ended. *Nice dreads! Great dreads! Wow, powerful hair, brother!* Remil laughed every time, did a dance, called out his thanks.

In the lot outside of the Portland show, Little Lucy, one of Remil's friends (he later told Jane that they grew up together, their parents travelling in the same caravan), an impossibly thin girl with massive blond dreadlocks and blue eyes speckled with silver, offered them some acid. Jane hadn't dosed in years, but she gleefully accepted the two tabs, carefully chewing as they walked through the stalls, swallowing the masticated paper just before going into the venue. Five hours later, they were in the van, driving towards Seattle, nothing between Jane and the world—she and Remil were holding hands, leaning forward, talking as fast as their mouths would let them, plumbing the depths, the rubbed-raw steering wheel and frayed seatbelt the only things anchoring Jane to the road, the van's dashboard, the lights of the highway.

"Hey, hey," Remil sung out, "when this tour is over, we should go down south, meet up with my parents. We can help them out at the store, lend a hand during the weed harvest. You'd love them Jane; they're good people. Real people."

"Sounds great!" she blurted, trying to keep her smile from breaking her face off.

Remil just kept rolling on: "Have you ever thought about how much faith we have in the band, in Janice? We have to believe, deeply, deeply believe, that the music they are playing on that stage is true improvisation, that we are right there with them as they create history. Imagine if we found out they planned it all out backstage, were nothing but lousy Babylonian frauds? Imagine our devastation. But we do believe. Why? Because if it wasn't for the communal thrill of improvisational music, there would be nothing keeping us from the daily grind. Tension and release, dissonance and resolution, the deepest minor-key despair shooting up to the purest major-key joy, all carved out of the ether with careful abandon! Those Babylonians wouldn't know beauty if it kicked them in the nuts."

"Remil!"

He turned to her. He had started talking so fast that it was hard to follow the words, Jane travelling through them like she was caught in a slipstream.

They both burst into laughter, sacred seventh-hour-of-an-acid-trip laughter. The pine trees outside the window smeared together like toothpicks being rolled in paint. Later, at that night's show, the music peaking all around them like transitory mountain ranges, Remil would bury his face into Jane's and say, "I've finally found my home" into her ear, and Jane would grab his hand in delirious agreement, but for now, the day breaking all around them, they pulled into a Walmart parking lot and crawled into the back of the van. They would sleep till showtime.

By the time they pulled into the Gorge and were setting up camp, Jane was irrevocably back into the tour life. The driving, the community, living outside of the regulated pathways of civilization, the music. The real fans, those who lived without compromise, all the Remils and Little Lucys with their campers and tattoos and commitment to the tour life. Jane wanted to live without compromise too. Remil was right: life was to be lived, music experienced, people loved, the world explored. And even though a mere two weeks ago she had never even heard of Grizzly, was still sore from Phish's breakup, she now felt like she had been a devoted fan her entire life, like everything that came before was leading up to that first live chord from Janice's guitar. She had seen four shows, listened to dozens more in the van, all of them flavoured with Remil's bottomless reserve of story, rumour, fact, and lore, and there was still so much to learn, dissect, argue over. Jane was about to, once again, embark into uncharted territory.

During the encore of the first show of the run, Dave Matthews himself came out to guest on vocals. "These guys are pretty damn good, pretty damn good, whattayasay," Dave told the audience in his cheery mumble, ecstatic cheering rising to agree with him.

The feeling on lot was unanimous: the shows were excellent. The audience, most of them having never heard Grizzly before, was enthralled. Janice, Cody, Steve, and Paul took to the amphitheatre at the world's edge as if they had played there hundreds of times. The canyon behind the theatre crescendoing into the distance, the sunset setting the vista aflame, the stage perched on the edge of infinity, who could want a better setting for Grizzly's introduction to the wider jam-band world?

A rumour from the first night, started on the lawn and spread throughout the amphitheatre, shakedown, campground, and parking lot, had it that Dave had heard about the band after an intrepid Grizzly fan had thrown a CD of an early show at Dave when he saw him out for a pre-show jog in Chicago. By the afternoon of the third show, everyone was talking excitedly about the crazed fan who broke into Dave's winery in Virginia and left a whole *CD booklet* of shows on his kitchen table before stealing a placemat and vacating the premises.

However Dave caught wind of Grizzly, he had just helped them reach the next stage of their careers. "They'll be touring nationally in no time at all," Jane said the night after the last concert. She and Remil were selling veggie fajitas out of the back of Jane's van, Remil's pipes showcased on the table next to the grill.

"And we were there. We were there. We were there," Remil sung, changing the words of Grizzly's "Yes (Yes) No," scooping the veggies off the grill and loading the fajitas, handing them to Jane to wrap in tinfoil. "Fajitas! Veggie fajitas! Heady, heady fajitas!" he called out. The lot was still going strong. Only a few cars had started the slow snake towards the exit, their headlights catching in the grass. "The Dave scene isn't nearly so bad as people on Phish lot would want you to think," Remil said, holding his spatula, surveying the night's goings-on.

"Yeah, you're right. Just another brand of poison."

"Everybody's so *white* though," Remil said, giving Jane a little shock.

"Just as white as at a Phish lot ..."

Remil surveyed the fans passing by, and Jane followed his eyes. "Yeah," he said eventually, "but it's a different kind of whiteness, somehow."

"It's amazing how little overlap there is between the two scenes," Jane said, dumping another tub of chopped peppers and onions onto the grill, stirring the already sizzling vegetables. "I wonder if them playing here is going to keep the diehard Phish heads from coming aboard."

"Not if I have anything to do with it," Remil shouted, exchanging a fajita for a five-dollar bill. A line was beginning to form, and Jane started working faster. Remil continued: "Phish is over and done with—they're playing golf now, learning how to gourmet cook. They are over, over, and Grizzly is the future! The music never stops, Janey. You know that!"

The folks in line started cheering, the whooping and catcalling spreading through the lot. A car stereo started pumping out a Grizzly show. Jane recognized it as one of the shows they had listened to on the drive up, January 17, 2003, in Missoula, at the Pit, the college bar they had played nightly as they refined their chops. The tape was right in the middle of the rising first part of "Paper." The line having died down, Remil jumped onto the grass and started thrashing around, his dreads in motion like a many-winged bird in flight. Jane drank him in. How had she ever thought she could leave tour? This was where everything was happening. This was the place to be. Remil was right: this was home, this tiny space they'd carved for themselves outside of the corruption of the world.

An hour later, the lot quieted down, and Jane took a much-needed trip to the porta-potties. Once back at the van, she sat down in the driver seat to get some hand sanitizer. She opened the glove compartment, but, instead of grabbing the bottle of sanitizer, she took out her cellphone. She hadn't checked it in three days. There were six missed calls and fifteen text messages. The last text was an hour old. It was from Drew and contained bad news: her grandmother Rachel had passed away. The funeral was tomorrow.

Jane got out of the van, the night twisted inside out: Shadows ran in and out of the tents and trees. The moon was suspended in the thick night sky. The celebratory screams and laughter dialled down to a faint hum. A firework went off, heavy and slow. She watched Remil as he cleaned the grill, scraping it with the spatula. He looked up, his grin collapsing.

The rest of the night was a blur. Jane packed her bag, left the van with Remil, who couldn't stop declaring his love for her, hitched a ride with some heads to the Spokane airport, flew to Seattle and then Chicago and then Buffalo, where her brothers Rick and Brian were waiting. She hadn't seen them in almost a year, and after Jane got over the momentary disappointment of Drew's absence, she was pretty happy to be with her brothers again. "Nana didn't want to be buried next to Papa?" Jane asked as they left the airport.

"She did, but she also wanted to be with her living family," Rick said from the passenger seat. "We're going to have a ceremony for her in Jersey, maybe next summer, put up a headstone."

"She'll be buried in two countries!" Brian said.

"Makes sense to me," Jane said.

They crossed the Niagara River on the Queenston-Lewiston bridge, got through the surprisingly hassle-free border in record time, and started the long curve around Lake Ontario. The QEW was deserted.

A Jerry Garcia Band album played softly. Jane didn't start to cry until they could see the lights of Toronto in the distance.

2. Summer Tour

Jane sat in her parents' living room, surrounded by family. She hadn't slept since the night before she left Washington state, and, still connected to the tour through a string of uninterrupted waking hours, was feeling oddly out of time and out of place. The early morning drive to Toronto, the funeral, the drive to the cemetery in the limousine, all of it some strange tangent to where she was mere days ago, sleeping in a tent listening to live music on the opposite side of the continent. How had she ended up here, in the suburban house where she grew up, old people in suits and dresses milling around her, eating babka, bending down and very seriously shaking her hand?

While Jane was of course sad that her grandmother Rachel had passed away, she didn't know most of these people. Rachel had lived in New Jersey until a few years ago, when she moved up to Toronto to be with Jane's mother, her eldest daughter, and this meant that a lot of the family present were from south of the border and were nothing more than faces. The extended family trees and knotted geographies of North American Jews just didn't hold Jane's interest in the same way a song history or setlist stats did, and she couldn't help feeling disoriented, exhausted, a little bored. What Jane really wanted was to spend some time with Drew, but in the rush leading up to the funeral, and with the house full of family both familiar and strange, her attempts had so far proven fruitless. Drew was stuck in the kitchen with his wife and year-old son and was unreachable in the sea of condolence-givers and baby-oglers, and Jane sat alone in the living room, trying to figure out who was who, if the man with the cane was a second cousin or a third.

Over the next four days, Jane was introduced to a lot of family, met a lot of Cahills, Goldbergs, and Tradewskys, heard stories about Rachel's life in New Jersey, kept a running tally with her mom on the number of Styrofoam cups of coffee they consumed, ate a large amount of bagels, cream cheese, and baked goods, fielded questions about her life on tour—"Do you know the band?" "Aren't there lots of diseases in those places?" "Don't you get bored listening to the same thing over and over again?" "I don't understand, are you *in* the band?!"—spent the few hours in the late evening when her old friends would visit in relative bliss (Drew's ex-girlfriend Tracy, Danika's older sister, even came one night, and they listened to an early Dead show—December 1, 1966, the band still playing mostly covers, Jerry announcing matter-of-factly, "Welcome to another evening of confusion and high-frequency simulation," a line they used to say all the time—in the basement like old times), escaped to her room or the backyard when at seven thirty each night the adults would pray, heard, for the umpteenth time, about the great-great-grandfather that disappeared, never to be seen again. It was an ingrained part of the family story, polished to a high sheen, anything extraneous—names, dates, locations—thrown out.

At the end of the third day, Jane finally cornered Drew, alone, outside the basement bathroom. They went out to the front of the house and stood on the driveway, just outside of the streetlight's halo.

"So, I hear you're onto a new band?"

Jane couldn't deny that Drew looked good: trim, healthy, his sandy hair messy but passably professional. Being a husband and a father seemed to be working for him.

She laughed. "Yeah. I guess I am. But tell me, how are things with you? How's Jerry? I'm sorry I haven't been around much."

Drew smiled, his old, affable, toothy grin. "Jer's great. Crawling, eating, shitting. Work's good. Everything's good. Don't listen to much music these days, sorry to say. Not like I used to."

"Don't be sorry. It is difficult to comprehend, though. What do you do with all your time?"

"With Jer there isn't all that much time. Samantha and I watch tennis when we can. The few times I've visited Rick and Bri at a work site, they've had the Dead blasting, you'll be happy to know."

"Tennis?! My God, Drew, what's happened to you? We've got to get you to a show!"

Drew laughed, and for an instant Jane saw a flash of the old Drew, her brother who cared about nothing but witnessing Jerry, Bobby, Phil, Keith, and Mickey make music, who taught her everything she knew about tour and the wider world that was not tour. Only an instant, and then it was this new, oddly adult Drew Jane was having so much trouble getting used to. "So what're your plans now? Going to leave us for another year of amazing adventures?"

"I think I'll stay in Toronto for the winter. Vanessa and her boyfriend and my friend Remil are coming out here with my van. They should be leaving the coast in a week or two. I don't know; I'll probably try and get back into the restaurant, wait to jump onto Grizzly's next tour."

"Remil, eh?" Drew said, raising an eyebrow.

Jane smiled, blushing. (When was the last time the mere mention of a boy's name made her blush?!) "He's a great guy, Drew. He blows glass in the winter, works at his parents' crystal store, and in the summer he's on tour. He was conceived at a Dead show—can you imagine?! He really cares about the music."

"Just be careful, Janey. Don't fall in love. I know these tour kids. They're so hooked on the experience, once the fuzzy warm edge wears off, they'll just move on."

"What are you talking about, Drew? You and Tracy met on lot!"

Drew laughed, kicked the blacktop of the driveway. "Yeah, yeah, I know. But what happened with Tracy? We broke up. Besides, it's a little different—we met on tour, sure, but she's still a good old-fashioned Jewish girl from Thornhill. Things are so different now, anyways. With the Dead, there was always, what, this potential that we were creating a better world. What is it now but an excuse to get really high and dance?"

Jane vehemently disagreed with Drew's pronouncements on the post-Dead scene—what did he know about it, anyways?—but held herself back. Drew laughed, and the tension modulated into something approaching their old bond.

"It's all good, Jane, isn't it? Now, tell me more about this new band. Rick and Bri say this guy Janice can play like a monster."

Jane had been home for four weeks when she happened to glance out an upstairs window and witness the surreal sight of her own van pulling into the driveway. There it was, her van, ARKS 066, in all its sturdy rundownedness, its scratches and dents, the faint rust around the wheel wells like crow's feet on a worn, dependable face. Barefoot, she ran out of the house—there was her van, there were Chase and Vanessa in the driver and passenger seat, and, and ... and where was Remil? Vanessa and Chase got out of the car, and Jane's stomach bottomed out. Vanessa ran to Jane and took her into her arms; Chase went around to the back of the van and started unloading.

"He didn't come?" Jane said into Vanessa's hair.

Vanessa pulled back. She was still wearing the shell necklace, bright white against her tanned skin. Jane felt a pang of guilt; her own shell necklace was hanging off a nail in her bedroom. "Oh, honey, no. He called Chase a few days before we were supposed to meet in Vancouver—Chase could barely understand what he was saying— apparently he couldn't, or wouldn't, cross the border. Something about a passport, maybe? Anyways, we met him in Seattle, and he gave us the van. I'm so sorry."

Jane tried to keep down the emotion that was bubbling out of her stomach and into her esophagus. The thought that Remil wouldn't come to Toronto hadn't even occurred to her. She felt like an idiot. She heard Drew on the driveway during the shiva: *I know tour kids. Fucking tennis.* Her whole recent trip across the country ran through her body—the desert, the coast, the ocean, all leading to Remil, to Grizzly, an orange tent dwarfed by towering redwoods—and all of a sudden it seemed like the whole thing was a waste. How had she been so deluded?

Startled, she pulled herself out of her thoughts. Vanessa was beside her, holding her hand. Chase was standing next to the van, looking sheepishly out of place, his legs lost in a circle of backpacks and coolers and duffel bags and guitar cases. It was probably the first time he had been in the suburbs, and if Jane wasn't such a mess, she would have laughed at how lost he looked, a foreigner on alien soil.

"Can we crash here for a few nights?" Vanessa asked.

"Of course," Jane replied. Being with Vanessa, as always, was a quick-acting balm. "Hey, I was thinking of getting an apartment downtown, maybe in Kensington, near the park."

"We'd love to!" Vanessa replied. They went up the walkway, giggling, Chase not far behind, carrying as much as he could.

"Oh my God, Jane, I almost completely forgot!" Vanessa shrieked later that night, as the three of them sat in her parents' backyard after dinner. It was a mild night, and Chase was very slowly rolling a joint. Over dinner, Vanessa had told Jane and her parents how much trouble they had at the border: the van was searched top to bottom, the officers giving Chase a hard time about all of his herbal medications, bags of dried sage, crystals. His hair sitting in a big bun on top of his head definitely hadn't helped. Everybody except Chase laughed when Vanessa described how horrified Chase was. Jane watched Chase as Vanessa told their story: it was painfully obvious that he was not used to being around parents, or adults of any kind, and every little noise made him jump. He had barely said a word since arriving. He was an utterly different person than the gregarious, carefree gardener they had met on the coast. Vanessa was rummaging in her purse. "I can't believe I let it slip my mind—Remil gave us a letter to give to you!"

A warm, big chord of sound opened inside Jane. She grabbed the envelope Vanessa had just retrieved from her purse and tore it open. Inside was an unlabelled tape and a letter.

Dear Jane,
I hope you enjoy this collection of all-time Grizzly jams. The 2002-08-16 "Rainbow Bleach" is smoking!
Love, Remil

The letter was dated September 21, 2005. On the other side was a list of the tracks on the tape.

"What does it say? What does it say?" Vanessa asked, shaking in her chair. "Did he apologize? Is he sorry?"

Jane stared at the letter. She pictured his big, beaming face, his thick, sturdy arms and legs, his earthy, warm smell, his eyes when the music was good.

"Yes," she said. "He apologized."

After the improvisation of yellow and magenta leaves, the tension of brilliant, bright afternoons, and the release of thick, damp nights, the fall imperceptibly segued into the winter, which slowly built its progression of snow and ice and wind and piercing blue sky. Jane got her waitressing job back, but by New Year's was still living at her parents'. She had decided to tough it out until the summer, saving tips and eating for free. Chase and Vanessa moved in with some of Vanessa's friends in the city: Chase was visibly relieved when they packed up and left Jane's parents' place. Vanessa reported that he was much happier living downtown, was growing herbs in the kitchen, though he complained bitterly about the cold and the oceanless horizon. Jane worked and saved, waiting again for the announcement of Grizzly's summer tour, sedulously listening her way through Grizzly's back catalogue, three hundred and six recorded shows. She listened to the shows in her van, like the old days, snow falling outside the fogged windows, the setlist in her hands, her pocket-sized journal in her lap. Every six weeks or so, a letter would come from Remil. Jane eagerly wrote back to the first letter, to a PO box in Denver, telling Remil all about the funeral and the shiva and life in Thornhill, saying how much she missed him and couldn't wait to be back on the road with him, but when Remil's reply had nothing personal in it, just philosophical musings about tour, Jane decided that letters were not the place for her to tell Remil how she felt. She'd have to wait to see him in person.

During that whole fall and winter—ever since the Gorge shows—word of Grizzly had been spreading through college campuses and jam-band chatrooms across the continent, the neural pathways of tape trading and band news laid down by the Dead and Phish reactivated, burning red hot, which meant that when Grizzly announced their summer tour in the middle of March, to many it was as if the band was finally claiming their throne. "Their first East Coast tour, Van!" Jane enthused to Vanessa over the phone, reading the tour dates on her computer screen for the fifth consecutive time. "And it's almost all amphitheatres! This is like being with the Dead in '69 or summer '74 or Phish from '93 to '97!"

"Are they going to be able to sell out these venues? Who even knows of them out here?"

"I guess someone must have thought they were big enough. Who cares though! Fourteen shows and a festival, it's completely doable. Star Lake, Camden, NYC, a handful of shows in the South, Deer Creek, Alpine, Minneapolis for an indoor show, and, this is the best part, a three night festy in some place called Red Hook, South Dakota." Jane paused, realizing there was something guarded in Vanessa's voice. "You're in, right?"

"Well, I'll have to speak to Chase, see what he thinks. We might be heading back to California for the spring; Chase really misses the coast."

Jane swallowed. Tour without Vanessa? She really wanted her to get to know Remil, experience Janice's guitar. "Well, I really hope you come, V. The road wouldn't be the same without you."

The next day the jam-band magazine *Relix* arrived in the mail, with Grizzly on the cover under the caption, "The Jam World's New Heroes?" In the feature interview with Janice, he talked about the band's excitement for their first national tour, about the pressures of taking on the tradition of the Dead and Phish. He ended the interview with a long quote from Jack Kerouac, which Jane wrote out and pinned to her bedroom wall.

March 21, 2006

Janey, my sweet scarlet begonia. From a spot hovering just behind Janice's head into his conscious mind into his neurons down through his musculature into his fingers, collected by the vibrations of the strings, grasped hungrily by the pickups, converted into waves, through the cables and into the preamp, magnified into booming waves of sound pumping out of the speakers, into our ears, back out through our bodies, filling the venue, pouring back into the spot hovering just behind Janice's head, a complete circuit.

Love, Remil

In the first week of May, the entire city in bloom, Chase broke up with Vanessa. One day they were going to get married and buy some property in California, the next he had bought a plane ticket to

Australia and was saying his goodbyes. Vanessa was devastated.

"A few days ago, a week, I don't know, just out of nowhere, he started talking about teacher's college," Vanessa said, sniffling, she and Jane sitting on her parents' porch, smoking a joint and eating ice cream. "And then suddenly he's enrolled in school, says he needs to be alone for this next part of his life journey. I had no idea he wanted to be a teacher. He hates kids!"

"Why Australia and not back to Big Sur?"

"I don't know, Jane. He just freaked out. I think the suburbs, I think Toronto, I don't know, it just got to him. And Gavin sold his property and moved to an ashram or something."

"What? He did?"

"You know how they are. They just can't sit still. But, but, I still thought we had something, I don't know, special. I loved him, J."

Jane didn't know what to say. Being high for the first time since she left the States wasn't helping. She had never seen Vanessa so out of sorts. Vanessa was right to feel blindsided: Chase going to teacher's college was anathema to what Jane knew—or thought she knew—about him. It would be like if Remil decided to go for an MBA. Imagine how thrilled her mom would be if she announced she was going to teacher's college!

"You guys had a good run," she offered, scraping the bottom of the ice cream carton.

"Did we? The whole thing seems more like a lie now than anything else." Vanessa looked at Jane, wiped her eyes. "I don't know, Jane; I'm so tired of this."

"Of what?"

"Of boys. Of disappointment."

"Oh, V."

"Why couldn't Chase have been like one of your brothers? Why can't I meet someone like Drew?"

"We'll just have to find you someone on tour this summer!"

"Tour? I don't know, Jane. I'm not really feeling it right now. That's the last thing on my mind."

"Oh."

"To tell you the truth, I think I've outgrown it."

Jane nodded. She needed a glass of water.

A few weeks later, a letter from Remil arrived. It was only four words: *Grizzly Summer Tour '06*. She pinned it up on her wall, next to the *Relix* cover of the band and the map she had drawn of the tour, red marker for the highways, each stop marked with a quarter note and a little sketch of the venue.

Summer approached.

Every night before going to bed, Jane would stare at the hand-drawn map pinned to her wall, guessing where she would find Remil. In the salty Atlantic water of Jones Beach? In the expansive parking garages of Camden? Or (hopefully!) on the first night of tour, waiting in line for a beer at the concession stand at Star Lake? Definitely before the tour dipped south. Jane felt a wave of doubt, but she pushed it back. They'd meet up. They'd find each other. They already did once. And this time, Jane had no intention of parting ways—after tour she wanted to just go wherever Remil and the van took them. Maybe down to Colorado to spend the winter with his parents, regroup, and restock before the next tour.

The spring's rhythms intensified and picked up momentum; there was a slight pause, and the summer came blasting through on a whole new sonic plane. Jane gave her two weeks at the restaurant, spent all of her free time outside, read *On the Road* for the first time since she was thirteen, daydreamed about Remil, her very own Neal Cassady. Their departure was days away. Jane packed, repacked, and packed again, oscillated between four skirts or five skirts, finally settling on three skirts, rifled through her tickets in their white envelope. She had tickets for every show, an assortment of pavilion seats and lawn, plus the festival ticket, three nights of camping and two of music. On a cool, breezy Friday morning, Jane picked Danika up from the airport, and they spent three days catching up, driving the city listening to shows, gathering materials at MEC, Bulk Barn, various health food stores. Jane hadn't seen her in years. Except for the weight she had put on, she looked like the same old Danika, stringy hair and pimply face, loud and confident, quick to argue and quicker to booming laughter. Jane filled Danika in on everything that had happened recently—tour, Chase's sudden departure, Remil—and Danika told Jane about life in graduate school, the lack of love interests, the slower daily rhythm of Vancouver, her classes, her dissertation, which was on the happy endings of American road novels.

"That's perfect, Dan! This whole tour will be research for you!"

Danika laughed. "Maybe, maybe not. Of much more pressing concern is listening to some good music, reconnecting with my girls, taking some psychedelic drugs, maybe even finding myself my own little glass blowin' Tamir."

"Ha ha. It's Remil! But I'll keep my eye out for you." Danika—like Jane and Vanessa—had lost her virginity at some Phish show or another (funny how details like that she couldn't remember), but as far as Jane was aware, she had never had a real boyfriend.

Vanessa didn't come along for any of the preparation or material gathering, but promised she would be ready for tour. After they'd crossed the border, they would pick up Kelly, a friend Jane made at the Grizzly Gorge shows who was living in Chicago and working as a yoga instructor, the fourth—and, until they caught up with Remil, the final—member of the van, and be at Star Lake, Pennsylvania, the first stop of the tour, by midafternoon.

The day before they were supposed to leave, Jane took her van to a mechanic. She had been putting it off, fearing the worst, but the prognosis was much better than she had anticipated: an oil change, fluid top-ups, a new filter or two, a replaced battery was all that was needed. The engine was still healthy, the rad—replaced in Virginia the year before, when it had died at the top of a hill, and she and Vanessa had to spend a day at a Sears in the middle of nowhere—still purred, the timing belt was good for another twenty thousand. She drove to a gas station and took three loonies worth of time to vacuum the purple interior until it was bright, dust free, ready.

Tomorrow.

Kelly was running towards the van, waving her arms before Jane had come to a full stop in front of the Erie, Pennsylvania Greyhound station. Danika slid open the side door, and Kelly jumped in with her suitcase and rolled-up sleeping bag. She was wearing black yoga pants, a bright pink sweatshirt, and sparkling white running shoes with white ankle socks. She was beaming, bubbly, squeaky clean, her fruity shampoo quickly infusing the stale van. Jane put the car into drive as she made introductions.

"Oh, I am so excited for the show tonight!" Kelly exclaimed. "For all the shows! So, so, so excited!"

"This'll be Danika and Vanessa's first Grizzly show," Jane said as she merged onto the interstate.

"Ugh, you're going to love it! LOVE it! Janice is just going to make you melt! You'll see. I can't wait for his guitar to wash over me! I can't wait!"

Checking her blindspot, Jane caught Danika making a face. Jane merged onto the highway, and Vanessa turned the stereo up. They were listening to a Phish show, February 17, 1997—Amsterdam, from the beginning of their European tour, one of Brian's tapes. They were leaving the shore of Lake Erie and heading south through hilly Pennsylvania, towards Pittsburgh, where they would veer west just before the city, heading to the small town of Burgettstown and the amphitheatre. Soon there would be mountains, the music was good, Kelly filled the silent spaces with excited talk, listing all the aspects of the tour she couldn't wait to experience; the four of them eased into the space of the van, adjusted into their seats. They would be spending the next four weeks with each other.

"This town is called Moon Run!" Danika announced hours later, as they neared the amphitheatre on the rural roads.

"The people look pretty earthbound to me," Vanessa said, looking up from her lap and out the window.

"So, Kelly, how long have you been into Grizzly?" Danika asked.

"Oh, God, soo long. Hmm, well, the first show I saw was after a yoga retreat in the Napa Valley, and it blew me away. You guys are from Toronto, yeah?"

"Yup. I live in BC now, though."

"What was it like growing up in Canada's capital?"

"Ha ha, what? You're joking, right?"

"No!" Kelly said brightly.

"Toronto isn't Canada's capital," Danika said somewhat condescendingly.

"Oooooh, cool cool. I've never been outside of the States before."

"Really? Don't you have an interest in seeing the world?"

"Why see the world? Everything that's going on is going on here." Danika snorted.

Kelly smiled, unsure. "What?"

Danika's face was incredulous. "Nevermind," she said, turning the stereo back up. Jane glanced at Kelly in the rear-view; she was back to singing along with the song. Danika reached behind her seat and grabbed Vanessa's knee, and the two of them giggled.

When they joined the standstill traffic, they knew the amphitheatre was close. They waited in the stop-start line for ten minutes, heads walking by outside the window, showed their tickets at the gates, were guided into a parking spot by orange-vested staff, and tumbled out of the car, stretching their limbs. "Let's find some food," Danika suggested. Jane locked the van, and they headed off in search of shakedown.

"Hey, Archives!" They were still in sight of the van when Neptune Terry called out to Jane. She had known the old hippie for years, and he hadn't changed much since the last time they saw each other: a ponytail of white hair, an old tie-dye shirt, faded blue jeans, an infectious-yet-subtle excitement. He hugged Jane. "Archives and the sassy soul sisters! Hey, hey, do you guys know of any live music happening tonight?" Neptune asked, his face a huge grin.

"Oh, I don't know." Jane said. "What kind of stuff are you into?"

"Something spacey, something exploratory, something rocking."

"Well, I might be able to help you out then."

Jane noticed a woman, large, tie-dyed, with wire-rimmed glasses and short, grey hair, standing off to the side. Neptune Terry's wife. She smiled weakly at the girls. Jane turned back to Neptune.

"I should've known you were on board with Grizzly! I can't believe I didn't see you at Berkeley last summer."

Neptune laughed. "I was there, sister. Pneumonia wasn't going to keep me from those shows!" Neptune began walking away, his face still a huge grin. "We'll see each other again soon, Archives. You'll have to tell me what's good this season from the vault! Have a good show!"

"You too!" Jane called back, smiling.

"I love how he only ever speaks to you," Vanessa said sourly. As soon as Kelly had arrived, Vanessa's attempts to be in a good mood had vanished.

They found the shakedown and started to explore. There were tables of shirts, tables of buttons, tables of pipes. Food vendors offering pizza, burritos, grilled cheese, chicken chow mein. A table of alcohol. A woman in an oat-coloured sweatshirt surrounded by a gaggle of teenage boys with golden hair selling beer and dollar waters out of coolers of ice. Drugs both proffered and desired whispered in ears. Jane watched helplessly as a tour kid, dressed in blankets, already rolling, got dragged away by two police officers, who, while searching the shopping cart he was selling scarves and pins out of, easily found plenty of contraband. They walked the lot for an hour, ate some food as the crowds of happy show-goers grew, stopped at the van to make sure they had everything for the show, and went to wait in the throngs at the gates. They were patted down by security, their tickets were scanned, and they were inside.

They found a spot on the lawn, settled in. Danika unfolded the blue, white, and black Mexican blanket that had survived countless lawns of countless tours, Kelly went off to get some beers, and thirty minutes later, the house music faded out, and everybody jumped up and started screaming as Grizzly took the stage. Jane watched the big screens suspended from the roof of the pavilion, her heart galloping in eager anticipation. On the screen, Janice waved as he slung his guitar around his neck. Steve lit a cigarette. Paul calmly sat down behind his kit. Cody held her bass above her head to scattered applause. The show had begun. The first show of the tour—Jane's eighth, Kelly's fifteenth, Vanessa and Danika's first—had begun.

They weren't yet through the first song, but it was obvious how on they were, how well-practised, and Jane let herself expand along the pulsing swell of the music. The whole tour was before them, and any moment now, amongst the drug-addled university students, aging hippies, young families, t-shirt and veggie-burrito purveyors, and true fans, she would see Remil, brimming with life, riding the music like a surfer on a limitless golden wave.

With a nod from Janice, the band began "Mechanical Staircase," the song's simple, infectious riff getting everybody moving. Before the end of the first chorus, Jane watched as Kelly danced off the blanket and disappeared into the crowd. The song opened into the jam section, rising chromatically, climbing the staircase. Danika and Vanessa danced beside her, along with the thousands of other fans spreading out from Jane in the horseshoe of the amphitheatre, the band far below. The song got as high as it could get, and Janice switched on the overdrive and ripped a terrific burning hole right through it, the song's structure breaking away in descending bass riffs and fireworking piano, and Jane's thoughts fizzled away.

At the set break, Kelly came back, dosed on a hit of acid a cute redhead had given her after she snuck her way into the pit, even though she only had a lawn ticket. "Janice really took us into outer space, didn't he? I could actually see the sweat flying off his fingers! I'm going back in, girls! Let's go for waffles after the show, waffles and ice cream!" And off she twirled.

The second set started with a massive "Say Hi to Charlie for Me." The band hit all the complex changes, Janice's obtuse lyrics soared, Paul changed the tempo, and Jane opened her eyes to find that Danika was dancing with a bunch of fans in full-on bear costumes, the three bears dancing and shimmying around Danika, wide mouthed and soaking it in. Paul hit his snare hard, and the song veered sharply into unexplored territory, and Jane closed her eyes again. Janice's guitar swung along the rafters of Cody's bass, skipped along the waterfall of the drums, rose, and crashed on the storm of Steve's keys.

Fifteen minutes later, Jane was waiting in line for the bathroom. The "Charlie" jam had gone on for too long, and as soon as it lost her, she realized how badly she needed to pee, and so here she was in a long line of girls in peasant dresses and butterfly wings. She had one eye out for Remil, scanning the beer counter, looking at the faces of those passed out on the picnic benches. Where was that boy? The line moved a fraction. Jane seemed to hear it an instant before anyone else: Janice was weaving the opening melody of "Cadmium Red" into the aural soundscape the band had been trying to find their way out of for the last ten minutes. Jane closed her eyes, waiting for the slight pause before the burst of ecstatic energy when the crowd realized, regrouped, went apeshit crazy. She was happy. She had yet to hear "Cadmium Red" live. She was sure Remil, wherever he was, would agree: tour was off to a raging start.

In the swirl of people, noises, smells, and sights of the after-show lot, Jane kept a lookout for Remil. Several times, she saw a short boy with thick dreads from a distance that turned out not to be him. Maybe he didn't make it to Pittsburgh. Camden, for sure, then. Back at the van, Danika used masking tape to spell out *Moon Run* in a big masking-tape heart on the back window. Kelly had bought a sparkly blue skirt from a vendor and had put it on over her yoga pants. Jane opened the trunk, tossed out the folding chairs, took the lid off the cooler, and they sat in the dewy grass as the parking lot emptied around them, smoking bowls of the Pittsburgh hydroponic someone in the pit had given to Kelly in the night's cool post-show blossoming.

They loaded up and left the venue around two in the morning and drove straight to Camden. They passed Philadelphia shortly after dawn, the skyline glowing as the highway filled with early rush-hour traffic. They crossed the Delaware, entered New Jersey, were lost for twenty minutes, found their hotel, woke Vanessa, and went to check in.

The hotel lobby was filled with sunken-eyed fans in Baja sweaters, half of whom were holding coolers of various colours, all of whom had just completed the same drive. The energy was at its lowest possible vibration, but there were still a lot of nods, a lot of twinkling eyes. The four girls climbed into the two beds in their room, the curtains creating a heavy, artificial darkness, and quickly fell into the deep anonymity of hotel sleep.

Jane thought that the two Camden shows were excellent. At the start of the first show—and from then on at every subsequent show on the tour—the band members each hit a sustained note on their instruments, light, fast drumming from Paul, the notes modulating until they were in tune, swelling at the end, pulling together the bandmates and the audience, forming a snug sonic knot. Kelly, beside

Jane on the lawn, closed her eyes and started humming *om* along with the mass gyration of electric sound, a huge smile on her face. She was wearing the sparkly blue skirt, but had taken off the yoga pants. Vanessa and Danika, on Jane's other side, put their hands out in mock-Buddhist prayer and started laughing.

After the first show, they partied in the hotel until the small hours of the morning, the lobby, patio, and every floor a different tableau of joyful revelry. Before the second show started, and at the urging of Kelly, all four of them jumped the barrier and snuck into the pavilion. They were now that much closer to the stage. Jane spent the entire night dancing with her eyes closed, only opening them once to take in the sea of heads in front of her washed in red light, the band on stage working away, the towers of speakers, the scalloped ceiling, the much larger sea of heads behind her, thousands and thousands of minds coursing along the same track of sound, finally looking down at her sandalled feet stationed on the cement, the crumpled water bottles and beer cups, before closing her eyes again and rejoining the river of music. After the show, they discovered someone had stolen their back licence plate. "I guess you're not the only ARKS 066 out there now," Danika said philosophically.

In the lot before the second show, a man with cotton-candy-blue hair and two full sleeves of Dead tattoos, whom Jane remembered from the Eugene show, came up to her, said, "Here ya go, sister," and handed her a letter: it was from Remil and said that he was tied up helping out with his parents' store, wouldn't be on tour for a few shows yet. When Jane looked up after reading it, the blue-haired man was gone.

"At least if you had a phone number, you could call him, see what his deal is," Vanessa said, after Jane had read her the letter. Jane, for one, felt only relief. She hadn't realized how wound up she had been waiting for Remil to appear. Vanessa, on the other hand, had been skeptical of Remil right from the beginning, was still burning from Chase's desertion, but Jane, riding high, shrugged her negativity off.

During the encore of the second show, which had blown Jane away, especially the twenty-nine minute "Paper" that closed out the second set, Janice came up to his mic and addressed the crowd:

"Thanks for coming out everybody. We're really excited for this tour, and we hope you are too. We thought it would be a good idea to talk a bit about the different kinds of jamming that happen up here, for those who are following a band like us for the first time. It's really pretty simple. There's type-one jamming, which is when we improvise over the chord changes and structures of the song. Like this." The band fell perfectly into the chorus of "Spunos," and Janice and Steve laid down a two-part solo, ending tightly. "And then there's type two." Here the crowd went completely nuts. "That's when the structure of the song is left behind, and everything being played is new, unknown. Like this." The band fell into some ambient weirdness. "Follow along at home!" The band went back into "Spunos" and brought down the house.

"So, how do you feel about the first three shows?" Jane asked her tourmates as they sat in their seats, waited for the venue to clear out.

"I can't wait for more!" Kelly shouted.

Danika laughed. "It's good to be back chasing the music, I guess," she said. "I'm seeing things in a very different light than I did when I was a teenager," she added thoughtfully.

"Like what?" Kelly said.

Danika stared, thinking seriously. "Well, lots of things. The class breakdown of the lot, the deified counterculture of the sixties, guitar players as godheads. Dreadlocks as cultural appropriation. What else. Baudrillard—this brilliant French theorist, ya know, the America is Disneyland guy—says that gift giving and death are the only two things that escape capitalism, and therefore are the best weapons against them. Being here, witnessing this, it's obvious that Baudrillard missed one: music."

"Wow," Kelly said. "He-a-avy."

Jane looked away.

They slowly migrated to the exit, Vanessa kicking empty beer cans as they went.

The carnival sets up its temporary enclave and moves on. That night, shortly after dawn, they left Camden for Manhattan, crossing into the city just after eight in the morning. They hadn't slept since the first

Camden show—except for Vanessa, who crawled under the covers as soon as they got back to the hotel the night before and didn't emerge until everyone was packed and ready to go. Jane was suffused with a diluted, contented exhaustion, and when they got out of the van and into the New York City morning, skyscrapers rising into the sky, the street corners pooling with businesspeople and students, she floated up like a balloon caught in a jet stream. They pulled into their midtown hotel at 53rd and Lex ("We're going to have to sell a shitload of fajitas to pay for this room!"), left the van with the hotel's valet, left their luggage with the concierge, walked around till they could check in, slept till three, and spent two hours showering and getting ready. Danika braided some beads into Kelly's hair, Vanessa went to the lobby to use the internet, and before they knew it, it was time to roll.

Before leaving the city for Jones Beach, they went to see a pot dealer someone had told Danika about the night before. "His name's Taylor; he came all the way from California with pounds of West-Coast weed." He was staying in a hotel smack in the frenzied centre of Times Square. They ran through the tourists and into the hotel's lobby, scrambled into a waiting elevator. Danika pushed the button for fifty-two. "Penthouse suite," she said. Moments later, they found themselves in front of Taylor's door. They all looked at each other, and Kelly knocked.

From the moment they entered his room, it was apparent that Taylor wasn't your ordinary tour pot dealer, standing in the middle of the shakedown holding a fat bud in his hand, patchwork knapsack full of half-quarters, sprinting at the first sign of law enforcement. This man was running a successful business: he was sitting relaxed on one of the many couches in the large, fancy suite, his golden knees spread wide, a bat of an unlit joint in his mouth. Grizzly was on the stereo. They were still standing at the door when Jane noticed the four boys who were in the process of paying Taylor's dreadlocked female associates for their weed, and her heart sank into her stomach. Dave, Brad, Dave, and Phil: she had gone to high school with them, and though she knew they were into Phish (even if it was in that superficial way Jane hated), the thought that they would be on a Grizzly tour had not crossed her mind. Three of them were wearing Blue Jays hats, one of the Daves a Maple Leafs toque.

"Hey, Jane!" Phil called, noticing them. "Dan, Vanessa. Wow! It's been a long time."

Jane gave a small-mouthed smile. She had dated Phil for a stupid week and a half in grade ten. Even then he was brimming over with arrogance, thought he deserved the whole world, spent most of their time together downloading Phish shows song by song on Napster as Jane sat on his bed listening to the latest acquisition. He stared at her before exclaiming his surprise again. "Chives! What are you doing here? In town for the Grizzly show?"

"Yeah, I am. We've been on t—"

"That's awesome, it's great you made it down!"

Jane felt herself cringe.

"Did you guys hear about Taylor from the message boards too?" Phil asked, picking a tooth with a nail. "Quite the operation, eh? You know, we were thinking, we should bring some weed down on the next tour. We could make a killing, I'm sure. The only thing is the border of course, but—"

"No," Jane said, cutting him off, "we heard about him from a friend at Camden."

"Oh. Oh. What did you think of last night? Were you guys there? Not the best, eh? They definitely need to redeem themselves tonight."

Jane blinked. She didn't want to get into an argument with Phil about the intricacies of last night's show, but she also didn't want to let him get away with such a poor assessment of the concert. Saving her from making a choice, Kelly sprung up from the weed smelling and skipped over to them. "Hiya," she said.

Jane loved the stunned look that came over boys' faces when they first saw Kelly, and Phil, Brad, and the Davids' dumbfounded expressions were no exception. Jane felt elated to have Kelly with her, in her posse. Phil blinked twice. "Oh, hey, uh, what's up? We were going to roll a joint or two before we bounced; you ladies want to get high with us?"

"Sure, please!" Kelly said, skipping back to the couch. Everybody followed.

"Jane, you have to smell this," Danika was saying, holding out an open Tupperware. "What did you say it was called, Taylor?"

Taylor glanced at the container. "That one's Soul Fingers. It's an indica-sativa blend, with some nice floral undertones, more of a body stone than a mind stone. It just makes you want to dance."

Taylor gave a loose, affable grin, raising his hands and shaking his fingers. Taylor screamed a certain kind of clichéd California: shoulder-length tawny hair, skin tanned a healthy chestnut, the taut muscles and laid-back glow of a lifelong surfer. You'd see guys like him on tour now and then, the kind of West Coaster who moved easily between different countercultural scenes. He reminded Jane of the coast, of the ocean, of Remil. (Jane wouldn't realize until later how he must have reminded Vanessa of Chase—was that the cause of the terrible mood V would be in for the rest of the night?) "Now this one," he went on, retrieving another container from the stack, "this one I wouldn't touch till after the show."

"We'll take an eighth of each, please," Kelly said. "Want to roll us a joint, Taylor?"

"Sure thing, sister. Hey, Chloe, can you find the rolling papers?"

"So how did a collective of organic weed farmers such as yourselves get turned onto Grizzly?" Danika asked. Jane turned her eyes from the pot she was smelling. Danika was talking to Taylor, but she was watching Chloe—the woman with blond dreadlocks who had let the girls into the apartment—grab the papers from the windowsill and come to the couches. Taylor took the bat-sized joint out of his mouth, tapped it against the table.

"Ears to the ground, mostly. We'd pretty much drive the entire state to catch a Phil and Friends show, or Ratdog, and of course when Phish was still playing, we'd see everything we could. Grizzly is just the next car in the train. Where else can you get such a collective experience, such an immediate hookup with your fellow humans? We had a really good crop this year, so we figured, why not come out east and share the wealth?"

While he was talking, Taylor had rolled three perfect, identical joints, now lined up on the table like sharp little pencils. He picked them up and passed them to Danika, Phil, and Chloe. A pack of matches materialized in his hand, three of which he lit, handing them to those with joints.

"You know," Danika said, taking a deep toke, "Baudrillard says that gifts and death are the two ways to disrupt capitalism. He forgot about music, though."

Jane and Kelly looked at each other, looked away.

"What about you folks?" Chloe asked in response to Danika, passing her joint to Jane. "You heard of Grizzly all the way up there in Canada?"

"Actually, Janey here discovered them when she was living on the coast," Danika said. Vanessa, who had ended up with two of the joints, one in each hand, coughed. "V was out there too, of course," Danika added quickly. "Jane is a musical genius. She can remember any show pitch perfectly after hearing it once. It's like an aural photographic memory."

Phil raised his head from his bags of weed. "Yeah, she's some kind of mutant!" he exclaimed, his friends laughing.

Jane smiled. "It's a blessing and a curse."

Taylor looked at her mock-skeptically. "Oh yeah? Let's see if your friend here is telling the truth, or just trying to impress us gullible beach bums." Chloe laughed at this, looked towards Danika. Taylor paused for effect. "What show is *this*?" he asked in a rush, as if pouncing in a surprise attack.

Jane didn't even have to stop to listen to the song before answering. "'Terrapin Station,' June 15. The Greek Theatre, Berkeley. Before that was 'Roses Are Free' from the '98 Island Tour, before that 'Paper' from two nights ago. Janice flubbed twice in the composed section but more than made up for it in the jam."

Taylor laughed a golden West-Coast laugh. When "Roses" had come on, Jane had been flooded with memories: she and Rick and Brian had gone to all four Island shows; when Phish announced in late February that they were going to play two shows on Long Island and two on Rhode Island in early April, Jane knew that nothing was going to keep the three of them from going. The shows were still among Jane's top shows of all time. They had even convinced Drew to fly down for the fourth show; it was the last time all four of them were together at a concert.

"Fuck yeah!" Phil said. "If only you could monetize your strange gifts, Archives, you'd be made in the shade!"

"If only," Jane said. She was more or less ready to leave, but Danika and Kelly showed no signs of readiness. They smoked a few more joints. Jane stared at the skyscrapers outside the window. Phil slid Taylor's guitar onto his lap and started noodling around. One of the Daves took an empty water bottle out of his knapsack and made a bong with it and his billy piece. After they were there for just over an hour, the phone rang, and five minutes later, Chloe let in four or five groups of fans, and it was time to go.

"Did you guys hear what happened at that Keller Williams show in Montreal where Janice surprise guested?" Phil asked as they were all standing at the door. "There was a huge after-party, and Janice was there, and he, he fucked Tim Stone's girlfriend in the butt!"

Tim was the fifth member of Phil's little group, and Jane had thought that it was strange that he wasn't there. "Ew, Phil, that's gross," she said, opening the door, leaving. "Have a good show," she said, spitting out the words a little harder than intended (but only a little).

"Later brothers, later sisters," Taylor said from the couch, not looking up, busy laying out batches of weed on the table. He had put the massive, unsmoked joint back in his mouth. "Tell your friends!"

The show that night was a letdown for Jane. No real improvisation, all the same songs they played in Camden, and worst of all, there was a serious lack of energy. The definition of an off night. It happens. (Phil probably *loved* it, she thought.) Maybe she was just too high on that Californian bud. They did go for a swim at the beach after the show though, floated in the cold, salty ocean under the dark blue sky. On the drive back through Queens, Manhattan growing larger in the windshield, they talked and laughed about high school, about Jane's ill-conceived stint as Phil's girlfriend, wondered if Janice had really had sex with Tim Stone's girlfriend.

"I used to have a big crush on Tim Stone," Vanessa said as they drove over the Queensboro Bridge. Jane was happy to see Vanessa squealing with laughter; she had been almost catatonic the entire night.

"Oh my God, V, that could've been your ass!"

"What's with the sheepish look?" Danika said to Kelly, still laughing. "What? You didn't sleep with Janice, did you? Did you? Oh my God, look at her face!"

"What? It was nothing." Kelly's cheeks had gone a deep crimson.

"I was in the front row—this was last summer, by the way, not, like, last night or something—he looked at me at the end of the second set, and a crew member came out to get me, and we met backstage. The sex was great, and no, he didn't put anything anywhere it wasn't supposed to go, jeez!—but afterwards all he wanted to talk about was books and stuff, like Dostoyevsky and shit."

"You're sure full of surprises," Jane said, laughing.

"That's not the only thing she's full of," Vanessa said. Danika snorted with laughter.

"You don't believe me? That's fine." Kelly's face had returned to its normal shade. "I'll tell you girls one thing, though: his hands are even *bigger* than they look! They are *soo* big!"

This had its desired effect of breaking the tension, and the van fell back into laughter.

"What do you think would happen if Cody pulled random dudes out of the audience to fuck them?" Danika asked after the laughter died down.

"They'd call her a slut," Vanessa said.

"I'm sure Cody gets plenty of dick," Kelly said.

"Kelly!"

They were back in Manhattan.

They had a full day and night in NYC before pushing off for North Carolina and the South. They shopped, smoked the rest of Taylor's weed, drank cappuccinos, sat in Central Park, went to the MOMA, gossiped about the people they knew on tour, speculated further on Cody's sex life. Jane thought about calling the relatives she had in the area, but didn't want to leave the girls. Her tour family was family enough.

After the two-day break in New York, the Southern shows went by in a syncopated rhythm of gas stations and hotel rooms and parking lots and conversation and music. There was a lightning storm in Alpharetta. Kelly picked up a Southern accent as soon as they crossed from

Pennsylvania into West Virginia. In North Carolina, a bunch of fans were wearing t-shirts that said *Cody Sucks*, but by the next night *Cody Drops Bombs* shirts were also in circulation. Danika bought a *Drops Bombs*, loudly scolded anyone in a *Cody Sucks*. (When Kelly showed up at the van in a *Cody Sucks* t-shirt, she and Danika got into a loud argument, Danika calling Kelly a misogynist, Kelly accusing Danika of not knowing how to have any fun. The fight didn't resolve, just petered out, continued in sarcastic comments and dirty looks.) They made fast friends with their lot neighbours at Alpharetta, two guys and a girl from Buffalo, nineteen years old, wide eyed and in love with the scene, with tour, with Janice. Bobby, Samuel, and Tess, Samuel's sister. They spent the next two nights together. Bobby was obviously into Kelly; Tess was obviously into Danika—and, to Jane's surprise, Danika was obviously into Tess—and Samuel seemed to keep switching between being into Vanessa and Jane, though Jane purposefully mentioned Remil numerous times. On the second night, Jane woke up to Kelly riding on top of Bobby in silhouetted silence, the glitter on her shoulders catching what little light seeped through the curtains, and some time later she woke, again, to the sounds of Danika having noisy, nasally sex with Tess. Annoyed, Jane still fell back to sleep with a smile on her face. The next morning at breakfast, the Buffalo crew departed, Kelly and Danika whispered to each other, giggling, sudden best friends.

An hour outside of Atlanta, on the way out of the South, Danika driving, Jane tore a sheet of paper out of her notebook and wrote Remil a letter.

> *Dear Remil,*
> *Hey, buddy, where are you? Missing one hell of a tour. I saw Little Lucy last night. It reminded me of our Northwest run last year. Here's last night's setlist:*
>
> *Set I:*
>
> *Birds/Turkeys*
> *Yes (Yes) No*

Yellow Blue Red
Forest for the Trees
Tautologies
Light Snooze
Quantum Mechanics
Anna Meets Vronsky for the First Time (!)
Bracketing the Referent
Rainbow Bleach

Set II:

Mechanical Staircase >
Cheesecake
Red Herring
CTT >
Video Game Medley >
Toot Toot Toot >
CTT
Spunos >
Paper

E:

Winterland >
Fireworks

Anyways, Tour's not the same without you.

   Janey

Jane looked up from her pad, the pen tight in her hand. When Jane saw Little Lucy in the lot before the show, walking through the cars holding a board spilling over with hemp jewellery, she was shocked to see that she was even skinnier than before. She was wearing the same overalls, though Jane noticed she had a new pair of sandals. Lucy screamed in excitement at seeing Jane, giving her a huge hug.

"Where's Remil been?" Jane had asked, surprising herself. "I've been waiting for him to show up since Star Lake. Last I heard, he was stuck helping his parents at the store."

Something flashed behind Lucy's eyes before she smiled widely. "You know Remil! He can't stay at home for long. Here, take a bracelet, any one."

Only now did Jane think about what Lucy had said. Can't stay at home long? What does that mean?

There was too much sun and wind and noise for Jane to think too long about it. She read the letter back to herself. His kind of letter. She looked out the window. She was eye level with a tractor trailer's massive wheel, their van reflected back to her in the spinning silver hubcap, their whole world floating in miniature.

It took them two days to drive the six hundred miles to Indiana. They camped in a loud, hot forest in Kentucky, got lost on the Indiana backroads, listened to the Big Cypress New Year's Eve midnight set in six straight, comprehensive hours. As they were passing through the outskirts of Louisville, the van's speedometer stopped working, the gauge falling to zero even though Jane's foot hadn't left the gas pedal.

"Don't worry, this's happened before," Jane said. "It's a few hundred dollars to fix."

"Should we go back into Louisville and find a mechanic?" Kelly asked, peering over Jane from the backseat.

"Nah, it's all right for now. Just watch your speed when it's your turn at the wheel, don't go faster than the speed of traffic. We should be fine."

"And if we get pulled over, just smile that winning smile," Danika said to Kelly, her voice sugary-sweet with sarcasm. Kelly didn't seem to notice.

Deer Creek was one of the only amphitheatres left in America that still allowed camping on the premises. They arrived the night before the concert, set up their tents in the light of the van's headlights, wandered around the grounds until they found a bonfire to whittle away the rest of the night at. Sitting on a log close to the fire, Jane looked around at the flame-lit faces. She didn't know any of them, but they felt like family: the eager faces, the clothing, the dreadlocks, the marijuana smoke, the very visible markers of road and music. They weren't there for more than twenty minutes, were only just easing into the conversation, when the air cooled enough to raise goosebumps on Jane's exposed arms; minutes later, without any preamble, it was raining, thick and loud. By the time everybody grabbed their sandals, sweaters, guitars, and pipes and ran for cover, the fire had gone from roaring to half-mast to glowing embers to a soup bowl of muddy ash. When the four of them made it to the van, they were soaked through, howling into the wet onslaught. They spent the rest of the night in their tents, while outside the Midwest unleashed huge amounts of water on them. Jane barely slept, tossing and turning, wet and sticky and uncomfortable. The tent getting thrown around on a roiling sea.

The next morning, everything was wet and shiny from the rain, the sun a sizzling kick drum in a crisp blue sky. The girls took it easy, spent the sweltering afternoon in the shakedown, ate flatbread pizza for lunch, went into the venue for the seven o'clock doors. All four of them were sticky and grumpy; Jane, who had been tired and low energy the whole day, had a splitting headache. Last night's sleepless, rainy night was one more sleepless night than she could handle, and she was once again getting antsy about Remil's absence. For the first time in her life, she was looking forward to the show being over—and it hadn't even started yet!—so she could go back to the tent and get some sleep.

The band came on a little after eight, and Jane lethargically got to her feet along with everybody else. After the sonic tuning, the show started off with "Light Snooze," which they had been opening with quite a bit lately. After a short jam, the band ran through a series of covers that they had never played before, the start of each one eliciting cheers from the audience: "St. Augustine," "I Feel the Earth Move," and "Third Planet." The set was now showing some promise, though the chance of paradigm-bending improvisation was slight, especially after Steve skipped the jam section after "Sweet Kicks"—which was blazing nonetheless—instead segueing flawlessly into the ambient weirdness of "Cuttlefish." After some funky washes courtesy of Steve's Wurlitzer pushed Cody to bounce into a clean major-key riff, Janice soon catching on, things got interesting. The whole band was now tightly locked into a bubbly, fuzzy groove, thirds and sevenths ricocheting off of each other, digging into the progression they had found (or that had found them). Despite her earlier mood—or maybe because of it—Jane's body and mind had metamorphosed into a blemishless ball of focus. Tour, the girls, the heat, and her exhaustion forgotten, even her longing for Remil faded into the background. The groove was getting bubblier, fathoms of energy swishing massively just underneath hearing. The entire amphitheatre was about to blast off into a novel journey to the heights, twenty-five thousand keyed-in beings along for the ride—Jane felt the imminent explosion deep in her core; with everything she had, all her considerable listening apparatus, she honed in on Janice's swerving, bouncing guitar, knowing instinctively that the first blast, the first kiss of the spark with the fuel, would come from him, when, in the exact exquisite moment Jane's entire being fused with the music, Janice began to slowly downstrum a single chord, very clearly signalling the end of the jam. Jane's focus relaxed along the rake of the chord, making room for the letdown—he was ending it too soon! Too soon!—except, except: the chord didn't end things at all, but, instead, crashed right through the floor of the music, pulling the entire band with it, everything modulating as it crashed further and further down, the poppy major-key bubbles flattening out into slow ethereal minor-key darkness, Cody opening up huge planes of trembling bass, Steve sitting on low, grumbling chords, Paul drumming an odd, shifting rhythm, the crowd yanked through the rabbit hole with them, the night majestically twisting inside out.

They were deep in the basement of the universe. Through the floor and into the basement. It was the darkest place Jane had ever been, aural or otherwise: large heavy pipes, dripping dampness, mold, darkness, rot, fear, a slow, tossing rhythm accentuated by the night's cool breeze. The necessary counterpoint to light, love, joy. The band explored this new territory for over ten minutes, everyone around Jane in lockstep awe, before they started to build their way out of it, triumphantly coming up for air with a set-closing "Mechanical Staircase." For the rest of the show, right through the second-set "Toot Toot Toot" into "Yes (Yes) No" into "Toot Toot Toot" marathon and the "Elliott Smith Buys Some Shampoo" encore, the band was able to dip right back into the strange new sonic space they had opened up, as if on command, and then climb effortlessly out into the sunshine, each excavation pushing a little deeper, probing the mystery a little harder. Jane was in a delirious daze. This was what it was all about: that sense of communion, of all of them discovering deep pockets of truth and joy together, the surprise, the newness of it. The sudden plunge into cold darkness.

After the show, Jane ended up alone with Vanessa; Kelly and Danika had gone off together at set break and were nowhere to be seen. They managed to leave through the wrong exit and had to walk the long way around the amphitheatre to their camp site, against the tidal rush of excited fans. Jane was buzzing like a tuning fork, tripping over herself in her excitement.

"I can't believe what just happened! Remil's going to kill himself when he hears what he missed! Van, were you there? Did you experience what I just experienced?"

"Yeah, I was there, Jane. It was just music. Just like every other night."

"What? What do you mean?"

"You can be so tiring—do you know that? Always needing to see things in the music. It's just a bunch of guys playing their instruments, making money, sleeping with their adoring fans. It's just music. There doesn't always have to be something there, Jane."

Jane's mood, expansive, connected to the entire parking lot and amphitheatre, integrated with all the fans coursing past them, collapsed into a needle. A dagger.

"Hey, V, just 'cause you're all depressed and shit about Chase doesn't mean you have to pull us all down with you. Get out of your fuckin' head for one minute. You should've slept with Samuel. Maybe that would have ended your soul-sucking funk!"

Vanessa laughed cruelly, as if she had been waiting to hear that all summer. "What about you, Jane? Maybe *you* should have fucking slept with Samuel, maybe that would have snapped you out of *your* delusions! You've been hung up on that asshole for over a year! I knew from the minute Remil walked into Gavin's house on the coast he was no good. He's a tour rat, Jane, a dirty tour rat!"

Jane was knocked speechless, but only until lava-hot anger gushed into her throat.

"You're a fucking bitch, you know that? Just because your relationship didn't work out, doesn't mean you have to shit all over mine!" Jane paused, took a breath. "And if he's a tour rat, then so am I!" she yelled.

Vanessa scoffed. "You. Are. Ridiculous." She bit off each word slowly, finally.

Jane felt tears coming on, but the last thing she wanted was to validate what Vanessa was saying by crying in front of her. She rubbed her eyes, a little calmer. "Why are you being like this? After such a special night. I was having the best time."

"You might be having the best time, but guess what, Jane? Some of us aren't."

They were back at their tents. Who the fuck knew where Kelly and Danika were. Jane ripped open the tent she shared with Vanessa, grabbed her sleeping bag and pillow, and stomped into the van.

That night, she dreamed of Remil. He had come after all, had been there from the very beginning: they were in Jane's tent, late-afternoon sunlight filtering through the orange nylon, dreadlocks and naked limbs akimbo. They had been making love, frenetic and soaring like the blistering peak of a jam; now they were still, Jane's head on Remil's chest, the powerful kick drum of his heart. The tent heavy with the sun's heat, Remil whispering wild stories into her ear.

Jane woke with a start, lying across the front seats, the gear stick in her back, drool on her pillow, the wet warmth of the dream still pulsing along her cortex. She closed her eyes to fall back asleep, but she was inescapably awake, already sweating in the morning heat. She got out of the van, groggy, sore, and parched, and plopped into a black folding chair. As her mind slowly turned to the bathroom, to a cold bottle of water, her eyes were pulled to something catching the sun in the yellow grass. She got onto her knees and grabbed it: it was a gold earring, in the shape of a little bean. Jane stood up, held the earring up to the sun, turned it in her hand. It looked like real gold. She was pretty sure it didn't belong to Kelly or Danika or Vanessa, and no one was camped near them. How long had it lay hidden, waiting for somebody to see it, for a storm to tamp down the grass and reveal its hiding spot? A physical piece of some lost show, some long-ago relationship. Jane opened the car door, dropped the earring into the cup holder. Okay, Janey. Time to pee and find some food. She started walking. All around her, folks were waking up, collapsing tents, singing their morning songs.

It was a hard, tense drive to Alpine Valley. Jane's dream stayed with her for the duration, as if she and Remil had really spent the morning together in her tent. They made it to East Troy in four hours, checked into a Red Roof Inn fifteen minutes from the amphitheatre, sprawled on the two double beds. An hour of rest before the van, lot, showtime. The next day, repeat. Onwards.

First night Alpine, as far as Jane was concerned, was a disaster. The jams ended abruptly, changes were messed up, some of them even mangled. "Rainbow Bleach" was aborted. "Spunos" was dreck. "Paper" lacked all the energy it usually had in abundance. Compared to the purveyors of the previous night's revelation, this wasn't even the same band. Usually able to shake off an off night like this, see it in the wider context of the tour, watching the band fumble through "Crowdsurf Tangerine" far up the expansive lawn, Jane's mood plummeted.

Jane saw for the first time in forever that they were just humans up there, humans with their flaws and tempers and flagging energy. Was Vanessa right? Did Jane overthink the music, invest far more meaning than there actually was? Jane looked around. Everyone was stoned, pounding beer, checking their cellphones. A group of college boys three blankets over were cackling like hyenas. She looked up at the screens broadcasting the band, all the way below them in the pav, unreachable. She watched as the camera panned the front row: a white guy in a Native headdress—Jane could only imagine what Danika would say about that—one of the rare black fans, a shirtless guy with an American flag draped over his shoulders (and there was Kelly behind them, dancing with abandon, a liquid painting). Jane started to feel claustrophobic: she was surrounded by bodies, by American bodies, on American land. Jane was a foreigner, an imposter. A fraud.

What was she doing here? What was she doing with her life?

After the show, Jane went right to the van, lay down in the back, and waited for Danika and Kelly to show (Vanessa had said she wasn't feeling well and sat the show out, staying at the hotel; Jane sold Vanessa's ticket for twenty dollars to the first fan she saw with their finger in the air), which they did just after midnight, talking and giggling. As soon as they returned, Jane slid into the front and turned the engine on; Kelly and Danika immediately stopped talking and got in, the van strangely silent as they slowly exited the parking lot, the noise of celebration streaming in through the open windows. Jane needed to take a shower or a bath or have a very long sleep. They drove out of the venue, through the dark farmland night, the air thick with manure. They pulled into the motel without anyone having spoken the entire drive, without a show on the stereo.

Jane smiled meekly at the girls and headed for their room.

Vanessa was feeling better in time for the second night, and so was Jane. On lot before the show, the four girls each took three shots of tequila from a bar set up in front of a hippie couple's aquamarine Volkswagen, Jane relishing the salty bite of the golden liquor. The eight hours of sleep had revived Jane's mood, and with the stimulant of the tequila, she was feeling good. It was a warm Wisconsin afternoon, Frisbees were flying over their heads, the crowds jostled with the promise of the upcoming music. After the second shot, Jane realized that she hadn't given herself enough space to really let go this tour. She had become too focused on waiting for Remil; it had made her uptight. That wasn't the kind of relationship she wanted; she had to take a step back, be more present at the shows, in the van, with the girls. As the friendly woman with bright red lipstick and rainbow-coloured hair poured out the third round, Jane glanced at Vanessa. They still hadn't said a single word to each other, which, considering Vanessa had barely uttered a full sentence since leaving Indiana, wasn't a particularly momentous accomplishment. Danika had a pav ticket, and with Kelly's help, stubbed everyone down from the lawn. From their seats, they had a terrific sight line of the band. It was the polar opposite of where they were on the lawn last night:

Jane felt like she was actually occupying the same physical space as Janice, Steve, Cody, and Paul. The difference between the seats of the pavilion and the blankets of the lawn had never seemed so stark; no wonder Kelly always wanted to be as close as possible. A man sitting behind them, with messy hair and a greasy beard, had a giant Ziploc of candy and was handing some out to everybody in the vicinity. The band opened the show with "M-Theory," a first. Jane felt herself sliding back into the music. Whatever had caused last night's weak performance—a bad mood, a cold, a fight, the musical gods— had obviously abated: the four of them were locked in, listening to each other, playing well. Cody had a huge smile on her face as she pounded out her ever-changing rhythms. Steve led a tremendously funky "Tautologies" jam. Deep in the chugging groove, Jane glanced at Vanessa: her eyes were closed, and she actually had a smile on her face.

Post-show, very drunk from the tequila and the two beers she had gorged on inside the venue (not to mention the sugar high from all the Tootsie Rolls and gummy worms), she and Vanessa wandered the shakedown. They ate cold sesame noodles, watched a fight break out between a vendor and security, listened to everybody's opinion on the show, and bought a pipe, a medium-sized bubbler with red glass spiralling inside, to give Danika for her upcoming birthday. Someone with a guitar was sitting on a hill overlooking the shakedown, belting out an assortment of Dylan and Neil Young tunes.

Vanessa looked at Jane. "You know, I never told you this, but after Chase broke up with me, he sent me a YouTube video of Joan Baez singing 'Don't Think Twice, It's All Right.'"

"What? What a bastard."

"Such a childish thing to do, eh? I was so embarrassed, I cried for days."

Jane thought for a moment. "I guess he thought maybe it would help you?"

"He's just like all the rest," Vanessa said, grabbing Jane's hand. Jane wanted to disagree but held herself back.

At the end of the shakedown, they stopped at a jewellery stand manned by an over-aggressive, pale redhead in a straw hat. Jane picked up two glass pendants on thick hemp and held them to their necks. "I'm sorry," they both said at the same time.

They were on their way from Alpine Valley to Minneapolis when they got pulled over by the cops. They were a half hour past the 90/94 junction, it was around three in the morning, and Jane was driving to a rocking Grizzly tape, when the state cruiser pulled up alongside them before dropping back and turning on its lights.

"Shit, Jane, the cops!" Danika exclaimed, looking at the swinging lights out the back window. Jane put her turn signal on, the cops bleeped their siren, and Jane pulled to the side of the highway.

"What were we doing?"

"How fast were we going?"

"I don't know. I don't know."

"I saw him look right at us!"

"It's okay. We don't have anything on us, right? Right?" Danika had turned around and was looking at Kelly. Kelly half smiled, half shrugged. Danika was about to say something else when there was a tap at the window. Jane cranked it down.

"Yes, officer?" she said, trying to sound complacent.

"Can you please turn the music off?" the cop asked angrily, bending down and shining his light on everybody's faces.

"Yeah, sure, sorry," Jane blurted. She turned the volume knob down to zero.

"Do you know how fast you were going?" When the light left Jane's face again, she looked at the officer: he was no older than Jane, crew-cut hair, a small, thin mouth, a meanness around his eyes. She was close enough to smell his breath of coffee and beef jerky. There were two more officers standing behind him.

"Listen, I'm so sorry. Our speedometer broke a few days ago, and we haven't had a chance to take it to a mechanic. I, I didn't think we were speeding." Jane tried to smile pleasantly.

"Licence and registration," the officer said, ignoring Jane. She bent over Kelly into the glove compartment, pulled out the envelope with her documents and tickets, and handed the whole thing to the cop.

"Stay here," he said, pulling his light out of the van and disappearing.

It was tense in the van, but before anything else could happen, one of the other officers came to the window. "Would you ladies please step out of the vehicle?" he asked, his tone softer than his friend's, but not without menace.

The girls awkwardly got out of the van and stood on the side of the road. It was a cold night, and Jane had left her sweater in the van. Her heart was racing. The two officers who were still with them were both men: the one who asked them to get out of the vehicle was about the same age as the first one, and the other officer was older, maybe in his forties. They were beside a dark field, no houses or lights; the highway was empty. Jane swallowed loudly, her throat raw and dry. If only Remil were here to sweet talk their way out of this.

"We're going to search your vehicle for contraband. Is that all right?"

Jane nodded. She felt Vanessa shoot Kelly a dirty look. What did she have in there, Jane wondered—pot? Pills? LSD?

After a few minutes of the girls standing silently in the chilly night, the first cop came back from the cruiser. He was holding Jane's ticket to the festival in his hand, but not the envelope or her registration. His mouth opened into a sickening smile.

"What are you girls doing out here in the middle of the night?" he asked, shining his light from face to face.

"We're on our way to Minneapolis to see some concerts," Kelly said, adding "sir" when it was obvious her charm wasn't hitting its mark. For the first time since Jane had met her, Kelly's beauty had no effect. If anything, it seemed to make the officer more aggressive.

"Isn't it a little odd, the four of you out here like this, all alone, a van full of, of all things, tape cassettes? And *Moon Run*, what is that about, some sort of hippie-dippie drug thing?" He put a lot of emphasis on the *about*, saying it like Canadians on US television would say it, *a-boot*.

"No, sir, it's a town in Pennsylvania," Danika said. Jane was startled to hear that she was crying. At that moment, the other two cops came back from searching the van, and Jane filled with relief. It didn't look like they had found anything.

The first cop's smile collapsed into a tight frown, and he started yelling at them. "What makes you think you can come into *our* country, drive on *our* highways, eat *our* food, corrupt *our* youth, have sex with whomever you please, and drive thirty miles over whilst high on drugs? Hmm?! This is a small, family-oriented county, and we don't need your bad influence here, no way, no ma'am."

Jane suddenly found her voice. "I'm sorry we were speeding, officer. Like I said, our speedometer broke. We'd be happy to pay the speeding ticket. I don't see what else we were doing wrong, though; we have rights like everybody else. We aren't on drugs. We weren't being reckless. We're just music fans. We're just good people."

The officer's eyes lit up. "Oh yeah?" he said, smirking. "Just music fans, is that right? Just good people, huh?" He held up Jane's festival ticket and deliberately, making a show of it, ripped the ticket in half, then into quarters, throwing the yellow pieces into the air like confetti. "What are you going to do *a-boot* that? Let me tell you what you're going to do *a-boot* it. Nothing. There's nothing you can do." He stared at Jane, daring her to say more. Jane stared back at him, her face set in defiance. Danika was shaking beside her.

The headlights flying towards them ended the confrontation. The car slowed down when it saw the swinging police lights, and the seven of them turned as it crawled passed: it was a green Volkswagen Westfalia with Louisiana plates and was obviously on tour—a guy and girl were in the front seats, their tie-dye shirts clearly visible, their mouths agape at the odd tableau awash in the cruiser lights. As the car drove away, a dreadlocked head popped up at the back window. Remil. It was Remil. Jane's mouth opened in surprise. Remil's momentary face was unreadable, and then it was gone.

"Clay, that's enough, take it easy," the older officer said, coming towards them. He had the rest of Jane's documents in one hand, a yellow speeding ticket in the other. Jane hadn't even noticed he had gone back to the cruiser.

Clay laughed, threw up his hands. "Fuck it, whatever."

They slowly got back in the van. "You girls have to be careful out here, all alone," Clay said, back at the window, smiling that same lecherous smile. Jane noticed under the coffee and the jerky the unmistakable smell of whiskey. "Y'all have a good night, now." Jane cranked the window up. Her hands shaking violently, she carefully pulled back onto the interstate. The cruiser continued sitting there, red lights swirling. The stereo was left off.

In the bustling post-show streets in front of Ye Old Fashion Music Hall on Washington Avenue in downtown Minneapolis, Neptune Terry placed a hit of acid on the stuck-out tongues of Kelly and Danika. Vanessa and Jane both declined. It was a great show, everybody, band and audience alike, relaxed and looking forward to the festival. The night before, they had pulled over at the first rest stop after their run-in with the authorities. It took a few hours, but after some coffee and chocolate bars, Kelly's favourite Grizzly show, and much laughter, they had mostly managed to shake off the jarring experience, though, when they were back on the road and Danika said, "It could have been worse. Imagine what would have happened if we were black," there was a tense silence. They spent the rest of the drive and all of the next day talking about it, about the arrogance of Americans, the fear of state-sanctioned violence, and, of course, the Remil spotting. They decided that if it was him, they would definitely run into him at the show.

"We'll catch up to him, sweetie," Vanessa had said, putting her hand on Jane's arm.

Danika, Vanessa, and Kelly offered to pitch in for a new ticket for Jane, but she insisted it was her fault for pushing back; the cost of the ticket was on her. Now all she had to do was find one.

After the show, in a lot full of dollar grilled cheese and celebration, Jane took two caffeine pills, a gooball, and drank a coffee: they had a lot of driving ahead of them. Danika peeled off the Moon Run tape and stuck a *Cody Drops Bombs* sticker to the bottom right corner of the back window. At around one thirty in the morning, the lot thinning out, Kelly back from wherever she had been, her eyes all pupil, they piled into the van and, after a long, disorganized stop at a large, bright grocery superstore for food and beer, eased out of the city.

For the first two hours of the drive, they sung and screamed along with the stereo, the landscape dark and fast through the open van windows, everybody's hair whipping around, Jane careful to go the approximate speed of traffic. Somewhere before the South Dakota border everything shifted: the windows were rolled up, the show they were listening to (the Dead, May 7, 1970) ended, and Jane slid in a new one (May 8, 1977—the show that supposedly never occurred). Danika unspooled her dosed mind to bug-eyed Jane, whose pulse was pounding as she leaned over the steering wheel and watched the road roll up into the van's ever-hungry engine, Kelly and Vanessa holding each other, foreheads knocking, one of them in a deep acid sleep, the other just plain asleep. Jane laughing as she drove, everything Danika was saying ringing beautiful, ringing true. She had gotten used to Danika's theorizing—it was just how she related to the world, and tonight she was making a lot of sense. "What gives us the right to access such heightened musical sensation? Such rarefied halls of creation? We are among the world's luckiest people." Yes. Yes. Yes! This was it. Pushing through time and space in the flatness of middle America in the holiest holy of the summer night, plugged in, aflame. She couldn't help it. The bliss was torrential.

A few minutes into dawn, half the sky veiny pink, Danika now asleep, snoring loudly, Jane pulled off onto a regional road and hit the lineup of cars waiting for the festival gates to open. The car came to a hard stop—what felt like the first true stop in three weeks on the road—and Jane's mood flipped. Her caffeine high crashed into her exhaustion and combusted. She was suddenly sick of the van, tired of the girls, of Danika's bubbly academese, of Kelly's effortless beauty, of Vanessa's tour-long torpor, apologies and recent perk up notwithstanding. Not to mention she needed to find a ticket to the sold-out festival. So it was decided: she left the keys in the ignition and slipped out of the van. Hopefully one of them would wake up when the line started to move. The cars snaked ahead until they were lost in the distance; there were low undulating fields on either side of the two-lane road, behind her the line already another fifty cars deep and growing. People emerged from their vehicles into the golden morning light as if from a long, restful hibernation. Jane walked into their midst.

The gates would open in three hours.

3. Festival

Thursday

Even with the thousand or so cars that had been in front of them in line, they had arrived early enough to grab a great site to set up camp. According to the colour-coded map the festival staff were handing out at the gates, their home for the next four days was at the back right of the grounds, in a gentle, grassy dip in the prairie. When they had pulled into their spot, Danika and Vanessa lay down on the grass, and Jane and Kelly started emptying out the van before getting to work on the tents. When Jane was about to stomp in the last tent peg, a black SUV with Massachusetts plates pulled up into the spot next to theirs, and a group of guys piled out, beer cans already in hand.

Before the gates had opened, Jane had spent the morning walking along the road looking for a ticket. "Extra, extra, who's got my extra?" Everyone she spoke to either had just seen someone with tickets or said there weren't any around. "Who's got my extra?" She walked past a rusty Subaru with the front door open, a bald man in a sky-blue bathrobe asleep in the driver's seat, Phish's June 18, '94 blasting out of the speakers and into the early morning. A red Pathfinder full of college boys watching a basketball game on the car's television. A group of children, nine, ten years old, playing in the tall grass. Folks on skateboards zipping past. Folks throwing Frisbees, thermoses of coffee resting on car roofs. Skinny hippies in ripped hemp pants clutching necks of acoustic guitars. The sunrise behind her large and gooey, the sun performing its pink and golden heat for an ecstatic audience of clouds.

"Extra, extra!"

Jane eventually found someone with a ticket to sell, a man with curly silver hair standing next to a rented silver Civic, smoking a cigarette, a woman sleeping in the passenger seat. Jane talked him down from a hundred and fifty to a hundred—plus the promise of free burritos if he found her on the festival grounds—and they smoked a bowl to close the transaction. Jane was on her way back to the van, taking in the broiling cars, the fans streaming past in every direction, the gently undulating hills, the murmur of expectation, the hot coin of the sun, when a faint noise rose up from the front of the line, started coming closer. Cars were turning on one by one, a giant zipper of engines. Folks running in both directions back to their vehicles. Slowly at first, the line started to move, and within a few minutes the cars were zooming past. Jane stepped a bit off the road to watch them. There were a lot of Volkswagens, a lot of campers, but also a fair amount of SUVs, shiny new sedans.

A break in the stream of cars, a snagged tooth in the zipper. Jane heard honking, followed by a car starting up belatedly, and she watched as her van appeared over a slight rise. Vanessa was driving, and Jane could see her face was set hard. She looked pissed. Danika was in the passenger seat, rubbing her eyes, bewildered. As the van approached, the side door swung open, and Jane watched Kelly's stunned face as they drove right past her without even slowing down. Jane turned and watched it go. Either Vanessa hadn't seen her, or she had and was angry at Jane for leaving them asleep in the van. Either way, here she was, too tired and high to feel anything except slight amusement at her current situation. She stuck out her thumb, and a minivan stopped immediately for her, barely giving her time to jump into the overcrowded vehicle before taking off again. Jane fell back and then was tossed forward, bashing her lip on the headrest. The van was full of men in overalls, crying babies on mothers' laps, guitar and banjo cases. They were at the gates in ten minutes. Jane said a quick thanks and got out, her lip thumping with dull pain. Spotting her van pulled over behind the ticket booth, idling, she started towards it. A sign over the gates said, "Welcome to Grizzly Fest. We Will Do Our Best to Please You." Vanessa got out of the car and, without looking at Jane, went into the back. Jane got into the driver's seat and shut the door.

When Jane and Kelly finished putting up the two tents, Jane's orange one next to Danika's blue one, they tossed their sleeping bags inside and organized the site, setting up chairs, repositioning the van. They woke Danika, sang "Happy Birthday," and gave her the bubbler, Danika excitedly vowing to keep it packed and burning the whole weekend. Vanessa woke up as they were smoking the inaugural bowl and wordlessly joined them.

They set off into the festival grounds, Jane and Danika barefoot, Vanessa still half-asleep, Kelly twirling along in front of them. The shakedown and the food vendors were set up in the middle of the grounds in a big ring identified on the map as "Festy Central," with the campgrounds branching off from it in four sections. A wide dirt path led to the concert grounds, which were nothing but a large, flat, fenced-off field, the stage on the far end. As they walked along, the campground was filling up fast; festival workers in orange vests were directing traffic, waving batons, trying to keep the planned roads and paths between the sections of campsites and cars clear. Tents were blossoming, tarps were being hung, canopies staked, chairs opened, music of all kinds playing from car stereos over the background chatter of friends reuniting, of stories being told and drugs swallowed, smoked, or inhaled, everywhere a rising, rippling excitement. The smell of diesel, of meat grilling, of patchouli (with wafting hints of Old Spice and Herbal Essences). The sickly sweet smell of the porta-potties, every two blocks another townhouse row, glowing aquamarine in the sun. The smell of burning marijuana on a hot afternoon on the prairies. A temporary village was ecstatically going up around them, the entire mad caravansary laying transitory root, claiming ground, staking out a communal basecamp for the impending assent to musical transcendence.

Festy Central was encircled by a ring road of food, band merch, clothes, crystals, jewellery, and book vendors, trucks and vans pulled up close behind the tables and tarps. About half of the vendors were already set up, the rest in the process of unloading their wares, organizing their tables, setting up their grills and ovens. The girls traipsed into the muddy field, a hand-painted wooden sign, like you see on saloons in cowboy movies, saying "Welcome to Festy Central." Aside from an old barn and a fully operational Ferris wheel, there was nothing but sky and sun. State police stood around, some on horses, drinking coffee and watching the colourful folks with detached interest. The girls ate and walked around the booths. Besides the usual things on offer, there were also a number of tables stacked high with used paperbacks. As the morning went on, the shakedown filled with people, unending streams of people. Shirtless boys playing guitars, children covered in mud, old hippie couples, smug college kids, women in costume, and every single one of them was shockingly familiar to Jane, as if she knew them from deepest childhood, from a powerful dream, as if this were a big family reunion.

"I am very high," she said.

The local fire fighters had set up a table, beefy men and sturdy women selling burgers and coffee. Next to them were the Charlie's Groove people, a support group for those wanting to remain sober during the shows. Jane was pleasantly surprised to see a table with a sign that said, "Rainbow Bleachers: Fans of Color," two black girls, a South Asian man, and two tie-dyed Japanese teenagers lounging around it. In the southwest corner of the market was the jet-black double-decker bus of the Believers, the radical Christian group that came to shows and festivals to proselytize and convert, to get followers to move to their compound in the Colorado mountains. If they were here, it was a telling sign that Grizzly had made the big leagues. They had a table set up in front of their bus and were giving away free cups of coffee and virgin apple cider, their faces big smiles. She gave them a wide berth as she traversed the square. There were plenty of other groups like the Believers who looked for donations and members at festivals and concerts: Jane saw the Kurtains, the End-of-Worlders, and the Free Folk, a group with a string of communes in the Sierra Madre Occidental mountain range in Mexico; every summer, they sent one representative to travel the States, and he was standing near the Ferris wheel holding up a sign that said, "Ask Me About Belonging." Jane often felt a twinge of curiosity about these groups, but never actually talked to any of them. They entered the barn, which housed the official band merchandise booths, selling clothing and CDs and posters, as well as a small bookstore, a farmers' market of local produce, and a juice bar. When the four of them got to the fence at the far end of Festy Central, they drank their lemonades and surveyed the concert grounds: there were speaker towers every fifty metres, beer vendors and porta-potties along the perimeter. The stage was still being built, a bevy of semitrailers fanned out, workers unloading road cases and trusses and stage decks, other workers high up on twenty-storey scaffolding. Behind the stage was where the band and crew would be staying. It didn't seem possible to Jane that by tomorrow night the stage would be ready to go.

They were on the other side of Festy Central, heading towards their site, when someone started calling Jane's name. It was Phil and his crew. They were lounging beside a semitrailer that was parked behind the barn, taking advantage of the enormous rectangle of shade being made by the cabless trailer. "Chives! Chives! How you doing?" Phil jumped up; his friends stayed by the trailer. It looked like they were asleep.

"It's so great you made it out!" Phil exclaimed.

"Thanks so much!" Jane said, playing along with Phil's ridiculousness. She looked at the boys by the truck.

"Oh, them?" Phil said, following Jane's eyes. "We ate some bad quesadillas, been yorking all night." It was true, Phil did not look good: his face was green, his eyes milky, and there were yellow stains on his white t-shirt, which said *Grizzly* in Hebrew letters above a cartoon amphitheatre stage. Phil waited for Jane to say something, but she was suddenly too high to think of the proper response.

"Did you hear what happened to Taylor?" Phil asked, leaning in, conspiratorial. The girls shook their heads. "He got arrested!" Some colour was coming back to Phil's face. "Their hotel room in Atlanta got raided, and he got charged with intent to sell over five and a half pounds!"

"Shit, that sucks."

"What about Chloe? Did she get arrested too?" Danika asked. Phil looked at Danika as if seeing her for the first time. "Chloe? Oh, you mean his chunky assistant? I heard he cut a deal with the cops so they wouldn't be charged. I guess they're on their way back to Cali."

"What an honourable thing to do," Danika said, ignoring Phil's rudeness.

"It was stupid, if you ask me. He should've fought in court!" Another impasse. Vanessa coughed. One of Phil's friends, maybe a Dave, moaned.

"Oh yeah," Phil said, somehow interpreting the noises. "Do you guys have an empty water bottle for a billy?"

"Nope, sorry."

"Well, we're off!" Kelly said.

"Good seeing you, Phil. Have a good show!"

"You too! Hey, did you hear Trey's been spotted? He's for sure going to come out tonight, trade off guitar lines with Janice. We're in for something special tonight! Enjoy!"

Jane smiled, and the four of them moved off. Phil went back to the trailer and lay down. One of the Daves moaned again, rolled over.

When they got back to their site, it was late afternoon. They immediately slumped into their folding chairs, sunned and sore; another string of sleepless nights was catching up to them. Their neighbours from Massachusetts were sitting in front of their SUV drinking beer, the grass around them already piled with empties and garbage. They had yet to set up any tents or otherwise make their small piece of land home. Jane caught them staring at Kelly as she unloaded the coolers from the back of the van. She was wearing a peasant skirt, a tight white halter top, and had a feather in her hair, her skin a dark brown from the three weeks spent outside. She had stopped wearing her white running shoes somewhere around New York and was now either barefoot or in a pair of flip-flops. The Southern accent, while not absent, had diminished, mellowed out into a calm, quiet *right on*, though the bouncy cadence of suburban Chicago was still nowhere to be seen. Kelly was an utterly different person from the yoga-clad girl they picked up in Erie.

They were making dinner when one of the neighbour boys ambled over. "Hey, do you girls have a can opener we can borrow?" He was in his early twenties, in baggie jeans and a sweatshirt, his brown hair short and mussy, his face affable, hungry, American.

"Yeah, sure, over there on the cooler?"

"Cool, cool. I'm Jon by the way, that's Jake, and that DEUTSCH back at the tents is Jeff. If you girls need anything, anything at all, don't hesitate to ask."

Kelly choked back laughter as Jon introduced his group, but he didn't seem to notice. "Where's Jonah, Jeremiah, Jill, and Jacklyn?" she asked brightly.

Jon looked at her, confused. "It's just us guys," he said.

The girls laughed as he walked away, his boxers showing over his low-slung jeans.

They devoured a pasta dinner, and for dessert they started on their beers. The music didn't officially start till the following afternoon, and the whole festival grounds had settled on a single goal: to party. The girls complied, drinking and recalling stories from the tour as the sun sunk into the prairie, filling everything with a comforting orange warmth. Tim Stone's girlfriend, the hole they almost drove into in Indiana, the thunderstorm in Atlanta, the stand-out jams, the look on Jane's face when Remil may or may not have been in the back of that green Westfalia.

"I am so over him," Jane said, surprising herself, knowing it wasn't entirely true. "I have my girls, wooo! I have the music—I don't need anything else!" She was already drunk, excited, expanding with possibility.

"Hey, let's go talk to our neighbours," Danika said at midnight. They jumped up and trooped over. Jeff, Jake, and Jon were sitting low in their lawn chairs, dumbly watching a fire burn in a blue plastic bucket. They all had big jeans, big t-shirts, scruffy hair. They were definitely on something, dosed or rolling or a few lines into an eight-ball. As soon as the girls approached, they snapped out of their funk, sat up straight, tripped over themselves in offering chairs, food, beer, joints.

"Hey ya, roll up a couple of joints, sugar pies!" Kelly said.

Jane was behind a pane of alcohol, the thick glass keeping the whole aquarium from spilling out and drowning her. She watched as one of the boys—Jeff, she thought—took a water bottle out of a half-gone twenty-four pack, twisted the cap off with a ripping plastic crack, and crushed the entire bottle over his hands, rinsing them with the water before tossing the bottle into the bucket fire. Jane gave a squeal of shock when he mashed the bottle—what arrogant disregard for the world!

"Did you hear that, Janey?" Danika shouted, full of incredulous glee. "These boys—sorry, sorry, these MEN—are about to join the army!" Danika stood up straight, a lit joint in her mouth, and gave a crisp salute.

Jon, the one who asked for a can opener—who goes to a festival with cans but without a can opener?!—coughed. "Actually," he said, "we've already 'joined' the army; we've gone through basic and everything. We ship out the day after the festy."

"We're out on one last hurrah!"

"One night we're dosing, listening to great music, hanging out with stank-ass hippies—no offense, ha ha—and the next we'll be hanging out the back of a plane sighting missiles!" Jon added with pride.

All kinds, Jane said to herself, half watching Kelly and Jake as they started making out, falling off their chairs onto the dewy grass. They come in all kinds.

The joints went around. The boys talked more about their impending army service. Vanessa got up, said she was going to go explore, maybe find a dollar grilled cheese. Around three in the morning, someone nearby started blasting a Grizzly show at full volume, the whole neighbourhood screaming with joy.

Jane was closing up the van, about to get into her tent, when she saw Vanessa walking towards the site in the fresh dawn blue. She was holding two hemp necklaces in one hand and a pamphlet from the Free Folk in another, and Jane could tell that something was wrong.

"What is it, Van?"

"Oh hon, I, I saw Remil. No, wait. He was on the Ferris wheel. He was with another girl, Jane. They were quite obviously … uh, involved."

Jane blinked. Vanessa gently lifted up Jane's hair and put the necklace around her neck. "I'm sorry," she said.

Like the suddenly recognizable sounds of the next tune coming together through the disassembled fog of the one before, a memory. Last summer, Gavin's cabin near Big Sur. Already a year ago. Remil and his crew had been there three nights already. Jane was going up to Berkeley with them the next morning. Eight or nine of them sitting on bleached-out logs of driftwood around the beach bonfire, the full moon illuminating the shoreline, the salty coastal world blue and white except for the brilliant orange of the fire, huge and hot and crackling. Chase and Vanessa snuggled together in the sand, Gavin feeding the fire, his dog, Pigpen, at his side. Pigpen suddenly agitated, stalking his way onto the rocky lowtide shoreline, barking madly at the dark blue surf. *Bark! Bark bark!* Gavin making his way towards him, dreadlocks down to his ass. "What's wrong, boy? What are you barking at? What, that? It's nothing. It's only a rock. See? See?" Throwing a stick at the imaginary threat. "See, boy? See?" Jane watching the beautiful moment between the best friends, deeply touched. "How cute," Remil said, without a trace of sarcasm or irony in his voice, just straight earnest appreciation, and Jane felt connected to him like she had never felt connected to any person, place, or collection of sounds before.

Friday

Scrambled eggs and red pepper, chairs and laughter. Jane catches Jeff looking at her, she smiles and turns away, around noon the girls head to Festy Central, check out the merch, wander through the barn, a hot sun with two-note chords of cloud, the grounds bustling with happy happy people, folks in rolled up jeans waiting in the mud for a vacant porta-potty, the walk to the venue, thousands of fans streaming towards the stage on a wide dirt road beer and lemonade vendors, people whispering drugs into your ear, a woman entirely in red sitting on a cooler trilling out "Mushrooms! Mushrooms! Red Bull!" the first set of the festival Jane drinks three beers before accepting a hit of acid from Neptune Terry the music is inquisitive low-key holding back patient Janice wearing a *Cody Drops Bombs* t-shirt Jane has lost the girls the acid rises through her stomach through her throat into her eyeballs after the set Jane is alone she is playing slap bag with a bunch of Midwesterners someone holds a bag of wine up in the air and you slap it as hard as you can and then you drink from it slap bag the sun sets Jane's trip slips away from her she hasn't eaten since breakfast she doesn't go to the second set finds herself at a bank of payphones in Festy Central the Ferris wheel lit up against the dark sky she is talking to Drew crying sputtering Drew is saying can you find some water can you find some milk he was my Cassady Drew he was my Cassady yeah but what happened to Cassady he hurt everybody he ever loved and died alone on the train tracks she's back in the venue the final set of the night the crescent moon a punctuation mark hanging above the stage the stars she is near the front off to the side twirling her skirt mooning out from her body "did you hear that ghost tease" somebody whispers in her ear the music is extravagant emotional an ocean Janice's guitar searching the starsky for release for meaning Cody's bass a rumbling powerful engine trotting drum licks high octane piano surges the music carving out its own place in the cosmos with careful abandon reaching reaching reaching grabbing at what it almost has it focus it rises pumping climbing it's almost there it's almost there I want to believe I want to believe so badly I do believe I do crash crash back to earth the set is over Jane is tumbling an encore of "Django Djuna" and "Yo-Yo" Jane is in the midst of shakedown it is very late scary men with mean faces selling nitrous the ghostly sound of the heavy orange tanks everybody holding red balloons faces stupid Jane sees a nasty fist fight somebody yells "it's whiter than a mid-eighties SNL cast party in here" and it is it is what a stupid scene a scene of middle-class white kids getting drunk and stoned why is she even here then Grizzly starts blasting out of a Toyota June 3, '04 an early Missoula show the first time they played "Paper" and she remembers it's the rising it's the falling it's the attempt always the attempt for meaning for knowledge for grace for belonging Remil Remil I believed you when you said you had finally found a home Remil I'm not going to let you ruin the music poison this world we've made I was wrong about you but there are some things I know I'm not wrong about you can't have a family without sacrifice you can't have release without tension goodbye Remil so long she's walking past the True Believers drum circle they're smiling and dancing singing about Jesus this the Jesus Freaks somebody yells walking by ha ha yeah Jesus s you sometime later Jane is standing just on the outside of a arp overhang listening to a bluegrass band play to a small crowd bass guitar banjo mandolin wearing overalls and straw hats who gave her a lift that first morning lifetimes ago the female er is tearing it up it is raining lightly and Cody is standing the fans make way to let her under the tent Jane grabs her you I love you so much she says Cody smiles shyly now the gone it's early morning Jane is lost wandering through the ws of tents and campsites looking for her tent her campsite nd it how long has she been looking hours minutes she is lost a teenage girl with short brown hair a bulging stomach and many piercings hands her a big red balloon pregnant with nitrous and Jane takes a big inhale and then another her brain calving into fine feathery pillows of tingling idiotic joy tents and tarps and half moons of empty chairs she sits down with some men, clean-shaven businessmen types but heads true fans she knows she just can tell they are talking in hushed tones about the music about what tomorrow will bring I'm lost she says not anymore sister handing her a beer a cold PBR, an old man with rolling eyes half his head shaved the other half very long wearing a *Cody Sucks* t-shirt with a penis and balls drawn under it in black marker walks by Jane throws her beer can at him, it sails through the air hosing beer lands harmlessly on the road dust puffing into the thin blue it's dawn the campground eerie quiet unreal, the chilly start of a new day Jane is falling asleep, it's bright now, already hot, people are emerging from their tents, she sees Kelly skipping past dark-skinned busty unbearably gorgeous Kelly her best friend in the whole world Kelly how did you find me Kelly Kelly Kelly

Saturday

"Want to get out of here for a little while?"

It was late afternoon, after the first set of the day; the band had played *Colors*, their first EP, in its entirety. Even though Jane had drunk nothing but tea all day, and her head was raw, her bruised lip sore and pulsating, she had changed into her red skirt and a clean black tee she had found at the bottom of her rucksack, had brushed her hair in the van's mirror for the first time since Wisconsin, and was standing i front of Jeff, who was slouched in his chair watching the smoulderi plastic bucket, wearing a Grizzly tour shirt and khaki shorts. Behir him, their two Walmart-bought tents sagged like sandcastles sie the tide.

Jeff looked up. He looked a lot like Jon, but with a smalle less smooth features, less overarching confidence.

"What? What do you mean?"

"Let's take the van, go for a drive."

Jeff looked confused.

Jane laughed. "I've had enough of this. I need a break."

Jeff's face lit up. "Oh, uh, yeah. Uh, sure. Let me grab my wallet."

On their way to the van, Jeff grabbed the last remaining water bottle from the totalled pack. Jane was about to cringe, but instead of using the bottle as a one-serve hand wash, he jammed it into his shorts pocket. They climbed into the hot van, Jeff throwing a pile of Kelly's bras off the seat and into the back. "Your friend and Jake seem to be hitting it off," he said.

"What? Oh yeah, that. I hope he's not taking it too seriously."

The car, roasting in the prairie sun, hadn't moved since Thursday. The engine turned over slowly, finally spluttering into gear. Jane flipped over the tape that was in the deck, put the car into drive, and slowly picked her way onto the road. The sunset was still a few hours off, but some of the fans were already heading towards the stage—there were folks everywhere, not one of them caring about a van slowly rolling to the exit. "I don't know how we're going to get back here after," Jane said. Jeff laughed nervously.

Jane manoeuvred along the edge of the campground and onto the main festival road, which still had folks streaming across it but was clear enough that they could maintain a more constant speed. They drove past the RV camping, the day parking, through the main gates and back out into South Dakota. It was a twenty-minute drive into Red Hook and, once they left the festival grounds, Jeff spoke almost non-stop the entire way. Jane had him pegged as quiet, even a little stupid, but he was anything but: Away from his friends, away from the frenzy the festival, the contours of tour, Jeff was a different person. For rters, he knew much more about the music than he'd let on. They e about Janice's guitar tone, early Phish, if Hornby or Pigpen was er keys player; to Jane's surprise, he thought Cody was a better yer than Mike, "more fearless," he said, and though at first it ous that he was a little intimidated by Jane—which, she was to lie, made her feel worldly, beautiful—as the prairies rolled kly found his voice.

ere talking about how lucky we were to post up next to you e are lots of hot girls at these show, but most of them have or aren't interested in ..." Jeff stopped himself.

at?" Jane said, laughing. "In putting out?"

Jeff's faced turned sheepish.

"Do you ever think about the geography of these venues, these festivals?" he said, trying to redeem himself. "We plant ourselves into the land, make it our home. It's very American, isn't it?"

"I guess I've never thought of it that way. I always think of us more as temporary sojourners, gathering for the night, revelling together, dispersing after the music."

"That's a little wishy-washy, don't you think?"

Jane laughed. "So, why the army?" she said.

"The army? Easy. To protect dirty hippies like you!" As soon as Jeff blurted this out, Jane saw his face go aghast in the mirror. "Sorry, really. I forgot I'm not with Jake and those guys." Jeff took a deep breath. "Honestly, I was always going to go into the army, ever since I knew what it was. My father was an officer, my grandfather and great-grandfather foot soldiers in both world wars. I love this country with all my heart. Where else could something like this happen? You want to spend your life following live music around the country? Spend your life following live music around the country! You want to have your own little micro economy, not pay taxes, barter and negotiate? Have your own little micro economy, don't pay taxes, barter and negotiate! It truly is the land of the free."

"I'm not used to hearing people speak so positively about this country."

"They just complain because they're able to complain. America is the best place on earth. Period. Yeah, it's had some growing pains, even its share of original sin, but what place hasn't? The least I can do is stand up and fight for it. What, you don't feel that way about Canada?"

"No, not really."

"Hey, what's wrong with your speedometer?"

"Oh, nothing, the gauge is dead. It's happened before. I'll [ ] to a mechanic after the festy." She decided not to tell him abo[ut] run-in with the police.

They passed an open-pit excavation of some kind. Jane[ ] usual sense of disgust and was about to voice it, but Jeff st[ ] speaking first. "Did I tell you I have a degree in geology? Af[ ] army, I'll probably go into the engineering corps. Nothing sounds better to me than damming rivers, building reservoirs and bridges, creating drinking water, turning the land into food and energy. I live for it."

Jane had nothing to say to this. Silence.

"What do you live for?" Jeff asked.

"What do I live for?" Jane honestly didn't know. She instinctively turned the stereo up, just as Jerry relaxed into his noodling, poignant guitar solo. "I live for New Year's Eve '95. I live for the Island Tour. I live for the sun blasting us into the new millennium at Big Cypress. The wefted beauty of Jerry's guitar. The eighty-four shows of '97. The first time I heard Grizzly."

Jeff smirked, about to give a smart-ass response, but then something on his face changed.

"All very good things," he said.

They parked on Red Hook's main street. It was a small, cozy-looking town, and they walked from one end to the other in fifteen minutes. The old-fashioned stone inn, with red colonial window shutters and flower pots, had a hand-painted sign that said, "Welcome Grizzly Fans!" At the end of the street, abutting a grassy park of tall oaks and benches, was a squat, plain-looking building with a Jewish star engraved over the wood door.

"I can't believe there's a shul here!" Jane exclaimed. They walked over to it, and Jeff read from a plaque affixed to the building: "This ornerstone was laid in August, 1912 by the mayor. The construction the building was supported by a generous donation from Mr. ham Klein, head of the first Jewish family to settle in Red Hook major benefactor of the town."

the synagogue courtyard was a small Jewish cemetery. They hrough it, Jane reading out the names on the headstones.

amily has been in the States since the 1700s," Jeff said. k to my great-great-great-great-great grandfather, all buried e graveyard an hour outside of Boston."

Jews move around too much for that, ha ha. There is this family, though, probably apocryphal, about an ancestor, the patriarch, disappearing into the American night. "

Jane suddenly thought about how her grandmother had been dead for almost a year already. She remembered with a pang of regret that last night Drew had told her that she had missed the unveiling of the headstone, and that her parents were none too pleased. She should really call and apologize.

Jane remembered telling Remil her grandmother had died, beside the van at the Gorge, the sky a dome of cold blue. The change in his eyes, a film between his pupils and her. Was that when he decided to drop her, when the real world—the world of death and struggle and commitment, the world of Babylon—intruded on the dream he had found, fenced off from everything else, and never wanted to leave? Jane looked at Jeff. Besides the music, he was the opposite of Remil in every possible way.

Back at the van, Jane opened the trunk, empty except for Vanessa's guitar case and some blankets, and slid in, throwing her sandals out behind her. Jeff, hesitating slightly, soon followed.

By the time they got back to the festival, drove past the deserted security hut, through the gates, found a place to park in the day parking lot, and walked into the concert grounds, Grizzly was a good way into the final set of the night, of the weekend, of the tour, of summer. The two of them stayed near the back, holding hands, the stage very far away, thousands of bobbing heads washed in the swinging lights, the night sky huge and open, the air warm and sweet. Without the crush of being deep in the pit, there was more room to dance: fans were twirling, spinning, gyrating. They had found a laid-back little pocket. The bear-suit guys from the first show of to were there, dancing with their paws in the air. The three wise be A young family, the father with hair down his back, the mother a floral-print dress, the boy blond and wearing tie-dye, a baby holster on the father's chest. A grizzle-faced man with dread that must have weighed five pounds each down to his knees raver girl with enormous black pants that belled out hugely, with an outsized hood, and skater shoes with white ankle s running and jumping, yelling things like "Grizzly is the best the world! We are the luckiest people alive!" every few min

And the music was good. It was the middle part of "Yes (Yes) No," and Janice's guitar was singing hot, Steve's piano wet with emotion, Cody keyed in, Paul's drumming loose, relaxed, ready for anything. The music icy cola in the warm, smoky night.

For once, there was nothing between Jane and the music.

They closed the second set with "Paper." At the end of the "Mulch" section and before the main jam, Janice introduced a fiddle player from Red Hook, Alvira Moffat. As soon as she hit her first, vibrant note, Jane knew it was the fiddle player from the tent last night, the one who gave her a lift the first day. Jane knew how good she was, and she did not disappoint—pulled up by the soaring lines of her violin, the music scraped the heights; the audience went crazy, screaming with release. In the break before the encore, lighters and phones held aloft, amid the swelling cheering of the crowd, the raver girl stomped by, yelling, "Thank you, America! Thank you, South Dakota! And thank you, Janice, for all the cum!" Everyone laughed, even the parents, and Jane joined in the refrain: "Thank you, Janice! Thank you, Janice!"

The band came back on to thunderous applause. Janice began to speak: "Thank you guys for a truly wondrous summer. Who would have thought we would be playing to you like this? What else is there to say? We love you all, and we'll see you soon." They encored with "Fireworks," actual red and gold fireworks exploding behind the stage. The moment the band walked off, the stagehands emerged, dissasembling the rigs, taking down the lights and the stage. There re dozens of them, crawling like ants, rolling out road cases, ping cable, rolling up Janice and Steve's carpets, eight or nine of ackling Phil's drum kit. The speaker banks slowly lowered onto e. Workers up on the catwalks unhooking lights, trucks with their flatbeds backing into position. Jane and Jeff stood ching the stage being dismantled as thousands of satisfied med past them. Two hours from now it would be gone. The er. There was no more music to chase.

Sunday

anika were sitting in their lawn chairs, watching the

festival vanish around them. Cars were driving past in every direction, the rows of tents and cars quickly losing their shape. The entire festival population had let loose all night. Jeff, Jake, and Jon had left shortly after the sun rose. Vanessa, too, was gone. Jeff's hair was sitting on the grass next to their fire bucket, where Jane had shaved it off with a pair of clippers in the cool blue predawn. The boys from Massachusetts had also left their tents, their cooler, and a wide range of crushed beer cans and garbage; the tents were collapsed, destroyed, sitting in puddles of rain, beer, probably piss. The three of them were now the official property of the US Army. Jane noticed her can opener lying on the ground. "I'm going to sleep for days," Danika said, pulling Jane out of her musings. "Days and days and days. It's going to be dangerous."

It had been a wild night. All the beer, weed, nitrous, and other ingestibles had to be finished, and they did their best. Danika had finally run into the Buffalo crew during the last set and had brought them back to the site, her and willowy Tess holding hands. There was immediate tension between the Buffalo and Massachusetts boys, especially after Bobby saw Kelly and Jake come out of Jake's tent together. Jane had come back from a nasty, drunken shit at the porta-potties to find Bobby and Jake yelling at each other, shoving roughly, Kelly standing off to the side. Jake was bigger and drunker than Bobby, and the whole thing would have tipped over into violence, everybody screaming, if Danika hadn't pushed her way in and man-handled the fighting boys apart. Jane had never seen Kelly look like that before, stunned, hurt, even—unbelievably—on the edge of tears; not at all like Jane thought she would look with two boys fighting over her. S stormed off into the campground, and Bobby ran after her. "Bitch Jake called, Jon and Jeff pulling him towards their SUV.

It must have been sometime after that that Jane had ma Danika go with her to get the van from day parking. As Danika drove, Jane rummaged through the van to find something to Jeff, some sort of keepsake: in the cupholder she found the bracelet she got from Little Lucy, the speeding ticket from V and the gold earring she had found in Indiana. Once they w back at their site, Jane gave the hemp bracelet to Tess, rip ticket into pieces and threw it in the fire bucket, and gave the earring to Jeff. In thanks for the earring, which he unceremoniously stuffed into his jeans pocket, Jeff shimmied under the van and fixed the speedometer; apparently all that was needed was to reconnect two wires that had come apart. And to top it all off, as the sun was rising Vanessa came back and announced that she was going to go with the Free Folk back to Mexico. "I've been looking for something more all summer," she said, her face the brightest Jane had seen it since they lived on the coast together, "and I think this is it." Jane watched, speechless, as Vanessa gathered her things. Jane filled with love for her oldest friend. "Write me as soon as you can!" she said.

"I will!" Vanessa said brightly, and was gone.

After a few hours of sleep, Jane and Danika sat drinking tea in the new morning, both of them keeping an eye out for Kelly, who hadn't shown up again since storming off.

"What are your plans?" Danika asked.

"I don't know. I think I'm going to head to the coast, maybe up to BC. I'm going to take a fallow year, lay low for a while, regroup."

"Can I get a lift?"

Jane laughed. "Of course."

"I can't wait to get back to Canada. Don't ask me how I'm going to get back into Ph.D. mode, though. I need a detox, a meditation retreat, and an intensive theory bender, and I need it soon."

"You should be all right," Jane said. "You seem to have had no problem keeping your mind sharp."

Jane had just finished brushing her teeth when Kelly showed with Bobby, Samuel, and Tess in tow. Jane noticed how tan they Samuel's skin, more or less white in Atlanta, was lobster red and They looked two years older than they did a mere week and . "Look who I found!" Kelly said, as if last night had never . She was holding hands with Bobby. Jane loved the light into Danika's eyes at the sight of Tess. Kelly was back in her and t-shirt, though she hadn't taken the braid out of her with the bags under her eyes she was beautiful. el and Tess's uncle lives in Chicago, and they were planning that way anyways—he's going to give me a lift!" she exclaimed, the Southern accent gone.

"What happened to you?" Samuel asked, noticing Jane's bruised and swollen lower lip.

"The music," Jane said, smiling.

"Do you think there's room for one more?" Danika asked, talking to Bobby but looking at Tess. "I can grab a flight to Vancouver from Chicago."

"Sure," Tess said. "We're going to spend the rest of the summer at our uncle's cottage if you guys are interested in coming along. We grow our own weed up there, are going to set up our instruments."

"Sounds interesting ..." Danika said.

Jane was laughing. "Girl," she mock-yelled at Danika, "you better have your ass back in school by September, or I'm going to come find you!"

Kelly and Danika arranged their stuff and said their goodbyes. Danika hugged Jane for a long time. "See you at the New Year's run! I hear it's going to be a five-night rager in the desert!" Kelly squeezed Jane tightly. "Thanks for the best time of my life!" she said.

Jane was in no rush to leave. After rolling up the tent and arranging the van, she walked the grounds. It was different, alien, covered in trash. Beer cans, broken chairs, tent poles, spilled food, paper plates, thousands of wrinkled red balloons. A wilted rose. The grass trampled, the soil exposed. The detritus of experience. She hadn't felt alone like this since they had left Canada, since before Remil. All of the questions that days ago would have been of pressing importance—how long had Remil been on tour? Who was the girl he was with on the Ferris wheel?—had shrunk in importance and pinged out of existence. She felt like she had struggled through a passage of tension, of disson of miscues, and was now on the other side, ready to live her life careful abandon.

Jane sat down. The end of tour was always a time to take s After tours, she usually fell into a recovery period of sadness, b didn't feel anything like that coming. At some point during the it had all become clear. Jane wasn't going to live for other peo anymore. She had the music, she had her van, she had her frie family in Toronto. She was going to be a nomad, a travelling w always moving, always changing, always chasing. No corporation or entrenched ruling elite were going to dictate how or what she was going to live for. That morning, after Jeff had left, Jane read through the Free Folk pamphlet Vanessa had left behind. Jane had to admit, it sounded pretty legitimate: they grew their own food, pursued their creative projects, held workshops and dances with the locals, had to vote unanimously on any and all community matters. If half of what the pamphlet claimed was true, they really were trying to live well, with each other and with the land. She was happy for Vanessa, who was taking a real chance. She would have to go visit her. Jane jumped up, started walking towards the van. A few feet from where she had been sitting, she noticed a fat bag of weed on the ground. She bent down to pick it up.

"Ground score!" Jane turned around to find Neptune Terry, looking old and bent over but with that same crazy grin on his weathered face.

"Neptune! What are your plans?"

"Oh, I don't know. I think we might head over to the Black Hills, join the protests at the Rushmore heads. Stolen Lakota land, you know. Our time is over. Native power is rising, and it's our turn to step back, get out of the way, be allies."

"I had no idea you were so political!"

Neptune laughed, his entire face beaming. "I don't know about that, sister. There's never been much difference to me between music and politics."

"Hmm. Maybe I'll tag along," Jane said.

"There's always room for one more."

"Meet me at the van; we'll smoke some of this weed."

"A gift from the land," Neptune said, nodding towards the weed good sign."

tune and his wife weren't leaving until the evening, and Jane aking a nap. For now though, someone had handed her a ag and pick and she was helping to clean up. She speared a rbage and dropped it in the bag. She speared another one. work until it was clean, she decided. She would scour the ould stay until any sign of their presence was gone.

ACKNOWLEDGEMENTS

"Ninety-Nine" appeared in *The Temz Review*. "Restaurants" appeared in *Grain Magazine*. "A/V" was shortlisted for the 2016 *Malahat Review*'s novella contest. Thanks to the editors and judges of these journals for including my work. A 2012 Writers' Works in Progress grant from the Ontario Arts Council allowed me to write early versions of many of these stories.

Thanks to Jim Nason, Heather Wood, and everybody at Tightrope Books. Thanks to my editor, Deanna Janovski, who pushed these stories as far as they were willing to go, and to whom I explained many things about jam bands, including what exactly those setlist chevrons mean. Thanks to the team at Diaspora Dialogues, where in 2015 I workshopped the collection with Lauren Kirshner. Thanks to Amanda Ghazale Aziz for her generative reading of "Restaurants."

Thanks to all my family and friends. To my parents, Cathy and David, my brother, Ben, my sister, Rachel. To Steph's family (aka The Korns): Mark, Susan, Jenn, Daniel. To David Huebert, friend, accomplice, fellow miller of rist. To Natasha Bastien, for the support, encouragement, and homemade ranola. To old friends: Dan Sadowski, Chris Bezant, Alex Smith, Sam stein, Adam Greenblatt, Jeff Ebidia, Jana Stern. To new friends: Myra m, Tyler Ball, Eric Schmaltz, MLA Chernoff, Kristina Getz, Tal Davidson. er, my canine companion on trails, riverbanks, and couches.

Thornhill, Montreal, Toronto, Victoria, Hornby Island, Kahshe re I wrote (or thought about writing) these stories. To everyone led into a car and driven over the border with to go to a music Phish concert, a New Year's run. To the Phish from Vermont, for or the joyful craft, for countless journeys into the unknown.

ks to Steph. My partner, my best friend. I couldn't ask for a ate.

ABOUT THE AUTHOR

PHOTO: Rick O'Brien

Aaron Kreuter writes poetry and fiction. He is the author of the poetry collection *Arguments for Lawn Chairs*. His work has appeared in various anthologies, magazines, and journals, including *Best Canadian Poetry*, *Ghost Fishing: An Eco-Justice Anthology*, the *Puritan*, *Grain Magazine*, and the *Temz Review*. *You and Me, Belonging* is his first book of fiction. He lives in Toronto.